THE COWBOY AND THE RASCAL

Also by Jackie North

The Farthingdale Ranch Series

The Foreman and the Drifter

The Blacksmith and the Ex-Con

The Ranch Hand and the Single Dad

The Wrangler and the Orphan

The Cook and the Gangster

The Trail Boss and the Brat

The Farthingdale Valley Series

The Cowboy and the Rascal

The Love Across Time Series

Heroes for Ghosts

Honey From the Lion

Wild as the West Texas Wind

Ride the Whirlwind

Hemingway's Notebook

For the Love of a Ghost

Love Across Time Sequels

Heroes Across Time - Sequel to Heroes for Ghosts

The Oliver & Jack Series

Fagin's Boy

At Lodgings in Lyme

In Axminster Workhouse

Out in the World

On the Isle of Dogs

In London Towne

Holiday Standalones

The Christmas Knife

Hot Chocolate Kisses

The Little Matchboy

Standalone

The Duke of Hand to Heart

THE COWBOY AND THE RASCAL

A GAY M/M COWBOY ROMANCE

JACKIE NORTH

Jackie North

MM Romance Author

The Cowboy and the Rascal
Copyright ©2023 Jackie North
Published March 29, 2023

All rights reserved. No part of this book may be reproduced, distributed, or transmitted in any form or by any means, electronic or mechanical, including photocopying, recording, or any information storage and retrieval system without the written permission of the author, except where permitted by law.

For permission requests, write to the author at jackie@jackienorth.com

This is a work of fiction. Names, characters, places, and incidents are a product of the author's imagination or are used fictitiously. Any resemblance to people, places, or things is completely coincidental.

Cover Design by Cate Ashwood

The Cowboy and the Rascal/Jackie North

ISBN Numbers:

Kindle Epub - 978-1-942809-78-4
Print - 978-1-942809-79-1

Library of Congress Control Number: 2023904724

For all those who know that love is love...

...and to those who look to the stars.

"Yours is the light by which my spirit's born: – you are my sun, my moon, and all my stars."
— E. E. Cummings

CONTENTS

1. Blaze — 1
2. Gabe — 13
3. Blaze — 27
4. Blaze — 37
5. Gabe — 49
6. Blaze — 61
7. Gabe — 67
8. Blaze — 75
9. Blaze — 83
10. Gabe — 95
11. Blaze — 107
12. Gabe — 117
13. Blaze — 125
14. Gabe — 133
15. Blaze — 143
16. Gabe — 151
17. Blaze — 159
18. Blaze — 167
19. Blaze — 177
20. Gabe — 185
21. Blaze — 195
22. Gabe — 205
23. Blaze — 215
24. Gabe — 223
25. Blaze — 233
26. Gabe — 243
27. Blaze — 251
28. Gabe — 261

Jackie's Newsletter — 265
Author's Notes About the Story — 267
A Letter From Jackie — 271
About the Author — 273

CHAPTER 1

BLAZE

When the door to Blaze's prison cell slammed shut at nine-thirty p.m. sharp, the hard clang rang in his ears as his eyes adjusted to the half-dark.

Of course, it was never truly dark in prison. The security lighting system stayed on all night, sending waves of half-light everywhere, even into the individual cells, as a kind of force field against anything undesirable that might happen during the night. Like an escape attempt, or a fight in a cell, or unnamable fears that stayed awake, unblinking, like nightmares from childhood, hunched in the dark, shadowy corners of each level of Wyoming Correctional, just waiting for their chance to strike.

That chance was coming, Blaze knew it was, whether it was day or night.

Blaze had been admitted to the state prison almost two years prior and had done his best to adjust to the schedule. But it was hard to settle into a routine teeming with so much structure, so hard he thought he'd go crazy inside of two weeks and throw himself off the level-two balcony just to get out of the routine, even if it meant, at the same time, that he'd be in the infirmary for who knew how many broken bones. Not to mention, he'd be under a lot more scrutiny in the infirmary than anywhere else in the prison.

His old life, though it was less than two years ago, seemed so far away. Back then, he'd slept in the upper bunk of whatever trailer the Butterworth family used at the time. Then he'd wake up sometime mid-morning to the sound of happy chatter through the half-opened window, the smell of charred hot dogs and the crisp, brisk smell of kettle corn fresh in the still, humid air. His favorite flavor of cotton candy was pink, and it was his favorite thing to have for breakfast.

His job, when he was very young, and they were working the carnival in summertime, had been to ride the kiddie rides. He was tasked with drawing in customers by looking like he was having a great time, even though the dragon coaster, for all its mini, kid-appropriate size, hurtled and jerked and usually made him puke, and the small Ferris wheel bored him to tears.

When he got older, he ran those rides, doing security checks in a slap-dash manner, and hurrying to the corn dog stand at the end of his shift. Then, after a break, his lips greasy with mustard, he'd help run the game booths along the main strip of the carnival, and smile as customers were cheated out of their tickets because he knew there was no way they could put the ring around the pole when the pole was tilted to one side, misaligned like all the other target games.

At other times, over the years, he'd been, as his parents had said, at liberty to pick pockets. In other words, *go get free money and bring it back*. Blaze had obliged and had become very adept at getting square wallets out of tight back pockets and rectangular wallets out of loosely secured purses and backpacks.

He went to bed when it got late, whenever that was, and woke up when he had to. And did his best, as he got older, to get along with his brother, Alex. Over time, Blaze learned it was best to stay out of Alex's way, which could be difficult sometimes, as they all lived in the same trailer.

It wouldn't have mattered so much to Blaze that Alex was their parents' favorite, if they didn't, at the same time, let him get away with everything, including the drugs. Alex was a mean shit to begin with and he had gotten worse with time, especially when he started snorting coke or whatever he could get his hands on.

Blaze's trouble really started the summer his parents decided to start working a driveway scam on rich old people.

The focus of the scam was on folks who lived in fifty-five plus communities and didn't seem to have the sense to know any better. During the first week they were doing the scam, he and Alex and Pop had driven door to door, with Blaze half hanging out the window so he could spot driveways that looked even the least bit ragged.

When he found one, they'd stop. Then Pop, in an old uniform shirt he'd bought at a thrift store, would go up and knock on the door while Alex and Blaze waited by the truck and, wearing similar shirts, rakes in hand, stand there like they were ready to go to work. The stage for the scam was set.

Pop would flash his ID and point at the badge on his shirt as proof that he had been hired by the HOA to come around and fix up driveways. Only there was a fee, you see, and did the woman of the house want to check with her husband about writing a check for the deposit? Which would be promptly refunded by the HOA once the work was done, of course. The old person would squint a bit, and hem and haw, and then write checks made out to Pop, following Pop's insistence.

Normally, Blaze had never minded working the shill at the game booths. After all, customers kind of expected that when they came to a carnival or a fun fair, they'd lose and lose and lose at those ring tosses and cap bottle tosses and the duck hunt because that was part of the carnival atmosphere. That and the oft-repeated *you could win big* line that every carny knew almost from birth. Only carnies could call themselves that, though, and hell help the man, woman, or child who referred to them as such.

Blaze had never minded most of his life as a carnie, either, but something happened to him during that scam, right from the start, as none of it felt right. This feeling of unease worsened from the moment the old lady at the fourth house they stopped at had peered up at Pop, squinting with her confusion. She'd wanted to know why, all of a sudden, after living in the community that provided so much for them, where she was being asked to resurface her own driveway, at her own expense, when her driveway looked perfectly fine and was practically new?

So many driveways have been re-surfaced in this neighborhood, ma'am, Pop had said. *I'm just trying to fit you into my schedule before all my slots are filled and I have no room for you. Is your husband at home?*

It turned out that she was newly widowed, and had just about started crying as she told Pop this. She wore a huge ring on one finger that glinted in the sunlight, and around her neck she wore pearls, so it was easy to see that she was loaded, and he knew Pop was salivating about it.

She might have been able to afford the scam, but as Alex dragged Blaze closer to the open doorway, perhaps to add bulk to the lie that they were hard-working men hired by the HOA to fix her perfectly functional driveway, it began to feel less and less okay to Blaze.

In her old faded eyes was confusion mixed with a desire to understand what was going on, and a hefty shine of soon-to-be-betrayed trust. Then she looked at Blaze with a kind of affection, as if he was her favorite grandson, and he just about lost it.

Had Blaze been born into another family, he might have had grandparents of his own, but he hadn't been. She could have been his grandma. He'd never had one, and they always seemed so nice on TV.

Had this been any other situation, he could have told himself the story that she *was* his grandma, then continued to help Pop and Alex pull off the scam. But not this time, so for reasons he could never fully explain to himself, either that day or ever, he dropped his shovel.

In the quiet cul-de-sac, the noise echoed off the walls of the other houses, and out of each one came old folks, sometimes alone, sometimes in pairs, seven in all. That was too many witnesses, especially for Pop, so he pulled out his phone, pretended to check a list, and told the old woman that he had the wrong house and could she excuse him for bothering her. Then they all got in the truck, and Pop zoomed off.

Later, for some reason, he didn't get called out for screwing up the scam. He did, however, make the mistake of expressing his opinion that the scam had been stupid from the get-go. Too full of risks and exposure were the reasons he gave to Mom, and Pop, and Alex, who had all looked at him with puzzled shock.

In his own mind, it occurred to him that he was meant for more than bilking old people out of their savings. Then, telling himself the story that his pretend grandma would be proud of him for finally getting his GED, he announced his plans to start studying for it.

He'd dropped out of high school four years earlier, so either his family thought he was joking or that he'd never succeed. Alex certainly made it more difficult to study, because every time Blaze would pull out his GED study guide, Alex would accuse him of thinking he was better than everybody else, smack the study guide to the floor, and generally be a dick about it.

Blaze soldiered on, doing his best to study beneath the single overhead light over the table in the trailer that everybody seemed to suddenly need to use when he had his workbooks out. The pleasure of his imaginary grandma dimmed day after day, but he was not going to give up.

Then, one hot August night, with his GED exam scheduled the first week in September, he'd been doing a practice test on a printout, as he didn't have a laptop, and the trailer had no wi-fi, his stub of a pencil smearing all over the place. Alex had come banging into the trailer, high on coke, nose red-rimmed with blood, staggering, fists swinging.

It had been all Blaze could do to avoid the blows at first, but when he'd steadied his stance and punched back, and the two of them had smashed out the front door, tumbling to the summer-dead grass with shouts and swearing.

Someone, perhaps their nearest neighbor in the RV park, had called the cops. It was astonishing to think of, even now, that a fellow carny would involve the local law, but that's what had happened.

When the cops had shown up, Mom and Pop, who adored Alex in

spite of everything, had pointed the finger at Blaze. They told the cops the drugs belonged to Blaze, and then the cops had taken Blaze away.

He should have known better than to attempt to go straight. At the very least, he should have read the signals his family had been sending him that whole summer that they did not approve of his attempt at self-improvement.

Why do you need that GED? Pop had asked. *What a waste of time.*

Don't yell at Alex, Mom would say. *He needed that money you've got tucked in that old lunchbox of yours. Here's five, go get yourself a corn dog.*

Go on over to Teller's ring toss booth, Dad would tell him. *The law is sniffing around, trying to figure out his scam, so you'll play and win for a bit until they go away.*

Still working on that GED? Alex would mutter, bumping Blaze hard with his shoulder. *What an idiot.*

He'd been an idiot not to protest when he'd been arrested, but after the quick trial, where his parents testified against him, he'd gone quietly into shock and let himself be fingerprinted, strip-searched, and hauled off to Wyoming Correctional.

When he'd attempted to call home on the prison landline during phone time, most of the time, nobody answered. That was because there was a recorded message that the phone call was coming from the state prison and his family was totally within their rights to refuse the call.

When Mom or Pop or Alex *did* answer, the phone call was terse, and Blaze always seemed to be in the wrong, with Alex, the innocent victim.

Typically, Blaze was turned down flat any time he asked them to come visit him, that or they ignored the question completely. But then, the Butterworths were good at ignoring what they did not want to acknowledge. Like the law, or what was right, or even the common decency to visit him. The shock of their betrayal made him feel numb, like he'd been pounded to the ground and simply left there to wilt in a pool of his own blood.

Now, though, he was getting out of prison, which would make the intense interview he'd had with the parole board worth it. The copious application paperwork for the Farthingdale Valley New Start program, had been worth it, too, along with the nerve-racking Zoom call he'd had with a guy called Leland Tate, who seemed to run the program, and who had an I'm-in-charge voice without even trying.

Blaze had gotten into the program by the skin of his teeth, it felt like, and he was pretty sure Mr. Tate hadn't exactly believed Blaze when he'd explained that the drug charges against him were false.

Who cared about that? Getting into the program would get him out of prison six months early, which would give him a chance at a new life, a new everything. He knew he wouldn't mind doing chores, taking care of horses, building paths, or doing whatever was needed if it would get him out from behind bars.

There'd been a week-long delay, however, in getting him transferred to the valley, for reasons nobody in the prison administration, including the warden, took the time to explain to him. But, of all people, Leland Tate took the time to call and explain to Blaze about the issue with the contractors not finishing in time, something about problems with the outbuilding for the kitchen, the plumbing snafu in the bathroom facilities, the platform for the tent for the dining hall that needed leveling, and on he went, so many details that Blaze had lost track.

Mr. Tate had seemed very involved in the explanation at any rate, and the whole thing sounded much more like summer camp than it probably was.

Blaze had never been to summer camp, but he knew that whatever the program had to offer, it would be a damn sight better than Wyoming Correctional. Once he was out from behind prison walls, maybe someone from his family would talk to him or even visit him at the camp, because family visits were allowed, weren't they? Or maybe they were forbidden, Blaze couldn't remember.

Added to his anxiety about the delay, was that they'd moved his cellmate to a different cell, so each night he was alone. He would be processed out in a few days, but until then, he was at risk each night.

Alone, he would be pretty defenseless against what was sure to come his way.

A pair of inmates on level two had somehow finagled the system or bribed a guard and had gotten hold of the master key to the cells. It couldn't be believed, something out of a black and white prison film, but there it was. The inmates liked to go into a cell where one guy was sleeping alone, and mess it up, taking what they wanted, maybe even attacking the guy inside, assaulting him, raping him.

Blaze had been smart not to sashay through the break room or the dining hall or even the yard and brag about his upcoming parole or the summer camp-like setting he was about to step into. He also knew better than to announce at dinnertime that he was alone in his cell every night.

Maybe he'd get lucky and the two goons would not know how alone he was. By the time they did figure out where he was, in a cell by himself, he'd be long gone.

Every night, what once seemed a well-dodged threat was now one night closer. If he didn't get to pack up his meager belongings in a black trash bag, if he didn't get to step into the white van with the prison's logo on the side, like, *tomorrow*, then he risked being mashed to pieces come the bedtime.

The little rape gang didn't have a proper name, so Blaze had always thought of them as the chance that was coming his way. Not a good one, for sure, and one he wanted to avoid at all costs.

Each night, he tried to keep his eyes open all night, all the way till morning, especially the night after they told him that yes, tomorrow he would be out of there. But that night, he heard footsteps in the corridor outside his cell.

He sat up in bed, eyes glued to the long window in his door, beyond which the half light from the corridor glowed. Sure enough, he heard the large turnkey in the lock, and the long bolt being pulled back.

When the door opened, the two goons silhouetted against the light, he was on his feet. But barefooted, wearing only boxers and a t-shirt, he could not fend them off and found himself smashed against the wall, then bent over by one goon as the other rifled through his meagre shelf of stuff.

"No commissary credits?" the goon going through his stuff asked. "No gum?"

"Gum?" asked Blaze, shrieking the word, not caring if he was loud enough for everyone to hear, including any guards who might be patrolling at that end of the cell block on level two. "Gum? You broke in here hoping to find gum? Are you that fucking stupid?"

With a growl, the second goon pulled him up straight, smacked him hard, then shoved him onto the lower bunk. Wincing, Blaze couldn't see the guy's face, but he saw the motion where his hands went to the snap on his prison-issued cotton pants. Because yes, for some reason, for this pair of dickheads, gum and rape went hand in hand.

The guy was on top of him, tearing at the elastic waistband of Blaze's boxers. Then, in a blaze of overhead light, he was gone, and there were two guards at the door. They made short work of the two gum assassins and, after giving Blaze a once over to make sure he wasn't bleeding from his ass, shut and locked his prison door, and switched off the overhead light from outside.

He was left in the dark, stifling a small shriek as he tried to breathe slower and then more slowly still. If that was it, he'd gotten off lucky. All he had to do was stay in one piece until morning.

Then suddenly it *was* morning. Blinking against the overhead lights as they came on, for a long minute, Blaze didn't know why his left eye hurt, or why his lower lip was split open, tasting tender and hurt. Then he remembered and vowed he'd just keep his mouth shut. Tell the release officer that he'd bumped into a wall, or whatever it took to get his exit papers signed.

He shaved as best he could around his sore jaw, and dressed, wincing when his left side screamed at him to stop.

Stepping outside his cell when the door opened, he stood for the daily count, and pretended like it was an ordinary day, rather than one where he was leaving prison, though whether to something better remained to be seen.

He looked up the line and saw that a lot of guys were looking at him. Even the banged-up guy just two cells down who'd run afoul of the rape gang a few days ago was looking at him like he knew something about Blaze. Well, they could ask him what had happened to him all they liked. As far as he was concerned, nothing had happened.

He staggered into breakfast with his block mates, ate the dull instant oatmeal and dull powdered milk, the water-thin orange juice, and had just decided not to eat the banana, which was too brown, when one of the guards tapped him on the shoulder and told him to stand up.

He got looks of sympathy, because it looked like he was being hauled into the warden's office for a good ass kicking. On the inside, he was doing fist pumps and hollering for joy, feeling like he was on top of the biggest Ferris wheel in the world and it had just stopped. Legs dangling, he could look out over the carnival, the festive smells and sounds rising up at him, and knew he was going to make it. He wouldn't let himself doubt that Farthingdale Valley would be more like summer camp than prison.

He moved patiently through the checkout process, which included receiving a black plastic bag to throw his things into. Then he was hauled into the medical office to be given a once over, after which he was finally able to get his wallet back, though his driver's license was out of date. They also gave him his duly received gate money, a whopping fifty dollars, which, on its own, couldn't do much for him.

A guard escorted him and three other guys out the front gate, waved, and then shut the gate behind them. For a moment, Blaze just stood there blinking up at a sun that wasn't banked on all four sides by a high cement wall topped with razor wire.

Then he looked at the three guys.

"You guys going to Farthingdale Valley?" he asked.

They all said yes, though they looked as uncertain as he felt.

Who cared about them anyway. When the van arrived, he would shine like a blaze of light, and lay on the charm. Then, while he sweet-talked his way through the summer, he could hold on to the hope that when summer was over and, certificate, resume, and recommendation letter in hand, he could make a new life for himself.

Or maybe he'd return to the Butterworth trailer, to follow the carnival calendar, and in the winter, help Pop with the driveway scam. He just had to decide which way his life was going to go, and he had five, maybe six months, to do it.

CHAPTER 2
GABE

The inaction caused by waiting for the prison van to arrive unsettled Gabe to the point where he got up to pace the tent, which was bigger than any army tent he'd ever slept in and about five times as comfortable. After five trips to each end of the tent, he sat down again and looked around him at his new life.

In outrageous luxury, the tent rested on the wooden platform, keeping it out of any dampness on the ground. The platform extended beyond the outside of the tent to provide a little uncovered front porch, though there was a canvas fly that could be put up as shade if you wanted to sit out there and not get scorched by the sun. As well, a wood rail on either side provided a place to lay wet towels or to hang wet boots from or anything that needed drying off.

Over the top of the tent was a cream-colored rain fly, and beneath, the tent itself was made of the newest, sturdiest pale green canvas that Gabe had ever seen. Inside were two cots, two little shelves, and there was a box under each bed, where Gabe had stored clothes and gear that wouldn't fit on the shelves. The cot on the other side of the tent would go unclaimed, as all the team leaders had tents to themselves, which was nice.

A flashlight had been provided, as well as, at Gabe's special request, a Coleman lantern, a box of string mantles and matches, and two quart-sized bottles of kerosene. There was an overhead light, and a power strip where he could charge his cellphone or his laptop.

To say he was sitting in the lap of luxury in the middle of the woods was an understatement, and he was on the verge of not regretting that he'd let Jasper, his old buddy from the army, talk him into signing up to be the first team lead in the ranch's new ex-con program.

At the end of the summer, Gabe would receive a five-thousand-dollar bonus along with a guaranteed job as a ranch hand for the next summer season, and all the benefits that came with it. In the winter, he'd probably go up to Greeley to work at the meat-packing plant again, as they promised him he could come back and work for them after the summer season was over.

This pretty much cemented the next twelve months of his life, which was both a blessing and a curse. He was all set for the next year but he also couldn't go anywhere else, as it would be rude, not to mention stupid, to up and leave such a sure thing.

Then again, he'd be working a whole summer alongside men who had made mistakes big enough to put them behind bars, and for whom doing grunt work to help complete a fancy resort for rich people had been their best option.

All of this felt like a very long way from his Kentucky coal-mining heritage, and the family that had rejected him because he'd chosen a different path for himself by joining the army. Marching in lines while wearing the uniform had seemed a much better prospect than taking a metal elevator into the depths of the earth every day, at any rate.

His first summer underground had been eye opening, to say the least, and the small cave-in that had kept them in the dark for seventy-two hours, while not a disaster, as no lives were lost, had scared the crap out of him. He'd never gone back, and his family had never forgiven him, seeing his choices as a rejection of their entire way of life. Still, even if he'd always be alone, on his own in the world, the life he had chosen was already better than the one he'd left behind.

His cellphone rang, and he picked it up from the shelf and clicked the answer button. The number was Jasper's, but the voice was coming in tinny, so he stepped out of his tent and went behind to the slope behind the row of tents, where the signal was better.

"Hey, my friend," said Jasper, and Gabe could hear him smiling. "You settling in?"

"Almost," said Gabe, a responding smile rising inside of him. "I feel like I'm at the Ritz or something. It's so fancy."

"Leland knows how to set it up to keep the cash rolling in," said Jasper. "But you were thinking of backing out. That still happening?"

"I'm just worried about doing right by these guys." Gabe rubbed his jaw, and looked out over the valley, the sparkling blue lake, the pine trees through which only slices of green and cream tents could be seen. Beyond the trees, though he couldn't see it from where he stood in front of his tent, was the jaw-dropping majesty of Guipago Ridge. "I have the best of intentions, but what if I'm not the right man for the job? What if somebody else could do a better job? Like Quint."

"Quint is no good around ex-cons," said Jasper, and he probably knew what he was talking about, since Ellis, his assistant, was an ex-con who had come to the ranch to do his parole. "He's got no patience for anyone that fails to live up—I mean, don't get me wrong, Quint's a good guy. But Leland chose you to be the first team lead in this program, 'cause he knows you're the only one who can start this thing off right. Right?"

"I guess so."

"Trust yourself," said Jasper, and Gabe could almost hear him nodding. "Do your best and you can't go wrong. Besides," Jasper added. "I didn't have any training when Ellis arrived, and you do. You've got this. So stop doubting yourself before you've even begun."

"Okay."

They said their goodbyes and hung up, and Gabe felt a little better, more bolstered by Jasper's cheerful talk than he could have expected.

Besides, he would still get to work with horses, because in addition to showing ex-cons how to be lumberjacks, he'd get to teach them how to be cowboys.

When he'd come to the guest ranch at the beginning of the prior season, his experience around horses was exactly nil. But with good coaching from his fellow ranch hands, he'd come to love any part of his job where he got to be around horses, grooming, saddling, anything where he could look into their sweet, long-lashed eyes and kiss their soft noses and, quite simply, shower them with all the affection in his heart, affection that had no place else to go.

Leland Tate had purchased around two hundred horses from a rancher who'd been wiped out by last summer's flood. The guest ranch, Farthingdale Ranch, would be able to make good use of about a quarter of that amount, and the rest would be sold to other ranches, or families, or to petting zoos, depending on their condition and training.

Which made Gabe feel pretty lucky, all things told, because he'd get that five-thousand-dollar bonus, have a promise of a job the following summer, *and* still work with horses. Which might even arrive as early as next week, if he was lucky.

When he'd worked at Farthingdale Guest Ranch, he'd lived in the staff quarters tucked up against the slope of the hill, and while he'd had a room to himself, he was pretty much shoulder to shoulder with cowboys and ranch hands and cleaning staff all day long. Now he was out in the woods with the fresh air all around, the dappled sunlight coming through the trees and not a bear in sight.

Not that he was worried about bears at all, though the camp was close enough to the mountains and far enough from the edges of civilization for wildlife wandering into the camp to be a very certain prospect. He had a hatchet tucked away in his bookshelf, but that was because Jasper had given it to him as a gift to remind him of his dream to one day own a small cattle ranch. *You'll need to get up at the ass-crack of dawn to chop at the ice in those water troughs you'll own one day,* Jasper had said as Gabe had unwrapped the gift.

Gabe had been unable to say thank you enough, and he appreciated the gesture because the dream was still somewhat new, and it was nice having tangible evidence of it. For now, all he had to do was be patient while he waited for the prison van to arrive.

That was the other thing. He'd be dealing with prisoners all summer, rather than ranch hands and wranglers and guests. He knew he'd be leading ex-cons into better lives, but, really, he had no idea what he was getting into, even after the two-week training at Wyoming Correctional.

Since the prison was eighty-eight miles and an almost two-hour drive from the ranch, he had stayed at the Holiday Inn at the edge of Torrington for his training. Not only was it only five miles away from the prison, the breakfasts were excellent and the sheets were soft, and he'd somehow ended up at the end of the top floor, all on his own, a bit of peace and quiet he'd enjoyed, even though it had made him feel alone.

Would he ever get to that state where he felt neither crowded nor alone? He had no idea, but as he heard the honking coming from the tree-free area in front of the mess tent, he stood up.

This was it. Five thousand dollars and an interesting summer coming right up.

The walk from his tent to the mess tent was short, but the path hadn't yet been cleared, so he had to wade through the tall, wild grasses and duck beneath pine trees and newly sprouted Aspen buds till he reached the tent and followed along the green canvas wall to the gravel parking lot that looked scraggly amongst the trees.

Leland Tate, the guest ranch's foreman, was just pulling up in a silver four-door truck with coal black tires and shiny chrome bumpers. Leland tipped his finger to his hat as he saw Gabe coming over to him, then turned his attention to the white van with the prison logo on the side that was just pulling into the parking lot alongside the truck.

"Hey, Leland," said Gabe with a nod of greeting.

"Hey there, Gabe," said Leland in return, straightening his shoulders and adjusting his cowboy hat in preparation for the new arrivals.

Gabe could see a driver and a guard and four rough-edged guys as they tumbled out of the van. There wasn't a handcuff in sight, not even a zip tie that had been used in an emergency. Which indicated to him that not one of the ex-cons had caused any trouble on their journey from Wyoming Correctional.

Well, that made sense, as the first batch of parolees this first week of the program, a warming-up period of sorts, had been personally vetted by Leland Tate. There wouldn't be any guy that had been involved with violent crimes. Just some shop-lifting, pickpocketing, hubcap stealing, maybe a little breaking and entering. No injuries or deaths had been caused by these crimes, so the criminals, while not exactly tame, would be easier to handle.

Not that *handle* was the word he was supposed to use. His two-week training had taught him that much. And also that he needed to be objective about any interaction, to be alert to sudden changes in mood or tone, and to never turn his back on a parolee, at least until they'd proven themselves trustworthy.

As for now, Gabe trusted Leland, and made himself shake off a sudden ruff of nerves that settled on his shoulders. He stepped up to the van, the driver, the guard, and the four men, who were standing with sloped shoulders as if they assumed that this was the type of work camp where they'd be forced into a chain gang, forced to wear a striped prison uniform, forced to work under a blazing hot sun for days on end.

Well, none of that was going to happen, and Wyoming was chilly and a bit rainy, still, in mid-May, as if hanging on with clawed hands to the ferocity of the winter that had just passed. Too chilly for a blazing hot sun, at any rate, though give it a few days and Gabe knew from experience that it would get a lot warmer in the valley, sometimes unexpectedly.

"Hello," said Gabe. He shook the driver's hand and the guard's, then took the clipboard the guard was holding out. "What's this?" Scanning it, he realized it was a release form, handing the parolees over to the project, and releasing the prison staff of all responsibility. "Oh, that's for him." Gabe gestured to Leland, who put up both hands.

"I'd say these are your men," said Leland, smoothly, shaking the guard's hand and then the driver's. "Who has a pen?"

It felt a bit surreal to sign the release form, though he enjoyed the

THE COWBOY AND THE RASCAL

weight of responsibility he felt settling around his shoulders. Leland trusted him, and Gabe was going to do his best to live up to that trust.

"How was the drive?" asked Leland.

"Uneventful," said the guard, as though, with someone like him, someone tough and experienced, that was purely to be expected.

Gabe knew that the previous year, when the ranch had hosted a single ex-con to test the waters, they'd gotten some delicious tax breaks. At the same time, the parolee, Ellis, had arrived battered and shaken from the abuse he'd suffered from the guard on the drive to the ranch.

Leland had been furious and there had been some shouting, it was said, from behind the closed door of his office. A door that was never closed, as everyone knew, which indicated how serious the situation and how mad Leland had been.

That hadn't happened this time, obviously. Still, the ex-cons, not at all relaxed, stood in a row, shoulder to shoulder, hunched, waiting, as stiff as if they were each nailed to their spots.

"Gentlemen," said Leland, turning to face the parolees. "I'm Leland Tate, foreman at Farthingdale Guest Ranch. You've all met me before, when you interviewed with me. At that time, we talked about the benefits of the program and what I'm trying to accomplish here. Let me now introduce you to your personal foreman—"

Leland paused, wrinkling his brow as though he was truly confused about the term. In reality, Gabe and Leland had agreed that the guy in charge would be called the team lead, which sounded much more inclusive and democratic than foreman. This little discussion about it, totally practiced beforehand, would hopefully help to create an environment where the parolees felt they could actually engage in the process of their own rehabilitation, rather than just following orders and clocking in hours.

"Team lead," said Gabe. "I prefer to be called team lead."

"Team lead," said Leland with a firm nod. "Gabe Westwell is your team lead for the next two weeks while the program gets underway. In about two weeks, there will be more parolees arriving, and another team lead. At that point, you might get moved, or ask to be moved to a different team, but until then, I'd like you to look to Gabe for direction, instruction, advice, and a listening ear. He'll teach you everything he knows, and it'll behoove you to pay attention. Gabe," said Leland with another tap to his hat in a kind of relaxed salute. "I present you your team. Good day, gentlemen."

Gabe watched Leland for about five seconds before turning his attention to his new team. For the majority of them, the word *behoove* had no meaning, but the guy on the end with dark hair and a split lip was smirking at Gabe as if to say, *That went right over their heads.*

Gabe dismissed the smirk, not giving it any more of his attention as he turned his gaze to the guards as Leland got in his truck and drove sedately away. He felt a rush of energy as he mentally stepped up to the plate, prepared to give the program his best.

"Do they have any gear?" asked Gabe, putting his attention fully on the guard.

"It's in the back." The driver waved Gabe closer, turning to unlock the back of the van.

Gabe gestured to the parolees to come closer, knowing that if he were in their shoes, he'd want to grab his own gear.

"Get your stuff and we'll head into the mess tent for a quick meeting," he said to the parolees.

He expected them to dawdle, but they hopped to, getting their stuff, a variety of duffle bags and backpacks and, sadly, one black garbage bag.

He hadn't read each man's file yet, as he wanted to make his own impression, a clean slate to start new relationships with. However, he had looked at each man's photograph and associated that with their names so he knew who was who, and had a name for each face—Kurt, Tom, Wayne, and Orlando—but he had no idea how they'd take to the kind of work they'd been assigned to.

The parolees in front of him in a line that stretched from the open back door of the van, all had their shoulders hunched as if they expected to get hollered at for lining up in the wrong place.

Part of this, perhaps, was from being in prison and having every moment of every waking day directed. Or it could be a bit of anxiety at being in a new place, a feeling Gabe well knew from his first days in the army, even his first days at the guest ranch. Well, he'd do what his old C.O. had done, and what his experience at the guest ranch had taught him: set the tone and be consistent about it.

"Thank you, guys," said Gabe to the driver and guard. "I'll take it from here."

For a brief moment, the guard and the driver looked like they wanted to stick around, like they expected to be backup for any inadequacies that Gabe had. Like they were sure he wasn't going to be as tough as he needed to be.

Gabe gave them a nod, a goodbye jerk of his chin, and walked toward the mess tent with a quick wave at the ex-cons, like he completely expected they would follow him.

"You're with me, guys," he said, turning his back on them for a second, just to see what would happen.

In the presence of the prison employees, who watched silently for a minute before clambering into the van, the ex-cons trotted obediently behind him, fearful under the prison employees' eyes or, perhaps, eager to leave prison life behind them, eager to start anew.

The green-canvas mess tent was built on a wooden platform like the housing tents, but lacked the outside wooden railing to hang things on to dry. It was roomy and long enough and wide enough to hold fifty people sitting at tables, with the buffet line at the far end, and the little library-slash-office area where the landline phone was up front and just to the left.

The mess tent was open at either end, allowing the crisp mid-May breeze to slide through, flapping the rain fly, twirling the ends of ties. With only the five of them, the mess tent felt quite roomy. The parolees stood like tent pegs in the midst of six ten-person folding tables, looking a bit adrift as Gabe glanced at his clipboard.

"Have a seat," said Gabe, pointing to the nearest table. "We're going to have a quick meeting, a bit of a tour, then I'll take you to your tents, where you can unpack your stuff and get squared away. When you hear the bell clanging, come to the mess tent here, and you'll get some dinner."

"What's for dinner?" asked Kurt, blurting the question.

"If you could raise your hand to ask questions when we're in a meeting like this, I'd much appreciate it," said Gabe. He didn't answer the question, but merely waited while the men looked at each other as if in reading each other they could understand where they stood with him.

Kurt remained silent, but Tom raised his hand.

"Yes, Tom," said Gabe, gesturing at him.

"What's for dinner?" asked Tom, amiably enough, though perhaps he was laughing at Gabe at the same time, testing the waters.

"Typically, they post that information on a little stand in front of the tent—and the menu changes every day—but the cooks are still gearing up. Today we are having tacos with all the fixings, and cinnamon sugar churros for dessert."

The men eyed each other again, and Gabe knew he'd not made the meal sound very exciting. But food was food, and, besides, he knew that what they would be receiving at the hands of cooks who proved their mettle at a high-end guest ranch would be a far cry from what they were used to in prison.

"Let's introduce ourselves, or rather, since you might all know each other, I'll introduce myself. I'm Gabe Westwell." Gabe pressed his thumb in the middle of his breastbone. "That's short for Gabriele, but I prefer Gabe. And you're Kurt, Tom, Wayne, and Orlando." Gabe pointed to each one in turn.

"Blaze," said Orlando, unexpectedly.

"Excuse me?" asked Gabe.

Blaze shook his head and raised his hand, like he was trying to be the most well-behaved student in class.

"I don't go by Orlando," he said. "I mean, my parents thought it was funny to name their sons after actual locations, but me and my brother didn't. That's why he goes by Alex instead of Alexandria, and I go by Blaze. I did go by Landry when I was a kid, but then I changed it."

The little speech came at Gabe like a freshet of wind and he almost laughed at the eagerness of the patter.

"That's a lot of names," said Gabe, aiming for lightness. "How many do you have?"

"As many as I need," said Blaze, and in that moment he sounded a tad defensive, as if he expected Gabe was going to tell him that he could only have one name at a time.

"If you prefer Blaze," said Gabe, speaking with more seriousness now. "Then Blaze it is." Then he said, "Let me go over the rules first, and then we'll take that tour."

The four men looked up at Gabe, the traces of prison living making their faces a little ragged, their postures stiff, their expressions wary.

Tom was distracted by the phone, as he kept looking at the old-fashioned landline at the six foot long table near the entrance to the tent. Kurt kept looking at the far end of the tent, where the skeleton of the buffet was sitting silently in place. Wayne was biting his nails to the quick, almost mumbling to himself while he did it.

As for Blaze, he was slumped with his hands dangling between his thighs, as if he didn't quite know what to do with them, and staring at his faded orange canvas slip-on sneakers that looked uncomfortable as well as unstable.

In fact, all the men were wearing clothes that looked as though they'd been donated and not something they'd pick out for themselves. Well, Gabe had the answer for that.

"In your tents you'll find new gear, including boots and hats, and anything you need. Maddy—she's the admin for the guest ranch—she's got your sizes and ordered everything, but if something doesn't fit, just let me know around dinnertime and we'll get you something that does."

He waited for acknowledgement or agreement or something, but it never came. Which, as might be expected, was due to the training, or rather conditioning, they received in prison. Theirs was not to wonder or question, but only to follow orders.

It was up to him, then, to make them understand that yes, they needed to follow orders, but that did not mean they couldn't ask questions, or make suggestions, or even object, when the occasion warranted it.

"I know this is all new," he said, keeping his voice quiet. "But you've done your time, and now you have a shot at a new chance, a new beginning. It might take a while for you to adjust, but this program is designed to help you reenter society with some skills and experience in your pocket."

"Is it true—" Tom stopped and raised his hand, then, when Gabe nodded at him, he spoke. "Is it true we get paperwork at the end of it to show we've done the work?"

"It's true, Tom," said Gabe. "Certificate of completion, resume, job placement assistance—"

"Do we get any money?" asked Kurt, blurting again.

"Excuse me, Kurt?" asked Gabe, arching a brow. Then he waited and saw Tom giving Kurt a good hard shove with his elbow.

Kurt raised his hand, scowling as if begrudging the whole exchange.

"Yes, Kurt."

"Do we get any money?" asked Kurt, his voice surly and testing.

"Yes, you do," said Gabe. "I'm not sure of the rate, but you do get paid. You won't be able to buy a mansion with it, but it's probably more than you have in your bank account or pockets at the moment."

Maybe he shouldn't have come across as chiding them or pulling them low, but he knew that this program wasn't like others he'd read about during his two-week training period, and then on his own, while waiting for the program to start. The way the program had been set up, courtesy of Leland, was better than the others, in that the men were going to be treated humanely, comfortably housed, and well fed.

"You are totally in your rights to leave at any time and do your parole a different way, but I think you'll find that while Farthingdale Valley is going to require hard work from all of us, me included—"

Gabe stopped, wishing he didn't sound so much like an out-of-touch CEO or a commanding officer of a battalion who simply had no idea what it was like to be in the trenches.

"It's a good program," he said simply, now. "And I know you won't regret having signed up for it. Now, shall we go over the rules?"

The four men nodded at him and Gabe did his best to keep it short, as the men were already starting to fidget. That is, except for Blaze, who was staring over Gabe's shoulder into the middle distance, as if he was really, really puzzled to find himself where he was.

CHAPTER 3
BLAZE

The drive in the white van from Wyoming Correctional to Farthingdale Valley took about two hours, though, it must be admitted, the driver took his sweet time, and used his turn signal obsessively until the constant click-click-click noise pounded its way into Blaze's head. He didn't usually get headaches, but he had one now and it was a doozy, a needle going right through the center of his forehead.

There was no sense asking the driver or the guard if they could pull over and fetch Blaze an aspirin or two, because he'd get the same response if he'd still been in prison. Headache? *Suffer.* Splinter? *Pull it out with your teeth.* Gouge in your thigh from a badly sharpened shiv? *Walk it off.*

Prison was that way and though, through the process of applying for the program, Blaze was led to believe that he was stepping into a glorious opportunity, his almost two years in prison had taught him that any glow of goodness was a false, tin-edged one, and even if the whole world proclaimed that ex-cons—or rather *parolees*, as they were supposed to call themselves—might deserve a break, in truth, it was agreed that they didn't deserve very good ones.

Blaze knew he was headed for bad things, his former optimism fading under the reality of being in a van headed to a future that felt completely out of his control. He still had a split lip and half a black eye, and his ribs hurt like hell, so he knew about bad things.

The van trundled through a small town, which in the middle of the afternoon, looked sleepy and quiet, but he and his fellow parolees looked through the rectangular windows, trying to catch glimpses of what was there. The rumor was that *trips into town* were on the agenda if they got their work done. If they behaved themselves. If.

A lot of how well the summer would go probably depended on how well they all got along. He'd not met Tom, Wayne, or Kurt before they'd all boarded the van, so while they seemed like regular guys, he really had no idea.

Kurt kind of looked like a skinhead, though if he had been, Leland Tate probably wouldn't have accepted him into the program. Wayne was a short, stocky guy, a little red in the face, who was biting on a hangnail and looking out the window as though he wished he was miles away. Tom was tall and quiet, and rubbed his wrists for the entire drive, as if trying to shake off the ghosts of handcuffs past.

"Another mile to the ranch and then a mile after that to the compound," announced the prison guard, who was sitting up front in the passenger seat as if he'd not a care in the world, though he had his hand on his side-arm, due to the fact that not one of the parolees was wearing handcuffs.

At any moment, they could leap and attack and stop the van and make brave escapes. But why? They all knew better, at least Blaze did, because the work camp was unguarded. Why hijack a prison van when, once they reached their destination, they could just leave whenever they liked?

There had to be a trick to this because it didn't sound right. Most chain gangs and work programs he'd ever heard of were highly guarded to make sure the cons did what they were told to, and at night, they were taken back by van or bus to the prison.

The situation he was headed to, currently, was described so much differently, he was sure the whole thing was a lie. A big, fat, greasy lie that he would have to stomach, just like he'd stomached the last two years of badly cooked, greasy, stringy, expired food in the prison cafeteria. Nastiness went with the territory, and when you had the ex-con label, you had it for life, so sure as heck nothing was going to change, no matter what the paperwork said. No matter what Mr. Tate had told him.

You'll be working in a peaceful, green valley, Mr. Tate had said. *You'll be given honest work to do and get three squares a day. You'll be able to start a new life.*

Lie upon lie, obviously.

When the van pulled up to a metal, green-painted gate, with an arched sign above that said *Farthingdale Ranch*, the guard got out, unlatched it, and stayed out while the van pulled through. Then he latched the gate and hopped back in the van.

They continued rolling along the curving dirt road for another mile that took them over a little hillock, dappled with trees, then over a stone bridge that arched over a wide, rushing stream. The driver took a left onto a dirt track that led the van up the slope to a wide grassy area where a new-looking wood cabin stood, all by its lonesome.

The van seemed to pause on the top of the hill. There was no one and nothing for miles, it seemed, just the waving summer-green grasses that were about hip high, beyond which there was a line of thick trees, mostly pine, that stretched all the way to the foothills. They were in the middle of nowhere, and still the van kept going. That was, until the driver steered to the left around a clump of tall green pine trees, and then to the right, and suddenly the nose of the van was headed downward.

"Keep it slow," said the guard. "Tate said it's almost a five percent grade here for a bit."

"Got it," said the driver.

The road was dirt and gravel, not paved, which meant that the van's wheels slid and skidded with stomach-churning suddenness whenever the driver put on the brakes. The road went for a long loop to the east, the trees thick on either side, still mostly pine, green and dark, keeping the van in cool shadow.

At the first turning, Blaze looked up and spotted a long valley, lush and wide and sloped at the sides, with green pine trees, and crisp-leaved cottonwoods leading down to a silky green, grassy valley bottom. He had a glimpse of a slice of shining blue that must be a river and then the trees closed in again, just as he gasped in a breath.

Beautiful was the only way to describe it, but he could not believe that it wouldn't get scary and rough and mean the second the van stopped and the driver told them *this is it.*

After a good ten minutes of consistently going downhill through the trees, the van broke out from the shadows into a sunlit area that turned out to be the only wide, clear space that Blaze could see through the van's windows. Everywhere he looked, he saw more trees, and more after that, until he was almost dizzy with it.

Wyoming Correctional was set on a flat area, surrounded by bare ground for miles around, it seemed, devoid of trees and any green thing, perhaps designed as a means of control, to leave the eyes hungry, for who would want to step into all the nothingness that surrounded the prison? Not him, that's who.

Someone touched his shoulder, and Blaze turned to look the other way and found himself staring at a large green canvas tent among the trees and realized that *this was it.* They'd arrived, and now his nightmares could all come true.

The driver and the guard got out and, on cue, all the parolees got out, as well. Blaze trailed behind so that he wouldn't be the first target that whoever was taking charge of them would see. That would give him time to dodge if need be or step sideways to avoid whatever nastiness was coming.

There were two men waiting for the van. One man, Blaze recognized as Leland Tate, whom he'd met on that one Zoom call.

In person, Leland was even more imposing than he'd been on the screen of the ancient laptop Blaze had been given to use for the purpose of the interview. Leland was tall and rugged looking, with intense eyes and an unsmiling mouth, like he was giving them all the once-over, like he had a list of criteria for each of them and each one of them had failed to muster up. Or maybe that was just the sunlight reflecting off his hard, blue eyes beneath the brim of his cowboy hat.

As for the other guy, Blaze had no idea who he was. One of Leland's henchmen, maybe, standing hard by his boss to deliver painful backup to whatever directive Leland handed out that he'd determined wasn't being followed fast enough.

Blaze waited, rocking back and forth in his thin sneakers while the usual greetings were exchanged between the man and the two prison staff, and the usual clipboard was handed over, assigning responsibility of them to Leland. Who, after a little speech, promptly handed over that responsibility to his henchman, Gabe Westwell.

"Thank you, Leland," said Gabe as an almost invisible veil of authority settled around him.

There was a bit of a pause as Gabe watched Leland drive away in his shiny silver truck, then he turned to look at Blaze and his pals.

"Get your stuff and we'll head into the mess tent for a quick meeting," said Gabe.

All of them hurried to do so, and then they lined up, because that was what you were taught to do in prison. Do the task, whatever it was, and then line up to be counted.

Blaze grabbed his black garbage bag, which was new, at least, and stood in line and waited, watchful like a stray cat at night, realizing that other than the guard, the driver, and Gabe, there was no security officer.

Then, without much preamble, Gabe dismissed both of the prison staff, like he wasn't at all concerned that he'd be left alone with four ex-cons without another human to assist him if things went sideways. So either he was oblivious or he knew he could overpower them all, four ex-cons with one blow.

And of course, right away, Gabe was looking them over with hard blue eyes, up and down, considering, taking the measure of each of them. As to whether he'd read all their files cover to cover, that was another issue. Blaze didn't know so he could only gather a few ideas to respond to the inevitable *So you're the drug dealer, eh?* questions that were likely to come his way.

As with anyone he met, Blaze did his best to catch up with the transfer of power, and updated his list of appropriate topics with which to woo his new overseer, ways to entertain that would deflect any unwanted attention.

All of Blaze's attention was now focused on Gabe, who was one of those guys who would have stood out in the prison yard, not as a victim, but as a top dog. He was the kind of guy who had hard muscles pushing at the seams of his shirt, but those muscles were from real work.

In the yard, had Blaze access to any cash, he would have paid a guy like this for protection, or even merely a glance in his direction, a gesture of inclusion that Blaze could sit with a powerful gang at lunch time, and then carry a cloak of *do-not-touch* around his shoulders for a good length of time afterward. Not that Blaze had lacked friends inside the prison walls, but those friendships were bought with Blaze's quick patter, flirty comments, veiled promises of commitment—all of which were gossamer thin and destined to fade at the first sign of adversity.

Not that Gabe looked like he couldn't resist all comers when tested, because he was tough all over. His dark hair was close cropped along the sides, all work and no play, but along the top, it somehow became a messy sprawl across his forehead, like a disarming trick meant to fool his opponents into thinking he was soft.

But he wasn't. His blue eyes, flinty and hard, looked them over much the way Leland's had, and found them coming up short, obviously. Which was too bad, really, because he had a nice smile, which he used on them all as if to gentle the moment when the real torture would begin.

"Come on inside and have a seat, guys," he said, then led the four men into the nearest green tent.

Gabe delivered a brief speech about something, but Blaze could hardly pay attention as he tried to absorb his surroundings as quickly as possible, feeling as though he might want to case the joint or perhaps just need a speedy exit. There came some brief talk about dinner and rotating menus, and then Gabe read off their names and pointed to each one in turn.

At which point, Blaze raised his hand, which seemed to be an issue in this place.

"Blaze," he said.

"Excuse me?" asked Gabe, his eyebrows going up.

"My name is Blaze," he said, smiling his best, friendliest smile. "I don't go by Orlando. I mean, my parents thought it was funny to name their sons after actual locations, but me and my brother didn't. That's why he goes by Alex instead of Alexandria, and I go by Blaze. I did go by Landry when I was a kid, but then I changed it."

"That's a lot of names," said Gabe, writing down a note on his clipboard with quite a serious turn to his mouth. "How many do you have?"

"As many as I need," Blaze said, meaning it as a joke, except now, instead of being a possible maybe, it was for sure that Gabe disliked him intensely and would be putting him on the worst work duty that could ever be imagined.

Blaze stared down at his prison-issued slip-on sneakers, mentally rocking a bit back and forth to distract himself, counting down the seconds until he was yanked to his feet or sent to the laundry, all his fears reeling upward through his skin, making him hot under his arms and on the lower part of his back.

"If you prefer Blaze," said Gabe. "Then Blaze, it is. Now, shall we go over the rules?"

Gabe's voice was reasonable and calm. At least *now* it was calm. *Soon* it would be raised. Soon the greasy, yucky bad stuff would start and Blaze would have two choices: run or submit.

"I see you've all noticed the landline over there in the office area." Gabe pointed, and they all looked. "There is only a table and one phone there now, but there will be a bookshelf with books, basic office supplies and that sort of thing, all of which is for your use."

"How long can we make phone calls for and when?" asked Tom, raising his hand at the same time he asked the question.

But Gabe didn't get mad. He just said, "Any time after dinner, and as for how long, that's up to you. We'd like to think you'd take into consideration your fellow parolees and keep your phone calls to a reasonable time, especially if there are men waiting in line behind you."

"That's a damn regular phone," said Kurt, without raising his hand. "Don't we get cellphones?"

"Raise your hand, next time, please," said Gabe. "Cellphone service is a bit spotty out here, hence the landline. But at the end of two weeks, if you've stuck with the program, you will receive an older model phone with six months prepaid service, courtesy of Wyoming Correctional's release support committee. At the end of the summer, we'll add another six months worth of prepaid service. How does that sound?"

Kurt seemed satisfied with this and settled into silence.

Gabe talked about when mealtimes were, how they were having tacos that night, how a bell would ring to call them to the mess tent. What the staff currently consisted of: two cooks and them, and that there'd be more parolees and team leads arriving in two weeks.

"We will have weekly group counseling sessions on Saturday afternoons, which we encourage you to go to, and individual counseling if you need it. Movie nights will be held in the mess tent on an as-needed or as-requested basis. And here are your shower tokens."

Gabe reached into his jeans pocket and pulled out four baggies, each with a name on it. Each baggie seemed to have a bunch of wooden disks and Blaze, for the life of him, couldn't figure out what they were, and he was usually very quick on the uptake.

"Sorry your baggie has the wrong name on it," said Gabe, smiling slightly as he handed Blaze his little baggie. "I can get a Sharpie and change that right quick."

Not smiling back, not even slightly, Blaze took the baggie and looked at the contents, rumpling the baggie in his fingers to look at the wooden disks more closely. They were simple and thin, rough-hewn, with a black stamp of what looked like a shower head spouting six delicate streams of water.

"What are these?" asked Blaze. He raised his hand quickly. "What are these, sir?"

"It's just Gabe," said Gabe. "They're shower tokens for the next two weeks. We encourage you to take daily showers. Two weeks from now, we'll give you fourteen more tokens, but if you need more than that, just ask."

That didn't make any sense. Blaze looked at his fellow parolees and they all looked at him and seemed to be mentally shrugging. They could all do math. One token equaled one shower, sure. But the *if you need more* part was throwing all of them, except nobody wanted to question the boss man.

Except Tom, who, apparently, had brass balls, and was raising his hand slowly, like a brown snake.

"Yes, Tom."

"How long are we allowed to shower?"

"Well, that's up to you, but again, you might take into consideration your fellow parolee and whether your indulging in an hour-long shower might leave him short of enough hot water for his shower. Do you see?"

Pulling his lips tight against his teeth, Tom shook his head, and didn't seem willing to put himself in front of the line for questions any longer, a feeling for which Blaze did not blame him, not one little bit.

"But for how long?" asked Blaze, raising his hand at the same time, which seemed to be enough courtesy for Gabe, who shrugged.

"How long is enough?" he asked. "Some days twenty minutes is fine and other days an hour is not long enough. One token equals a thirty minute shower."

"Thirty *minutes*?" barked Kurt, obviously too overwrought at the idea that they might even consider showering for that long because he did not raise his hand. "You're fucking kidding me. *Thirty* minutes?"

At Wyoming Correctional, the limit on showers was five minutes, maximum, enough time to wash your head, your pits, your junk, and then rinse off. The idea of standing beneath a warm spray for twenty or even thirty whole minutes was like a bit of heaven and just as impossible to reach.

Prison showers were short and dangerous, as well as lukewarm, so maybe Gabe was spinning a tale to keep them docile. Or maybe nobody on the inside had dreamed about hot showers as much as Blaze had.

"The tokens are just so that we can monitor how much hot water gets used, on average. We only have propane to heat the water at present, though we hope to install solar soon and be a bit more off-grid." Gabe's brow furrowed as he looked at them each, one by one. "The tokens are just to help us keep track, you see. There are no restrictions on how many tokens you get, so you can shower morning and evening if you like."

So. Okay. Blaze's confusion had just been added to. He stood up and without raising his hand, said, "So you're telling me that not only can we take a half hour shower every day, we can take *two* of them, if we wanted to?"

He squinted hard at Gabe, feeling like he was talking from inside of an echo chamber of sorts, where each utterance, his or Gabe's, went through a confusion blender before being received by the other guy.

"That's what I'm saying. We just want to keep track, hence the tokens. That'll help us calculate how many showers get taken each day, which will let us know how much more propane for hot water we need to order and have delivered."

It could not be as simple as that; it simply could not be. Or maybe the surface generosity and sense of abundance was just that, a glossy cover-up for the shitstorm of abuse that was to follow.

CHAPTER 4
BLAZE

As Gabe led them out of the mess tent and into the lushness of the undergrowth once more, he was going over the rules, or guidelines, as he called them. Lights out was at ten, lunch was at noon, dinner was at five-thirty, and so on. Do the work assigned to you. Ask questions if you don't understand. No guns, no drugs, no smoking. No fighting. And if you leave the valley without permission during the first two weeks, you will be considered AWOL and your parole will have to be handled some other way.

Blaze understood those rules, as they were much like the ones in the prison, but Gabe's voice was low and calm, which threw him.

Gabe didn't sound mean, and he wasn't shouting like he was trying to wrestle control before any trouble broke out. Rather, he was quiet, and Blaze had to follow close with the group so he could hear Gabe, as it wouldn't do to fuck up so early in the game. You had to know the rules of the game to play it.

"Here is the supply building," said Gabe, pointing to a Quonset hut, which was next to the wooden kitchen building. The silver-gray curves of its roofline shone dully in the afternoon sunlight. It had a pair of double doors that reminded Blaze of barn doors. "And here is

JACKIE NORTH

the cook's tent, and the team leads' tents. The first tent along this row is mine, if you ever need me."

Gabe pointed along a row of green canvas tents nestled among a line of pine trees, which were so thick the tents could only be partially seen, their green edges blending in with the woods, the paler canvas strung overhead looking like casually draped cream-colored wings. Wooden rails along the sides almost disappeared into the branches of the pine trees.

"What's with all the fucking weeds?" asked Kurt, kicking at the dense grasses and weeds they were currently standing in. "Sorry," he said, when Gabe calmly turned to look at him. "Raising my hand. What's with all the fucking weeds?"

"Thank you for raising your hand," said Gabe. "That's what we're here for. My team will clear undergrowth so that paths can be created. We'll also cut down old trees and dead bushes, and use a wood chipper to make mulch out of all that."

"With chainsaws?" asked Wayne, raising his hand with a grin.

"And axes, hatchets, hacksaws, crosscut saws, even clippers. Whatever's necessary." Gabe smiled, seemingly at Wayne's eagerness at the idea of it. "Next week, we'll have a herd of horses coming through, so you'll be tasked with helping to take care of them."

"Cool." Wayne smiled in return.

Blaze looked at his hands. He needed his hands soft and supple for picking pockets, though really he was too old for that kind of task. Besides which, his mom had been pushing him all year to start a floating poker game so he could take the game anywhere the law wasn't and scalp the players for all they had. Except he wasn't so good at poker, and if his hands were wrecked, there was no way he could even take on something like that.

"Do we get gloves?" asked Blaze, raising his hand. Only to find Gabe's attention fully on him as they stood in the knee-high damp grass.

In prison, to have the kind of attention Gabe was giving him would be bad news. But here? Blaze didn't know, so he held real still and put on his best I'm-harmless-and-only-asking-questions face.

"And hats and sturdy boots, whatever you need," said Gabe. "Your tents are in among the trees over to our left," Gabe gestured behind him. "But first, let me show you where the facilities are."

They hiked again through the grass, going between two lush stands of trees. Amongst the trees on either side, Blaze glimpsed a few more green tents, but Gabe was striding on, so Blaze hurried to follow. The hems of his jeans were damp through and his thin sneakers were soaked by the time Gabe stopped at a fence line, newly built out of wood, that was just a tad taller than head height.

"Toilets on the right, and showers are on the left," said Gabe. "Come on in and take a look, and then I'll drop you at your tents, where you can try on your gear, put away your stuff, and settle in a bit."

They clustered behind Gabe as he went through the open doorway to what looked like a large shed, open to the air, with a slanted roof overhead and a carefully laid flagstone floor beneath. There were five porcelain sinks on one side. Then, on the other side, were five free-standing wooden structures that looked like outhouses. But when Gabe opened the door to the first one, the inside was a little more upmarket than Blaze had been anticipating.

There was a bench made of wood, but instead of a simple hole, there was a nice white toilet seat with a lid, and there were metal vents high on the slatted wooden walls. And, perhaps best of all, stacks of soft-looking toilet paper, still wrapped in plastic and of a brand much, much nicer than the prison used.

"We're on a compost system," said Gabe. "There are five stalls, so no waiting. Once we get going, perhaps toward the end of summer, we'll build five more of these on the far side of the compound. And over here—"

Gabe shut the wooden door and led them along the flagstone path to another large shed, which had five wooden structures, each one with a thin door, which Gabe opened. Behind the door was a dressing area with a cement slab for a floor, and a little blue and white striped curtain that led to a rustic shower.

Except, when Blaze looked closer, he realized that the shower head was a high-end, brushed nickel kind, which was supposed to make you feel that you were standing in a rainfall. Definitely pricey. And definitely part of some big fake, because while everything looked rustic, he was starting to see that beneath the surface, the facilities were anything but.

"They're like sheds," said Kurt with a hasty wave that was obviously meant to stand in for raising his hand. "How come they're not like regular showers?"

"Yeah," said Tom, following suit, looking up at the slanted roof to where, through the gap all the way around, could be seen trees and sky. "It's like we're outside. How come we gotta be outside all the time?"

"The purpose of the valley is to create a retreat," said Gabe. "Up the hill from us, on the other side of that slope, is the Farthingdale Guest Ranch. They're expanding into this valley to create a retreat for people who want to check out from their hectic lives. But instead of, as with the guest ranch, having them go on cattle drives and take horse riding lessons, they'll be slowing down, having meals in the mess tent, taking long walks along the paths that we'll create for them. Doing a little bird watching or canoeing on the lake. Stargazing from the ridge, once we get some lookout towers built. We had contractors get the job started. Our job this summer is to help finish the retreat, to shape it. In future summers, we think, we'll have parolees like yourselves come out and further develop the valley, and also do maintenance on the paths and structures."

"So you're going to exploit us 'cause we ain't got any other options." Kurt's chin jutted out in a mulish way.

Gabe paused, his dark gaze fully focused on Kurt in a way that made Blaze shiver. Gabe might seem easy-going but it was clear to see, at least to Blaze, that you wouldn't want to get on this guy's bad side cause he'd rip you a new one before you could blink, and he'd never say a word to warn you.

"Just to be clear, Kurt, and everyone," said Gabe. "You voluntarily signed up for this program. Your other alternatives were the military, or to try to make it on your own with a parole officer you would check in with once a week. You chose this."

Gabe looked at them each in turn.

"I know what you're thinking," he said. "These are rustic living conditions, and in your view they can't be much better than in prison, but I assure you they are. I could stand here all day and try to convince you of that, but keep in mind this one fact: once the retreat is up and running, rich folks from the city will pay good money to shower with a breeze around their ankles, or to sleep in a tent with the scent of pine all around them. So do me and yourself a favor and consider what you think you need to complain about. Come next summer, there will be a waiting list to get in here, I guarantee you that. And if you have any complaints or concerns—real ones, I mean, not imaginary ones—then bring them to me and we'll work out a solution. Got it?"

When they didn't answer him, he asked again, "Got it?"

"Yes, sir," they all answered in unison, and when he gave them a glare, they said it in a different way. "Yes, Gabe."

"Yes, Gabe," said Blaze, smiling to himself because he'd gotten it right. The whole place was a big fake to let rich people feel like they'd gotten in touch with their frontier, old west, old time roots.

"Thank you," Gabe said. "Now let me drop you off at your tents so you can get settled in. And feel free to use your shower tokens before dinner."

Gabe slipped past them like he wasn't at all worried he was standing unarmed in close proximity to a group of tough ex-cons whom he'd just basically scolded like they were in the third grade and ought to be behaving better, and led them back along the barely there path among the grasses. At a big clump of trees, he pointed down another barely there path that seemed to lead right into the heart of the woods.

"Kurt and Wayne, you're in tent #1, just along there, and Tom and Blaze, you're this way."

Blaze felt a sense of relief that he'd get a break from having to listen to any more rules, or upbeat talk about what a wonderful opportunity they had ahead of them. All he could see was the space between the words where the truth was. That they'd be worked to death, punished if they stepped out of line, and on top of that, they'd have to shit and pee in outhouses, and take showers with a breeze around their ankles. Great.

Gabe stopped them at the other side of the clump of pine trees and pointed between the trees, where there seemed to be a bit less undergrowth, fewer grasses. But as for any kind of trail, there wasn't any.

"You two are in tent #4, so make yourselves at home. I'll see you at five thirty for dinner, when the cook rings the dinner bell. Okay?"

"In the mess tent, right?" asked Tom.

"Yes," said Gabe.

"Make myself at home?" asked Blaze, making his voice rise in a saucy way, as if there were better ways that Gabe could make him feel at home other than dropping him off at a tent in the middle of the woods. And regretted instantly drawing that kind of attention to himself.

But Gabe, perhaps made wise by some kind of training about how to respond to inappropriate remarks, just smiled and nodded.

"Everything you need will be in boxes on your cot," he said. "If you're missing anything, just let me know. Make sure you find your flashlights, as you'll need them when it gets dark. Okay?"

"Sure thing," said Blaze with his best insouciant shrug. "I'm sure we'll be deliciously comfortable."

With a wave, Gabe left them alone, tromping away through the grasses, perhaps to go back to his tent, or perhaps to get out his bullwhip so he could keep them all in line.

"This is us, I guess," said Tom.

"You want me to go first?" asked Blaze, seeing the hesitation in Tom's step.

"Snakes, man," said Tom, shaking his head.

"You'll owe me," said Blaze, knowing that he'd just gotten a few extra points by being the first one to do the other guy a favor.

That was how it worked in prison, an exchange system built on promises requested and then delivered. Or on goods delivered for a favor, or whatever. The barter system had been deeply entrenched in Wyoming Correctional, and Blaze saw no reason to dispense with it now, or at least until something better came along.

He walked in amongst the trees, crushing the grass and weeds beneath his still soaked slip-on sneakers. At one point, he was going to back up and find Gabe to ask for a machete or something to cut the undergrowth, but then, with Tom on his heels, they broke into a little clearing.

There, a green tent with a cream-colored cloth slung over it seemed to appear before them, as though it had been wished for. Blaze didn't remember making a wish, and besides, wishes were for fools.

The tent, though, was cunningly designed and laid out in the clearing, pupped from the green trees, perhaps, or like it had been waiting for them forever. The front flaps of the tent were tied back, and a thin screen was zipped closed. Looking at Tom over his shoulder, Blaze stepped onto the platform made of new wood and unzipped the screen, pushing it out of his way as he stepped into the tent.

Inside, the air was warm and still, and smelled like new wood and sun-drenched canvas, and though dim in the middle, was lit by the sun coming down through the pine trees, which could be seen through the screens at either end.

There were two cots, one tucked on each side of the tent, and between the cots were two shelves side by side. Blaze could see that there was something beneath each bed, but it was what was assembled on the beds that drew him close: two large cardboard boxes that were so full they couldn't be shut, and a smaller, but still large, shoebox.

Tom reached out and grabbed the shoebox from the bed on the right side and shook it at Blaze.

"Size twelve and a half boots," he said. "Guess this is my bed."

"Guess it is," said Blaze.

He went to the other bed, claiming it as his in his mind, and reached for the shoebox. It said size twelve, which was too bad, since he wore size eleven, but what did that matter now?

Blaze popped open the lid and stood there gawping at the brand new soft brown leather boots with spongy soles and bright yellow and black laces.

"These are Carhartts," he said. He looked at the lid again, just to be sure. "Yeah. Carhartts."

"So?" asked Tom as he rifled through his new things, like a kid on Christmas morning who simply didn't care where everything had come from or, even, what it was. That it had been given to him was joy enough.

"My pop used to run counterfeit clothes, everything from Carhartt to Prada. Expensive stuff, if it's real."

"You think these are real?" Tom held up one of the boots and stroked it with long fingers.

"Yes," said Blaze, quite sure of what he was looking at. "That's a Carhartt denim jacket, too. Worth over a hundred bucks." He traced the soft collar and then the bit of lining peeking out.

Then he and Tom looked at each other and Blaze knew that they both knew what the other one was thinking, and that neither one could help it. The boots and the jacket alone could be sold to buy a Greyhound ticket to simply anywhere, which meant they could be on their way before the dinner bell rang with nobody, not even Gabe, having any idea which direction they'd headed.

But that was stupid. Where would they be able to sell the goods? The town they'd passed through had been quite small, and he had no idea where the nearest Greyhound bus station was. Not to mention, if they left the valley without permission, they'd be considered AWOL and, at that point, it would be a bitch kitty to set up a new parole. So he nixed the point before he even voiced it aloud and put the shoebox back on the bed, and opened the first cardboard box all the way.

It contained so many things, all new, that he felt a little dizzy. Two pairs of blue jeans, Levi brand. A blue bandana, a leather belt, a pair of leather gloves. And three soft shirts with sleek white buttons up the front, one white, one dark blue, one a soft blue chambray.

The second box held five pairs of socks, five pairs of tighty-whities, a packet of v-neck t-shirts—all made of thick, sturdy cotton. A shaving kit. Shampoo and conditioner, three bars of Ivory soap, a small first-aid kit, a big bottle of sunscreen, and a bottle of bug spray. The promised flashlight and a pack of batteries, and other stuff besides.

Tucked along the side of the second box was a typed note. The only part of the note that had been personalized was the bit where his name had been written on a line in blue ink. The note read:

Dear Orlando Butterworth,

Welcome to the Farthingdale Valley New Start Program. In this box is pretty much everything you'll need to get started. Later this week, your team lead will bring you to the ranch store for a straw cowboy hat.

Wyoming Correctional didn't include your head measurement, so I couldn't get you one in advance. You'll also get to pick out your own cowboy boots.

If anything doesn't fit, check with your team lead as soon as you can. During your stay with us, should you need anything, or run out of something, please check with your team lead.

All the best,
Maddy Greenway

Blaze hefted the baggie of shower tokens in his hand. His skin itched with the thought of standing beneath the stream of water that, according to the evidence he'd seen with his own eyes, might not be lukewarm. Then he said to Tom, "Let's go take a shower. I'll lead the way in case of snakes."

Tom nodded vigorously and in tandem they gathered what they thought they'd need and, leaving the tent wide open, for there was nobody to steal anything, they hiked through the grasses to the shower building.

Tom picked the shower at the furthest end, put a token in the little slot in the little metal box on the metal counter above the row of porcelain sinks, then lifted the lid, peeking inside.

"It's not even locked," he said, scoffing.

"Who's going to steal it?" asked Blaze. He'd picked the first shower building in the row, and was about to strip to his bare skin in front of Tom, like he would have in prison because after the first few days you got used to being naked around guys you didn't know, and this was just another day of that, when he remembered that each shower cabin had its own private little dressing room. "It's not worth anything."

"This is crazy." Tom started stripping, but then, half-naked, well-muscled, lean, he paused as if he, too, remembered he had his own private changing room. He looked at Blaze as calmly as if they were both fully used to dressing and undressing in private and were merely socializing after Sunday morning church. "And it's all going to turn to hell the second Gabe wants it to."

"Yeah, it's crazy," said Blaze, doing his best to be amiable. But maybe it wasn't crazy? Maybe this was just how things were going to be? Kind of nice, and straightforward, unlike prison life, where secrets hid and codes had to be unraveled.

Blaze put his wooden token in the slot of the little metal box, too, then stepped into his changing area, securing the slatted wooden door behind him. He undressed quickly, shedding his clothes like an unwanted skin. Then he turned on the shower and stepped into the spray, which was warm, turning to warmer still, sweet Jesus, even in the wilderness. And it was soft, like a never-ending caress.

He washed his hair and soaped himself all over, still hurrying, despite knowing that he could take up to half an hour. When he was done, he turned off the shower, and stepped into the little dressing area, and then laughed, a hard bark.

"What's up?" asked Tom. The sound of his shower went silent.

"No towels," said Blaze, smirking. In prison, you never had a wash-cloth, but you did have a medium sized, rather thin towel to dry off with. Here, there should have been fluffy towels for after, maybe even some lotion, in keeping with the high-end gear that had been given to them. "They weren't in the boxes, so I thought they'd be here. That's a fuckup, for sure."

But he was able to dry off, mostly, with his old, dirty, foul-smelling clothes, and managed to get dressed quickly in his new clothes so that as he was stomping into his too large boots, Tom didn't have to wait long.

Then together, they tromped through the woods to leave their old prison clothes and gear in the tent. Then, as the dinner bell rang, a high-sounding, hearty clanging, he shook his still-damp hair, and followed Tom, suddenly now not afraid of snakes, on account he wore the armor of his brand new boots, thick jeans, and excellent quality chambray shirt, through the woods toward the mess tent.

CHAPTER 5
GABE

Cellphone reception was spotty, but when Gabe took a step out the back of his tent, he wandered across the dirt track on the other side of the trees, along the sloped hillside. There, he was able to call Leland so they could quickly discuss how it was going.

"They seemed surprised by the shower situation," he said, after he'd given Leland the rundown about how basic orientation had gone that day.

"Are they complaining?" asked Leland, sounding quite surprised, as well he should, in Gabe's mind.

"No, not at all." With a half-shrug, his free hand in his pocket, Gabe smiled into the cellphone at the memory of it. "They reminded me of shelter dogs when they realize they've found their forever home. Like they're surprised to find any kindness at all in this world."

"Well, it's a step up for them." A pause fell, as if Leland was thinking. "They've committed crimes, but they've done the time, and if a little kindness and human decency is all it takes to keep them on the straight and narrow, I'm willing to be the first in line to do what it takes to point them in the right direction."

"Same," said Gabe, thinking that sometimes Leland sounded too

JACKIE NORTH

good to be true, but in person, in real life, that was just the way he was, good and kind and decent, right down to the bone. "Well, that's the dinner bell. I'm taking it slow like you said. Next on my agenda is sitting down with them to dinner, rather than at a separate table."

"I'd like to know the dumb cluck who suggested that idea," said Leland. "Teamwork is what it takes, Gabe. Teamwork."

"Yes, sir," said Gabe. "I'll check in with you tomorrow, right?"

"Yes, please."

Gabe disconnected the call, and thought about stuffing his cellphone in his back pocket, but then knew he'd just be running down the battery for no reason because, for the most part, there was no cellphone access in the valley. Some discussion had been had about setting up a mini-relay tower for cell service, but that had fallen to the wayside, amongst all the other details that had needed ironing out.

He went back to his tent and plugged in his cellphone, and made his way along the faint trail to the mess tent. There, as he stepped through the breezy opening made by the tent flaps folded and secured back, he found Wayne and Kurt wearing their new clothes.

They looked a bit like they were floating in the material, as it was thicker than the clothes they'd shown up in, and their expressions told Gabe they didn't quite know what to make of everything they'd received without doing a lick of work.

The keyword was *yet*. They'd be working hard, but they'd be compensated, not just by money, but by decent clothing to work in, the good food, the counseling, everything. Smiling at them, wishing them well, he came over to them.

"Hey, guys," said Gabe, being casual, but on alert.

Wayne and Kurt had been standing near where the buffet tables were, eying the two cooks, Del and Neal, who were wheeling a metal tray out from behind the buffet line. Then they looked at him with the suspicion that he'd done something with their dinner.

Gabe waited for either Wayne or Kent to ask him about that, wanting to encourage questions at any time, but they remained silent, so he nodded to Del, and asked for all of them. "Hey, Del," he said. "Is the buffet not set up yet?"

"There are so few of you," said Del. "Neal and I thought we'd bring each of you a plated dinner."

Gabe stepped aside to let Del go by him, and looked up to find that Blaze and Tom were coming into the tent, both with wet heads, their shirt collars damp.

Tom's hair was short, so would dry quickly, but Blaze's hair lay slack against his jaw, making him look like a cat caught in a storm. He was shivering, his boots swimming around his ankles, but then he saw Gabe looking at him and straightened up with a happy smile as if all was right in his world and he didn't want Gabe to worry about a thing.

"What's going on with your hair?" he asked. "And your boots?"

"No towels," said Tom, plainly.

"Uh," said Blaze. "Wrong size?"

"Weren't there towels on the bed next to the boxes?" asked Gabe, a shard of worry rising up inside of him. He didn't think the parolees would revolt over such a small thing, but he rather did want the sense of comfort and plenty to continue. "Must have gotten missed," he said now. "Del, can you set up for Kent and Wayne? Tom and Blaze and I will be right with you. Okay?"

"Sure thing," said Del, as Gabe led Tom and Blaze out of the mess tent and along the ragged path to the supply hut.

There was a latch on the double doors, but only to keep the doors closed in the wind and to keep bears and other wildlife from getting inside and rampaging through the shelves of cotton socks and shirts and whatnot. He could see both Tom and Blaze eying him, as if they were storing away the idea that the hut wasn't locked and that they could take anything they wanted at any time. Or maybe not.

"If you ever need something," he said, stepping inside while flicking on the overhead light and grabbing the clipboard from the wall. "Just write down what you took. That way—"

"You can keep track," said Blaze, saying this as if it had been something he'd memorized by rote. And also like he wanted Gabe to think of him as a straight-A student, but in reality he was looking at Gabe like he was crazy to suggest that the parolees could just have whatever they wanted, when they wanted it.

"Exactly," said Gabe. "I'll get you some towels to dry your hair with, and you can take them with you to your tents and hang them up to dry. And Blaze, your boots don't look like they fit."

He handed them each a towel and waited till they'd ruffed their heads to dry their hair. When Tom headed out, still drying his hair, Gabe's attention was, once again drawn to Blaze for reasons other than the boots, reasons he couldn't explain to himself. Blaze, who met Gabe's gaze with what seemed like wariness, smiled as if he wanted Gabe and his attention to go away.

"There's nothing worse than ill-fitting boots," said Gabe. He made notes on the clipboard and hung it up on the nail sticking out of the frame of the double doors. "What size are you?"

"Eleven," said Blaze brightly, but he was chewing his lower lip as if contemplating that somehow that answer was the wrong one.

"I'm good, boss," said Tom, folding the slightly damp towel under his arm. "Can I go to dinner now?"

"Sure," said Gabe, wondering if the moniker *boss* was too chain gang for the type of environment he wanted to create. With half of his attention on Tom, walking away with his slightly damp towel under his arm, Gabe turned to Blaze.

"You'll need hand towels as well, but we can take care of that later. For now, have a seat."

Blaze seemed a little startled, his eyes wide, and it was only then that Gabe realized how it might seem to Blaze to be alone in a supply hut with a guy who held a great deal of power over him. But to have Blaze sit while Gabe helped get him a pair of boots the right size was simply what he would have done for any ranch hand or army buddy or anyone.

"Eleven, you said?" asked Gabe as he began scanning the shelves.

As most personal gear was ordered to suit each particular man, there wasn't a huge supply of new work boots on hand. Luckily, there was a box labeled size eleven, which Gabe pulled down, opening the lid as he turned to Blaze.

THE COWBOY AND THE RASCAL

Who was staring up at Gabe, eyes wide, fingers curled around the edge of the metal folding chair, like he'd been trapped there and was frantically trying to figure out how to escape his current situation. Well, there was one thing Gabe could do, and that was diffuse the tension in the air, which would hopefully make Blaze feel more at ease and erase the worry tightening his features.

Not that Gabe preferred the just about fake happy-go-lucky expressions Blaze had been displaying since he'd gotten out of the van, but the near panic wasn't an improvement. So he knelt down in front of Blaze, rolling his shoulders forward, making himself small. Not advice that Leland would have given him, or any guard at any prison, for sure, but it seemed to be what the moment called for, so Gabe went with his gut.

"Take those off and we can make sure these fit," he said, opening the box and putting the lid beneath it before putting the box on the floor. "Then we can both go get our dinners."

Blaze's dark hair, still drying, rumpled across his forehead, almost hiding one green eye. He seemed dubious, but he let go of the chair and bent forward to unlace his too-big boots. His fingers, just at eye level for Gabe, were long, graceful, as they unlaced the yellow and black laces.

Gabe reached to help tug off those boots, realizing, perhaps too late, just how close he was kneeling, how he was eye level with those long fingers, the curve of Blaze's knees, the length of his thigh. This close, Blaze smelled good, the scent of plain Ivory soap mixing with fresh pine-scent, with salt, the warmth of Blaze's skin.

Then Gabe saw the socks Blaze was wearing, obviously not standard valley-issue, as they were grimy on the bottom, with one of his big toes sticking out of a hole that looked like it had been created weeks ago and not just today.

"Why are you wearing old socks rather than the new ones you were given?" he asked, pausing at his task of putting new laces through the brass grommets on the smaller pair of boots, the boots resting on his bent thigh.

"I figured, you know, that I'd just keep wearing these," said Blaze, the words rippling and hurried, perhaps in an attempt to ease Gabe's irritation. "That is, until I can't anymore, and then I'd wear one of the new pairs. Save 'em till I need 'em."

Gabe nodded as he finished lacing the boots.

"I mean, I'm sure I'll need 'em. I'm sure I'll need a whole lot of things while I'm here. You know?"

The sensation of abundance had not yet kicked in for Blaze, that much was for certain, but perhaps for a man like Blaze, abundance was a faraway dream, and new socks, no matter how white and soft and sturdy, just weren't his to enjoy.

Gabe wasn't irritated, simply worried about how he was going to convince Blaze to simply stop putting on all these different tones, from apologetic, to worried, to flirty. It was exhausting and unnecessary.

"You'll need new socks inside boots like these, otherwise you'll get blisters," said Gabe, sticking to the practical. He placed the boot on the cement floor and stood up to grab a new packet of socks, sized nine to eleven. "Put those on and take the rest of the pack with you. I'll update the clipboard." Gabe watched Blaze put on the new socks, bending at the waist, his dark hair sprawling over the side of his face, pale beneath faint dark hair, a long length of muscled calf jutting from the shoved up hems of his crisp blue jeans.

"That's better."

Gabe knelt again, focusing on the task at hand rather than Blaze's feet, now tucked into new, white socks, warm beneath Gabe's hands while he helped Blaze on with the new boots.

"Sock, sock, then shoe, shoe, eh?" asked Blaze, head still down as he held his feet still as Gabe laced them up.

Gabe nodded as he pressed on the toe of each boot. "Get up and walk back and forth to make sure they fit."

Blaze got up and took a few steps in each direction, which satisfied Gabe.

"That's you, then," said Gabe, patting the ankle of each boot, the way he might with someone much younger, but the gesture felt natural and besides, Blaze might like to know that Gabe was done fussing over him, though it might remain in his mind as to why he was fussing quite like he was.

"And yes." He looked up with a laugh. "Sock, sock, then shoe, shoe. Or in this case, sock, sock, boot, boot."

Open-mouthed, Blaze looked like he was on the verge of laughing out loud, too, but because Gabe was his boss, perhaps he was holding it back.

In that moment, Gabe had a vision of how Blaze might be, in another circumstance, another life, maybe. Head thrown back, a laugh on the verge of his lips, as though someone had taken a photo of a candid moment. How Blaze might be if he'd not been a prisoner for almost two years. Not faking it, not going through the motions. Warmth in his face, green eyes dancing, looking out from the photo as if the person who had taken it was a good friend to him, someone around whom Blaze could drop his guard.

Gabe stood up, wiping his hands on his thighs, writing quickly on the clipboard, taking the box and putting it, lid tucked beneath it, on the long table near the door, in case someone wanted a box, because the boxes Carhartt boots came in were good boxes and not to be wasted.

All of which were thoughts he let fly free, rather than focusing on the unanswerable question of what the energy running at that moment between him and Blaze could be labeled as. Nothing, that's what. All his imagination, and besides, it was time for dinner.

"Grab your towel and those socks," said Gabe. "You can drape the towel over a chair while we eat."

Blaze followed Gabe out of the Quonset hut, patiently waiting while Gabe latched the double doors. Then he followed Gabe to the mess tent, perfectly silent, though it looked like he wanted to ask Gabe why he kept fussing with his damp towel. At which point Gabe would explain about how mold grew in dampness, and how it was easier to launder towels if they weren't also caked with mold. Which would have been a great conversation to distract Gabe, settle the odd jitter beneath his breastbone.

They arrived at the mess tent, and Kurt and Wayne and Tom had all been served and were just about to eat. At the sight of Gabe, they paused, looking at him with wide eyes.

"We were just about to start," said Wayne at the same time Tom said, "The food was hot."

"Not to worry," said Gabe, coming over to them. "We should have been quicker to get here."

Del was already on his way with the rolling cart that held two covered dishes. Gabe sat down in the empty seat near the still and silent buffet line, and Blaze, after he draped his towel on an empty chair, sat down across from him, grasping his cutlery in his graceful hands, then shifting back on the bench seat as Del placed one of the covered dishes in front of him, and then one in front of Gabe.

Gabe looked around as he unwrapped his own cutlery, rolled in a napkin, and smiled as Del made an overly dramatic gesture and uncovered both of the covered dishes at once. It was then that Gabe realized why the others had been unable to wait.

On the plate were three street tacos stuffed with meat and cheese. Swirls of grilled onion and fresh green onion sat snuggly on the plate with a mass of homemade refried beans and a pile of aromatic Spanish rice. And for a moment he forgot himself because, quite simply, he loved to eat.

Food in the army had always seemed a half-assed affair, but food at the guest ranch had always been excellent and it looked like food in the valley was going to be just as good, maybe even better. Though as he looked up at the four parolees, he wondered if they thought that this meal was a fluke and that the rest of their stay would be fortified by generic cans of creamed corn, frozen tater tots, hastily baked without enough salt, or dehydrated milk with enough water added to it to make it turn blue.

"Eat up, guys," said Gabe, pulling up one taco and inhaling the warmth and spices. He took a bite and hummed, maybe to show them how to enjoy their meals, or simply to show them that yes, the taco was amazing.

It took a little while for the parolees to start enjoying their meals as if they were not ex-cons freshly out of prison, that their lives had not been a Humpty-Dumpty mess up until this point. They would get used to abundance in time. Also, in time, perhaps they would get used to actually using their napkins, rather than crumpling them up after unrolling their silverware.

They finished dinner mostly in silence, but there were murmurs of enjoyment over the cinnamon and sugar churros. As well, the parolees copied Gabe's movements as he took his own plate and scraped off what little remained before placing the plate and cutlery and his plastic glass in the bussing tub that the cooks had left out for them.

Of course, the parolees had probably all bussed their trays in prison, having eaten cafeteria style, but Gabe, were he a betting man, could have bet real money that even if in the past they all had left something on their trays, they wouldn't be doing that moving forward, the food was just that good.

"What do we do now, boss?" asked Blaze, being bold, moving to the front of the little group, hands in his pockets, a toss to his head to show he knew how flirty he was being.

"Whatever you'd like," said Gabe, almost laughing at the shocked look on the men's faces, as though he'd yanked the floor out from under them, and the drop to any hard surface was about thirty thousand feet. "Too soon," said Gabe, half laughing to himself. "How about a little bonfire?" he asked. "The fire pit by the lake is ready for use, though the path is a little rugged. Why don't you grab your jackets and flashlights—"

"What do we need jackets for?" asked Kurt, in the rude way that every statement he made seemed to have.

"It can get chilly in early spring," said Gabe. He made a mental note to talk to Jasper, who had experience at this sort of thing, whether it was okay to simply not like someone you'd just met, because in this case, Gabe was supposed to remain neutral, but that was already proving to be impossible. "You'll be glad of it when the sun goes down, especially. As for me, I'll grab some wood and kindling."

"Get mine for me for me, would you, Tom?" asked Blaze. "And take this?" He held out his towel, which Tom took. Then Blaze turned to Gabe, his mouth in a tender curve as though he were on the verge of smiling, but was holding back. "I thought I'd give you a hand. I like bonfires."

As Tom and the others strode off to their tents, Blaze looked at Gabe, sweet-faced and not at all like a man freshly out of prison. Which, according to what Gabe had learned, could be a warning that Blaze was about to shift gears and become a little mean, which parolees could sometimes do, as it was said, to test the waters, to test their own strengths now that freedom was at hand.

It didn't feel like that, though. There was no meanness shifting from Blaze's stance, no sense of menace or malice.

"Sure," said Gabe, pleased at the offer, enjoying the moment between them.

He had to make himself start moving rather than doing whatever it was he was doing—looking at Blaze like they could be friends, that something more could grow between the two of them. Rather than what was supposed to happen, him guiding Blaze into a new life, with Blaze heading out on his own at the end of summer.

Together they tromped through the weeds in a mostly companionable silence, as if this wasn't the first time they'd fetched wood for a fire together. On the other side of the Quonset hut, tucked between the hut and the small building that served as a kitchen, was the log rack, currently only one-third full, though Gabe hoped to remedy that with his team's efforts.

"Grab about three or four logs, if you would," said Gabe. "I'll get the kindling and the matches." The kindling was in a small cardboard box, which would hopefully soon be replaced with something larger and more waterproof. The matches were in the kitchen building, stored on a shelf just inside the door.

Then, walking along the half-trodden path to the fire pit, Gabe led the way, inhaling the air that was quickly growing cooler as the sun slanted in the sky, half hidden by pine trees. At the fire pit—an elegantly rustic arrangement of broad stones surrounded by unpainted Adirondack chairs—Gabe built the fire, making his movements slow so that Blaze could get an idea of how it was done.

Kneeling by his side, Blaze watched him with as much eagerness as a Boy Scout on the verge of getting his fire safety merit badge. The closeness between their bodies felt right, as if Blaze was someone he'd known and liked for a good long while.

But he shoved those thoughts aside as he finished building the fire, and by the time the flames flickered up like orange and gold plants waiting to grow, he realized that he needed his jacket, too.

"I'll be back," he said. "Keep an eye on this for me, will you?"

Perhaps the manual would have told him never to leave a newly sprung parolee in charge of a fire out in the middle of nowhere, but Gabe knew that second guessing himself every step of the way would only hamper the parolees' transition into the real world. Besides, there was an honest glow of anticipation in Blaze's eyes as he picked up a loose stick and moved closer to the stone circle, as if he was proud of being left in charge like he was.

"Be right back," Gabe said again, then hurried back along the path, passing by Kent, Wayne, and Tom, who were looking over his shoulder at the fire, a reflective look in their eyes.

Maybe having a bonfire on the first night was a bit too much like summer camp, but he had a feeling it was the right thing to do. Besides, there was nothing better than sitting around a warm flame as the night grew dark.

Had any on his team looked up at stars growing bright in the night sky? He had a feeling the answer was no, and it pleased him to be able to give them this experience. After that, they'd have to see how the rest of the summer turned out.

CHAPTER 6
BLAZE

When Blaze had been a kid, there had never been any time for a bonfire or for just sitting around. There was always some crooked thing to do, something to steal, someone to con.

To have sat doing nothing would have been considered, in the Butterworth family, a colossal waste of time. So, to have spent a good two hours huddled in a new sherpa-lined denim jacket, his new boots snugly laced and tied, sitting in front of a small, glowing cascade of warmth and light of a bonfire seemed outlandish, at least at first.

Gabe had talked a bit more about the program, then pointed up at the stars, which glowed like pinpricks across a circle of dark blue-black, rimmed by the darker shadows of pine trees and cottonwoods.

He'd been explaining the different constellations when Blaze's eyes had started to glaze over. Not from boredom, but from the deep, whisky-soft sound of Gabe's voice. Which seemed to give signals to various parts of his body—pretty certain signals that, after a day of being moved from the scary world of Wyoming Correctional to this wooded place, he was allowed to shut down.

He couldn't figure Gabe out, though, Gabe who might or might not be hiding a layer of meanness below the more obvious niceness.

But his brain couldn't manage it and began giving into the sinking pull of exhaustion, and the last words he heard Gabe say as he tipped his head back to rest on the wooden slats of the Adirondack chair were something about Orion's Belt and the speed of light.

The next thing he knew, Gabe was standing over him, shaking him awake. Out of the corner of his eye, he saw the others tromping along together, flashlights sweeping over the darkness, reflecting off the tall grasses until, one by one, they disappeared.

Blaze sat up from his sprawl, rubbing one eye with the heel of his palm.

"You okay there, Blaze?" asked Gabe, his voice soft and low, sending a shiver up the back of Blaze's neck.

Of course, he was okay. Even if he wasn't okay, he was hardly going to tell the boss man, despite how nice Gabe seemed or how he smelled nice, too—like salt and dust and the smoky traces of the little bonfire, now out, sending invisible trails of thick wood char into the night air.

"Fell asleep," said Blaze. "Did I miss the ghost story?" he asked, doing his bit to make a little joke out of how the after-dinner entertainment had seemed a great deal unlike being on a chain gang and a whole lot more like summer camp.

"Don't know any of those, I'm afraid," said Gabe, humor warming his voice. "But the guys said they wanted to make s'mores, for sure, next time."

As for the guys saying anything like that, Blaze imagined that they'd been testing Gabe to see how far they could push him. They'd probably based their request on what they thought normal people would do around an outdoor fire, not because any of them had any special hankering for toasted marshmallows or any variation of that.

"Sounds good to me, too." Blaze scrambled out of his chair.

"Can you make your way to your tent?" asked Gabe, as he reached into his jacket pocket to pull out a flashlight.

"Sure," said Blaze, because the last thing he wanted to do was admit that he was already lost. With the fire out, the sky was dark

THE COWBOY AND THE RASCAL

overhead. A chill breeze swept through the pines, sounding a little bit like someone was moaning. "Piece of cake."

"We're going the same way," said Gabe unexpectedly. "Let me show you."

Blaze found himself following close at Gabe's side, bumping into him when the way between pine trees grew narrow.

At one point, he was sure Gabe was leading him somewhere he shouldn't be so that he could have what he wanted from Blaze with no one the wiser. But then Gabe led Blaze straight to his tent. There Tom, in the single overhead light, was sitting on his bunk, holding his pair of Carhartt boots in his hands, admiring them. On the little shelf closest to his bed, he'd placed his flashlight on its end, sending a circle of light to spin on the roof of their tent.

"Hey," said Tom.

"Thanks, boss," said Blaze to Gabe, who, after a pause, nodded and said, "Good night," before disappearing into the darkness.

"I don't think he likes being called boss," said Blaze as he bent to place his flashlight on its end, which created an additional circle of light on the green canvas.

"Why you think that?" Tom shimmied out of his clothes until he was down to his tighty-whities, then he decided again and pulled on a sweatshirt before slipping into his cot.

"I dunno," said Blaze, yawning hugely as he contemplated his own cot and the boxes and gear that sat on top of it.

He now owned a ton of stuff which needed to be put away. His mind was spinning as though it had been swept into the circles of light on the canvas overhead.

"I need to pee," he said. "Maybe even brush my teeth. Isn't that what you do at summer camp?"

"Fuck that," said Tom. "It's too cold and too dark." He turned his back on Blaze and faced the wall. "Turn off my flashlight, will you?"

Blaze clicked Tom's flashlight off and placed it on its side. Then he rifled through his gear till he found the toothbrush, brand new, and a cute little tube of toothpaste.

"I'll be back," he said, then grabbed his flashlight and trudged off into the darkness.

Which right away felt like a mistake, because without a bonfire, without Gabe, even, his puny little flashlight barely showed him the way. All around him, the darkness felt alive, with the wind in the trees, and the smell of woodsmoke weaving among the pine tree trunks. Somewhere, insects were making a small racket, and was that an owl hooting?

Doing his best to focus, he thought that the facilities were a straight shot from tent #4 through the trees. Or it should have been, but he bumbled around a little bit and ended up in the clearing that was the parking lot.

At least, at that point, he knew he needed to go left, so he did, only to hear a sharp branch breaking behind him, and when he turned, it was Gabe, carrying a huge flashlight, and dressed in a thick flannel bathrobe.

"Are you barefoot?" asked Blaze, coming to a stop, completely forgetting to put a smile in his voice, to be disarming because, frankly, he was simply too tired and on the verge of freaking out. "Is that a bathrobe? Aren't you freezing?"

"Did you get lost?" asked Gabe, coming up beside him. "And no, I'm not barefoot, I'm wearing flip flops, and yes, it's a bathrobe. I hate taking a shower and getting dressed back in the day's clothes. Where are you headed?"

Blaze debated whether to tell the truth or not about the fact that he was lost.

"I'm going to brush my teeth," he said, instead of anything else.

"We can go together."

They walked through the dark woods, and Blaze paid attention extra hard as to where they were, and about how many steps it took to get to the facilities. Then, as Gabe disappeared into the shower area, Blaze went to the row of porcelain sinks in structure with the fancy outhouses and brushed his teeth, wincing as the toothpaste stung the cut on his lower lip.

Leaning close to the mirror, better arranged and better lit than any

THE COWBOY AND THE RASCAL

in any bathroom that convicts used, he ran his tongue along the cut, then, with his free hand, gently touched the bruise along his eye, his temple.

His ribs on one side, his right side, ached, but that awareness had faded in and out during the transfer, during the excitement of being in a new place.

Giving himself a good shrug, he finished brushing his teeth, slowly, listening to the sounds coming from the shower area. How Gabe seemed to be humming under his breath. The clunk-clunk sounds as he arranged his toiletries in the little dressing area of his shower stall.

Noises were crisp in the cool air and seemed to float over the top wood railing to land in Blaze's ears. Of course, every man showered, didn't they. And Blaze was used to showering with up to ten other guys, all naked, with various levels of hardness of dick and the lack of compunction to keep them from staring at another man's junk.

Somehow, though, with Gabe hidden beyond the wall, the sounds he made came to Blaze, secret and intimate. Blaze had to shake his head to keep the ridiculous, exhaustion-inspired thoughts at bay.

He finished at the sink, quickly peed, washed his hands, and then tiptoed out of the facilities and slunk through the darkness back to his tent, not wanting Gabe to think he had to escort Blaze everywhere he went.

When he got there, Tom was fast asleep in the darkness beyond Blaze's small circle of flashlight, snoring slightly. There was a rustle in the woods, and Blaze stepped out, his heart hammering, thinking it was either a wild animal or it was Gabe. Either way, he was unprepared to battle or do small talk. After a moment, the woods seemed to settle down except for the ever-present breeze across the top of the pine trees.

Standing on the edge of the little wooden platform, he clicked off his flashlight and gripped it in his hand. And looked up at the arc of stars, silver and more silver, so bright and brilliant they were almost a solid mass against the blackness of the sky.

Was he looking at the Milky Way? It was hard to tell, since he'd never really seen it before, until, that is, he'd been sitting in front of the bonfire with Gabe and the others. All the events and carnivals he and his family had traveled to had been in the city or in well-lit Wal-Mart parking lots and stars had been faded to nothing against that.

The stars were beautiful now, though, even if the night was very cold.

Blaze stepped back into the tent, propped his flashlight sideways and stripped out of his clothes, shivering as he put a sweatshirt on over his t-shirt. He pulled down the end canvas and zipped it shut, then, for good measure, zipped the screen shut, too, cause who knew what bugs would be at them in the morning.

He barely remembered crawling into his cot, but he felt wide awake the second he opened his eyes. The tent felt warm and seemed to glow with sunlight. Tom was already up and dressed, and was unzipping the screen, and rolling back one flap of the tent.

CHAPTER 7
GABE

When Gabe finished with his shower, the day's clothes beneath his arm, his flannel robe warm around him, he stepped out of the shower, telling himself he wasn't looking for Blaze. Except he was. After sweeping his flashlight around the darkness to be sure Blaze wasn't waiting for help getting back to his tent, Gabe made his way to his own tent in the dark, silent and still beneath the starlit sky.

Turning on the overhead light, he pulled out his Coleman lantern, pumped air into the chamber, and lit the mantle. When the light was glowing and bright, a comforting little hiss in the background, he turned off the overhead light, and pulled out the file folders and laid them on the cot next to him, in a row. He figured now that he'd made his own impressions of the parolees, it was time to read the files to see what the prison system had to say about each man on his team.

Kurt had been arrested for stealing hubcaps and for using local 7-11s in Cheyenne as his own personal pantry. It had not been the first time he'd been caught, but it had been the first time he'd been arrested. Evidently Kurt'd had an attitude problem in jail, but that mostly amounted to him being mouthy with the guards and complaining a lot.

Tom had stolen diapers and baby supplies for his newly pregnant girlfriend, who, as Gabe read, was currently on her own with a six-month-old baby. This got to him because he could understand the theft of baby supplies in a case like that, though he hoped someone in the prison system had talked some sense into Tom about getting supplies a different way in the future. He also read that Tom had no visitors during his short time in prison, and that his sentence had been cut back for good behavior.

Wayne had a string of breaking and entering arrests, though he seemed to be on someone's payroll and had barely spent a year in prison each time. The written statement from the guards indicated that Wayne knew his way around the prison system and seemed unfazed by it all.

And then there was Blaze, whose file Gabe had been saving for last. Blaze seemed to be intent on making Gabe like him, as though he thought that was the only way he'd get through the program. This made the information in the file Gabe held in his hands seem that much more important, a way for him to understand what was going on with Blaze.

According to the file, Blaze had been convicted of dealing drugs and domestic violence, even though he looked, to Gabe's eyes, anyway, like he was completely surprised to find himself in the ex-con program.

But there were more notes in the file, so Gabe flipped the page, shock making him go still. The report was dry, but Gabe knew how to read between the lines.

There had been an altercation in Blaze's cell the night before he'd been released. Two other prisoners had somehow exited their cell in the middle of the night and, opening Blaze's cell, proceeded to beat him up.

Blaze had fought back, and the noise had alerted the guards on level two, who entered the cell, ended the fight, and made sure Blaze was okay before locking level two down for the night. The next day, Blaze had been pulled out of the dining hall during breakfast, processed out, then sent on his way to Farthingdale Valley.

As to why two prisoners would wait for the middle of the night rather than simply picking a fight in the prison yard, Gabe had no idea. His knowledge of how a prisoner's mind worked was very limited so far, though he imagined he'd learn more as they got deeper into summer.

What he did know was that Blaze had been acting like he wasn't injured at all. As if the cut on his lip and the marks on his face were from something else entirely. Maybe he was covering, or maybe he thought it didn't matter, but it was sure weird to Gabe.

There was more in the folder, copies of a surveillance report on Blaze's whole family from three years prior, when the Feds had been interested in an interstate ring of illegal gambling. Somebody had been sent out to take photos and keep an eye on the Butterworths, but they'd come up with nothing.

The surveillance had happened the year before Blaze had been arrested, and three years after he should have graduated from high school. According to the report, Blaze had been studying for his GED while in prison, but had never taken the test.

The photos of the family's trailer, even in black and white, showed the effects of a streamlined life that could be packed up in under an hour and scooted to the next place, and then the next after that.

Oddly, the file included photos of each of the family members. Gabe found himself looking at Mr. and Mrs. Butterworth, their faces lined and hard, their eyes sharp, their mouths thin. Alex, the older brother, took after Mom and Dad.

And then there was Blaze.

There was a blurry photo of Blaze hanging out of a truck window, beneath which was a short handwritten note, something to do with driveways and fake repairs, a scam to cheat the elderly out of money.

There was a sharper-focused, candid photo of Blaze when he was younger, his hair wild around his face as he stood watching the Tilt-a-Whirl, eating a corn dog, the pleasure of the moment making his eyes bright.

The Blaze in the photograph seemed much younger than the guy who'd gotten out of the prison van only the day before. Though there had been, in certain moments, flickers of that younger Blaze peeking out of an older, prison-hardened Blaze's eyes.

Gabe didn't know enough about prison psychology, and maybe Blaze's behavior was a big sham, and the effect on Gabe, the tenderness of his heart in reaction, would, in time, prove to be just as false.

Blaze's file made him shake his head. The whole Butterworth family were con artists, working the carnivals, the booths, working the shill. In reading Blaze's prison history, he could better understand the expression on Blaze's face. How he didn't quite fit in with the other parolees because, simply, he wasn't like them.

At least not in the truest sense, even if his whole family thought that stealing was the way to go about things. No specific detail of Blaze's time in Wyoming Correctional jumped out at him, but the photographs did.

The third photograph was a strip of square, black and white intake photos, with Blaze holding up the mugshot board. How stark and pale he looked. How dark his eyes. How much younger he seemed.

At the front of the file was his discharge photo, still black and white, the lighting overly bright. But it was enough to let Gabe see the difference between the man Blaze had been and the man he was now.

Some men were unchanged by prison. Other men were so changed that they turned into ghosts of themselves. In the older photos, Gabe had seen the ghost of who Blaze had been, the laughter in his eyes, the confident set of his shoulders, but which had been undone and then undone some more, and then again.

It wasn't his job to rebuild a man, merely to give him an opportunity to rebuild himself. But in this case, he wanted to try.

His friend Jasper often said, of the parolee he'd taken responsibility for, *I was the man in the field, and had to make my own decisions.* Perhaps Gabe could make his own decisions about how to handle Blaze. Only Gabe didn't know what to do.

Tucking the papers back in the folders and putting them on the shelf, Gabe slid on his boots over his bare feet and, still in his robe, he unplugged his cellphone and grabbed the lantern to take into the darkness.

The lantern spread a bold yellow circle on the grasses and the tree branches. When Gabe found the road, he put the lantern on a flat spot in the dirt and called his friend Jasper.

"This is Jasper," his friend answered.

"Is it too late?" asked Gabe.

"Nope," said Jasper. "Just let me step outside. How did it go?"

Gabe knew Jasper was stepping out onto the porch to his little stone cabin, which looked over a glassy river. Though there was no moon, Gabe imagined the stars lit up the sky, reflecting off the water of the river.

"It went okay," he said.

He filled Jasper in with the details of Leland's little speech, and then his hopefully straightforward presentation of the rules. He told the story of the tour, and the almost comical surprise of the parolees when they were given nice things to wear and had a gourmet-level meal of street tacos for dinner.

"I'm glad you suggested that I wait to read their files until I'd made my own impression of them."

"Yeah, that's what I did with Ellis," said Jasper. "I figured the prison system would have a slanted view, because that's who they are. I wanted my own view going in. I wanted to go with my gut."

"If I were to go with my gut—" Gabe paused, thinking that he was hearing bats whirling around the trees. Or maybe it was too late for bats and the noises were his imagination.

"Go with your gut," said Jasper. "What's it telling you?"

"Two of them I do *not* like," said Gabe with a small laugh, feeling bad even as he said it. "Kurt and Wayne. It's their attitudes. Maybe prison made them hard to the world or maybe that's just the way they are." He paused, shaking his head. "They act like criminals and they look like criminals and I just don't like them. Is that normal?"

"It's normal," said Jasper, in his calm way. "But just like at work, there are guys you instinctively don't like from the get-go for whatever reason. Doesn't mean you do anything about it. You keep your thoughts to yourself and maybe in time, they turn out to be not so bad. Or maybe you were right all along."

Gabe thought it over. "I like Tom. He stole baby supplies for his pregnant girlfriend. Didn't think it through, but my heart kind of goes out to him. There's a girlfriend in the picture and now a baby, who I don't think he's ever seen. I just want to drive him to wherever they are. Isn't that dumb?"

"Not at all." Jasper went silent and then said, "Sounds like Tom did a foolish thing, but you gotta feel for a guy who's that much in love. Go with your gut instinct and keep an eye out. You're the man in the field, so you have to decide based on the circumstances of the moment. You'll learn more about them as you go. You may find that Kurt turns out to be a decent guy who's full of anxiety about this program, and you may find out that Tom is a number one jerk. When you've experienced them more, you can shift your opinion or act on it whatever is needed."

"And then there's Blaze," said Gabe, knowing he left Blaze for last because Blaze was the most puzzling.

"Yeah? What are your thoughts about him?"

"Yeah. Blaze's real name is Orlando, but he prefers Blaze. He doesn't seem like he belongs with the others."

"Oh, yeah?" asked Jasper. "Why is that?"

"Don't laugh," said Gabe, laughing himself.

"Never me," said Jasper, and Gabe could hear the smile in his voice.

"My heart goes out to Blaze even more than it does to Tom. Blaze just looks lost, like he has no idea how he got here, and he's just holding himself in check until he's allowed to go free again."

"The parolees can leave any time, right?" asked Jasper.

"That's the way Leland wanted it set up," said Gabe. "There's no cage. No cage door, so their reasons for staying are *their* reasons."

"I do like the way Leland thinks," said Jasper.

"I know you do," Gabe replied. "You know that song by the Talking Heads? Blaze has got an expression like he's asking how he got here. I keep wanting to point him in the right direction, help him get his GED."

"How long was he in for?" asked Jasper.

"Almost two years," said Gabe. "The file said he studied for his

GED, but never took the test. Or maybe he did and the file's just not up to date. Or maybe they don't add that kind of information to the file. I don't know."

Two weeks of training in Torrington had prepared him, but not for everything. It certainly hadn't prepared him for what he was supposed to do when his own feelings crept into the mix.

He had sympathy for all the men on his team, even a bit for Kurt. But when it came to Blaze, his feelings rose into a different shape, surrounded by tendrils of woodsmoke from a campfire, with visions of a sleepy-eyed Blaze, for once not putting on a show or flirting with such intention it was obvious even to Gabe that it was a put-on.

But in that moment—when Gabe had woken Blaze up and Blaze had looked up at him—there had been the warmth of gratitude in his eyes to see Gabe there. Gabe, rather than, perhaps, a prison guard, or even his two attackers.

Gabe was making up the connection between them, surely he was, and going through some weird transfer of his own emotions onto a single prisoner, who probably wouldn't like Gabe even if they met on the street, and certainly wouldn't appreciate Gabe having less-than-professional thoughts about him.

"I have to get my head on straight," said Gabe, running his fingers hard through his hair. "Maybe I'm having problems because I'm the only one here."

"You are on your own, aren't you," said Jasper. "But you won't be for long. Aren't some of those horses Leland bought at auction coming through next week?"

"Yeah." Gabe sighed, dropping his hand, looking up at the stars beyond the glow of the lantern. "There was a delay in the paperwork, but we should get them soon. Are you going to shoe them down here or up at your forge?"

"That depends."

A bit of silence fell, and Gabe waited, letting Jasper think.

"On how many, and whether Ellis wants to come down there with me. I don't want him to. Don't want him to mix with the kind of guys he knew in prison, but he's his own man and gets to decide, so we'll see. As to your head—" Jasper paused, and Gabe thought he could hear Ellis' voice in the background. "Sure, keep it on straight, but that doesn't mean you can't let your heart have a voice in all of this. You're only human, you know."

"I am, I guess."

"You can only do your best, right?" On the other end of the line, Jasper yawned, and Gabe distinctly heard Ellis say *C'mon, Jasper, it's time for bed*. "Get some rest and just take it as it comes. I'm here if you need to talk."

"Goodnight, then," said Gabe, and he hung up when Jasper did.

He was lucky to have a friend like Jasper, who'd come from the army, same as him, and who had a level head on his shoulders. And he knew Jasper was right. He could only do his best.

But that advice, even as he walked back to the tent, turned off the lantern and crawled into his cot, wasn't enough to keep him from thinking about Blaze.

CHAPTER 8
BLAZE

"Didn't you hear it?" asked Tom. "It's the breakfast bell."

His eyes opening wide, Blaze sat up with a gasp, reaching for his jeans, which he remembered tossing at the end of his cot. There was a chill in the air, a sense of dampness. Outside of the tent, beyond the tied back tent flap, he could see a mist weaving among the tree branches. Above, somewhere, a bird was singing.

All of which seemed to be doing its very best to break through his sense of panic.

In prison, if you missed breakfast, the hours until lunchtime would stretch out so long you felt like you were going through hell. Not that the food was any good, but it was something, and at least in the cafeteria, with each man concentrating on his food, nothing bad usually happened.

Sure, fights sometimes broke out when one guy figured that another guy had already had his share of chocolate pudding, but Blaze always made sure to stay out of the way, in case a chest-shoving argument turned into one where secret shivs were pulled out and used with great energy.

He scrambled into his clothes, half-lacing his boots, scrubbing his eyes as he followed Tom along the grass-trampled path that was beginning to seem more familiar. And already he could smell something frying, fresh-brewed coffee and, along with Tom, followed his nose to the mess tent.

As he sat down at the table near the front, to be waited on by Del, he wondered why he'd ever balked at the idea of doing his parole at a place like this. Maybe the bad thing was still headed his way, but with the sun shining brightly, turning the air outside the mess tent to gold, he didn't think it would happen today.

Besides which, Gabe came and sat down directly across from him, bringing up memories of the night before, Gabe's smile as he built the little bonfire, his obvious pleasure as he gestured to his men that they should sit and relax.

And now, there seemed a little space around the two of them, where they weren't team lead and parolee. They were just two guys who happened to be working a summer job together, one of whom smelled amazing and looked freshly shaved and the other who had hair hanging in his eyes and wasn't quite awake yet. Blaze scraped his hair out of his eyes and looked up at Del as he poured him a cup of coffee.

"Uh, thanks," said Blaze.

"Don't get used to it, sonny," said Del in a jocular way. "And by that, I mean, by next week, we'll have a coffee urn for you to use."

"Okay." Blaze took a sip of the coffee, which was so good it made him sit up and take another sip.

"No cream or sugar?" asked Gabe. He was doctoring up his coffee until it was the color of coffee-flavored ice cream.

"No?" The response became a question, because in Blaze's world, the last two years of it, anyway, if the boss man decided that you should like your coffee sweet and soft, then that's how you would have it.

"Probably better for you that way," said Gabe. He took a sip of his coffee and sighed, leaning forward, his hands cupped around the white china mug. "But I have a sweet tooth."

"Oh." Blaze didn't know what to say to that. In prison, the less you shared about your personal life, the better. Back at the Butterworth trailer, they all already knew each other's secrets. But in the valley, what was the protocol?

Blaze was saved from having to think too much about this as Del brought out a platter of pancakes, and he could watch Gabe soaking his stack of three pancakes with enough butter and syrup to turn them to mush. Watching Gabe dig into his food was its own secret pleasure and, as his lips glistened as he chewed, he did not seem at all secretive or embarrassed. Or that he minded that Blaze was staring at his mouth—

Blaze looked away, at his breakfast, at the pile of pancakes and the three links of nicely fried sausage that were all his, and that didn't have any mold on them either.

He stole another glance or two or three at Gabe while he ate, but pretended he was more interested in who got one of the sausages that Wayne said he didn't want. In the fact that the butter dish held real butter, and that the offer of freshly brewed coffee was endless.

After breakfast, contented and full, Gabe led the way in bussing their table, and then took them to the supply hut for gloves and safety helmets and vests. Then they went out beyond where the fire pit was to an open space beneath the trees and just about right next to the river.

Blaze knew there was a river, he'd seen it through the trees, but to see it so glassy and blue and white as it tumbled over the rocks before smoothing out and feeding into a lake was just about the last thing he expected to see.

"This is Half Moon Lake," said Gabe. "Isn't it pretty?"

They all nodded because, yes, the lake was pretty, like a painting. Surrounded by tall pine trees, it almost looked fake.

"And that is Guipago Ridge," said Gabe. He pointed to the long, sky-edged hem of stone that cut across the blue, high above the foothills to the west. "It's named after the last principal chief of the Kiowa tribe, who probably passed through here, years ago, on their way south to Colorado."

Gabe's words sounded like something Blaze might have memorized for his GED test, a goal which he'd left behind him, long before his release from prison. But something about Gabe's pleasure in this bit of history sparked something inside of Blaze, because maybe he'd have a chance this summer to get that certificate. Or maybe he was just crazy, wishing for what he could never have.

"And this here—" Gabe led them to a dump truck, behind which huddled a long machine, covered by a tarp. Gabe pulled away the tarp to reveal a clunky machine.

"This is the wood chipper we're borrowing from the BLM. It's got 170 horsepower, enough to tear through a tree trunk or to rip a man's arm off. The truck will help to haul away woodchips. This here," Gabe pointed to the red bars along the opening and the orange and white stripes beneath that. "This is the feed intake. You don't ever want to stand in front of the feed while pushing trees and logs and branches in there or they could snag you and pull you in and you'll disappear without a yelp. Do you understand me?"

He turned to look at them each in turn, a hard, steady look.

"If I catch any one of you messing around this machine, or any of the other tools you'll be using, you are off my team. You won't get another chance. Whether that means you'll get kicked out of the program will be up to Mr. Tate, and he is not one to suffer fools gladly."

"Yes, sir," they each said, and then they all amended that to, "Yes, Gabe."

"Now, this morning, you only need to wear gloves, as we'll be picking up branches and chunks of wood from this area that the BLM already cut for us. This afternoon, we'll get a delivery of chainsaws and axes. We'll get started on doing our own clearing then. I'm also getting a map of the area so we can see how this project will progress over the summer. If you have any questions, just ask. If you get hurt, then stop working and let me know and we'll take you to the first aid hut. Got it?"

"Got it," they all said.

Blaze was glad for the slow way the day was starting. On a chain gang, or so rumor had it, you were handed a pickaxe or a shovel or whatever and were told to produce a certain amount of crushed rock or spread gravel or whatever, and by golly, you'd better produce or they'd come down hard on you.

Gabe put them to work, gathering branches and logs and strands of bark. Tidying up to make the place look nice and for no reason other than that.

The work might have been straightforward, but it was more physical work than Blaze had done in a while, his whole life, even. Bending over and straightening up, over and over again, to pick up branches and sticks, and then hauling them to the clearing made him sweat more than he ever thought he could.

It was nice, though, to look up and see the lake, or to look at the clouds rolling along, white and puffy and innocent, over the steel-gray ridge. Blaze was not an outdoor guy, but this was pretty, all things considered.

What was also nice, and totally unexpected, was that Gabe was working right alongside them. He didn't stand off to one side barking orders or finding fault. No, he was bent over, sweating beneath his armpits, just like they were.

He was in real shape, too, not muscle bound gym and weights shape, but real shape. Like he did hard labor every day, and he probably did. Blaze did his best not to stare, which was very hard, as the pull of muscle along Gabe's back, the strength in his thighs inside of his blue jeans, was very eye-catching indeed.

At one point, when mid-morning started warming up, Gabe took off his flannel shirt. Standing there in a clean white t-shirt that showed off his biceps and strong neck, he slathered himself with sunscreen, then handed the tube around so they could all join in. Then, without a word, got back to work. Making Blaze feel, unexpectedly, like he was part of a working unit, and not actually on parole.

He threw himself into the work, and did his best to keep up with Gabe, but it was hard because he wasn't good at it. They were all struggling with trying to keep up, looking at each other with wide eyes behind Gabe's back as if to ask, *Is this guy for real?* And as if to say, *This guy is a machine!*

Every hour, Gabe would stop and make them drink some water. The first time this happened, Blaze took a sip, not sure if he was thirsty or not, and then recapped his water bottle.

"Take a little more, Blaze," said Gabe. "Don't gulp it, but drink enough to stay hydrated."

Blaze did as he was told, and if that wasn't the nicest, sweetest swallow of water he'd ever had, Blaze didn't know what was. And he had no idea why Gabe was fussing over him more than the others.

At a point where it seemed the morning had hardly begun, they heard the bell clanging into the relative quiet.

"Let's go get some lunch," Gabe said, making it sound more like a suggestion than an order. "We can wash up first."

Together, like a team, they headed to use the facilities and then washed up, all in a row, like kids at boarding school, which made Blaze laugh because going to a boarding school would have been a kind of fantasy life for him.

Lunch was BLT sandwiches and potato salad with iced brownies to finish up with. When Del asked what everyone wanted to drink, Kurt, sounding like he was joking, asked for a glass of milk. Only thing was, he got the milk, and finished it in two gulps. Del brought him another serving, and Kurt drank that too, in record time, then wiped his mouth on the back of his hand.

"What?" he asked as they stared at him. "I like milk and the milk in the joint tastes like old cow jizz."

Blaze couldn't fault Kurt for being greedy about what he had missed in prison because everybody missed something on the inside. Blaze missed hot showers, and he missed a whole bunch of things he probably never even knew he'd been missing. One of which was the ability to sit around after eating a meal without feeling like they had to rush off. Certainly, Gabe wasn't in a hurry, having a second iced brownie and a cup of sweet, creamy coffee.

He looked up at Blaze as if he'd realized Blaze had been staring at him. Which perhaps he had been, though he needed to stop that shit right now.

"I'm waiting for the call from Maddy that says our other equip-

THE COWBOY AND THE RASCAL

ment is on its way," Gabe said, patting the two-way radio strapped to his belt. "When it is, then we'll get going."

A bit stupefied, they all accepted the sweet tea that Del offered them. Blaze drank his slowly, got a second glass, and though it tasted just as good, the question as to when the other shoe was going to fall kept leaping around in Blaze's brain.

Surely Gabe wasn't as nice as he seemed. Surely, Gabe secretly hated them all. And surely Blaze was being stupid, letting his brain go on like this, rather than being focused on just getting through the summer, head down, so he'd come out at the other end intact.

"I'm going to call Joanna," said Tom, getting up from the table.

Just then, Gabe's two-way radio squawked at him and he slipped it from his belt.

"This'll be Maddy," he said. "I figure you've got about ten or so minutes, Tom. All right?"

As Tom went to the phone, he looked at Blaze and rolled his eyes a little, as if to indicate, yet again, Gabe was not acting like they all expected him to. Blaze shrugged, and smiled back at Tom, because there was nothing to be done except roll with the punches and get ready to jump out of the way.

Gabe talked to Maddy, her voice coming in sounding a tad metallic as they went over a list of things that needed arranging. When a beat-up truck showed up in the gravel parking lot, it was without much fanfare, though Gabe tucked his two-way back onto his belt, and hurried from the mess tent to the truck, unlike his usual self.

The driver got out, a tall man with messy dark hair and a flannel shirt that wasn't tucked in. He and Gabe exchanged the handshake-back-pat greeting that Blaze had seen before, but the smiles on the men's faces struck him—they were truly happy to see each other. Blaze's curiosity raised its head as to who the man was and how he was placed in Gabe's life to bring a smile like that.

Gabe waved the team over, and Blaze put on his happiest face.

"Who's this, Gabe?" he asked in a saucy voice, meant to imply that the question was a jealous one, but that he was keeping a lid on it for now.

Still smiling, just about ignoring Blaze, Gabe gestured to the other man, presenting him.

"This is my friend, Jasper. We met in the army and then, when we got out, we both ended up working at the guest ranch. Jasper's the blacksmith there."

Jasper seemed pleasant and steady in the way that Gabe was, which was starting to make Blaze feel that every single person who worked at the ranch was decent and nice and hard-working, which would be cotton candy sweet and almost too much to bear if only the men he'd met weren't devastatingly handsome.

What would it be like to live in a world like that, where you washed your hands because it was the right thing to do? Where you were polite to everyone you met, and you didn't walk around thinking that the other guy was going to screw you over every other minute?

"Hey, guys," said Jasper, accompanying his smile with a little wave. "I hope it's going well, though I already know it is, seeing as Gabe is in charge." He turned to Gabe as though, now that they were all introduced and practically old friends already, he needed to get down to business. "Where should I take this so you can unload it?"

"Over by the fire pit," said Gabe. "I think you can get through the trees without having to go around the back way, and if you mash a few weeds along the way, that's okay with us. Right, guys?"

"Right, Gabe," they all said in unison, and Gabe smiled at them as if to reward them for calling him Gabe rather than sir, because he was just their team lead and not anybody special. He just happened to be in charge.

Following the truck, Blaze snorted to himself. As if Gabe was *just* an anything.

CHAPTER 9
BLAZE

At the site, the parolees helped Gabe and Jasper unload the power tools and safety gear. Then they watched while Gabe and Jasper set up the wood chipper and arranged the discharge chute so it pointed over the deep bed of the dump truck. After which, they waved Jasper off, and watched for a minute as he got into his truck and drove away through the trees.

"If we load this thing up with chips, we're never going to get it out of here," said Kurt in his rude way.

"There's a service road just on the other side of those trees that we'll take the truck out on," said Gabe, ever patient as always. "When guests come, the service road will allow the retreat to haul in supplies or haul out trash, and so on. Which will keep everything tranquil, which is what they'll be paying for."

Kurt grunted under his breath and turned away, as if insulted at how coddled future guests would be, but Blaze thought it was smart.

A lot of things Gabe said sounded smart, like when he broke down the guidelines for the afternoon's work, giving each man a task. No yelling, no threats, just clear instructions. Of course, this could all be a smokescreen and Gabe could turn out to be a grade A asshole at the end of the day.

JACKIE NORTH

"Aren't you worried we're going to hurt you with these tools?" asked Kurt as he tapped one of the axes with the toe of his boot.

"Well," said Gabe after a pause long enough to have them all fidgeting. "I look at it this way. If you wanted to hurt me, you could have already." With a small shrug, he turned away from Kurt and gestured at the tools.

"I'll need one man bringing branches and limbs over here in a pile. I'll need another man on the chipper. And two of you will go with me and I'll show you how to use a chainsaw."

Blaze raised his hand for the chainsaw even though he'd never used one before, as that sounded like it would involve a whole lot less bending and stooping. And besides, he'd get to work with Gabe and Tom, who was also raising his hand.

As soon as Gabe showed Kurt and Wayne how to use the chipper, he took Blaze and Tom a little way into the woods and next to the lake, where there were several picnic tables made of newly cut pieces of wood, so new, the smell of sap was sharp in the warm afternoon air.

Gabe showed them the different parts of a chainsaw, how to start it, how to hold it. Blaze paid rapt attention because Gabe had broad shoulders that strained against his flannel shirt. And he smelled nice, the sweat on the back of his neck a faint gleam, his eyes serious through the face shield of his safety helmet.

Tom settled his helmet, ear guards, and face guard, pulled on his gloves, and reached for one of the chainsaws. At Gabe's direction, he went up to the first tree with a plastic yellow tie around the main part of the trunk and lopped it down to the stump with one swipe. Sure, the tree was old and dead and thin, but Tom did it like a natural.

Blaze tried to copy him, but by the time he was holding the chain saw, it felt heavy and unbalanced in his hands. He didn't want to be handling such a dangerous piece of equipment, after all, and would Gabe get mad if he asked to switch places with either Wayne or Kurt?

"Let me show you a better way to hold that."

Blaze looked up. Rather than hollering at him like a prison guard would that he was a dumb fuck and ought to know better, Gabe, of course, wanted to be helpful in that steady, serious, Gabe-like way of his.

Not that Blaze should get used to being treated with kindness, oh no. Soon would come the moment that Blaze cut down the wrong tree or sliced off the wrong branches and Voila. He'd be in the doghouse.

"Use your right hand to support it and guide it. Use your left hand to turn the brake on and off."

Gabe placed his hands gently on Blaze's hands, standing out of the way of the round, more deadly end of the chainsaw. Up close, he smelled like sweat and there was a leaf on the back of his neck. A small one, bright green, and Blaze had to tear his eyes away when Gabe looked at him, a steady, blue-eyed smile.

"Like that. You'll be more in control now. Does that feel better?"

Blaze nodded, speechless, unable to reach inside of himself for any flirty patter or even a witty comeback. It felt as if pieces of a shell were starting to break apart and fall away, but with Gabe being the way he was, focusing on what Blaze needed, rather than on anything else, would it be okay to not rebuild that shell?

Tom had moved off to a series of thin, dead trees, his face all concentration, his hands steady on his chainsaw. Gabe tugged Blaze in that direction.

"Wait till he's moved on, then make sure the area around the felled tree is clear." Gabe used his own chainsaw to demonstrate how to use it to trim dead branches away. "Trim anything that might get caught when the log or branch falls to the ground. Then start slicing through the trunk. About twelve to eighteen inches is standard for a wood stove and a good size for fireplaces, as well. We'll trim to size whatever Tom is cutting down, then we'll all stop and stack so the wood can age and dry properly. Later, we'll use the axe to split the logs into quarters. Sound good?"

Blaze nodded, gripping his chainsaw more confidently this time around. But what really sounded good, oddly, and in the middle of the low burr that he could hear through his ear protection, was Gabe's voice.

Seriously, with a voice like he had, Gabe could read a plumbing supply catalog and Blaze would be leaning forward to learn as much as he could. The sweat on Gabe's chest, a small bead of it, was slipping down to his t-shirt, and all Blaze wanted to do was lean in and then lean in some more. Which was stupid because no matter how nice Gabe was, he was still the man, still in charge, and he could do pretty much whatever he wanted to with any of them.

Blaze believed that, had believed it from the first moment he'd stepped foot inside of Wyoming Correctional. Only now, he wasn't there anymore, so should he keep thinking like this?

Maybe not, especially when he was working side by side with Gabe, in tandem, copying the strokes he made with his chainsaw, standing with his left leg forward, like Gabe was. Stopping to take a drink of water when Gabe signaled they should. Being, in short, the man's shadow. Only it wasn't cool and lonely, it was warm and sun-drenched, and Blaze shook his head, trying to rid himself of foolish thoughts.

He did his best, but it was hard to stop focusing on Gabe like this, especially when they were pretty much alone with each other while they worked amidst the spicy smell of the pines, beneath the bowl of blue sky overhead.

Halfway through the afternoon, Gabe signaled that they should stop, even though it hadn't felt like they'd been working very long.

"Let's switch off, so you can get some experience with the chipper," said Gabe, after he'd turned off his chainsaw. He pulled off his headgear, holding it against one canted hip, knee slightly bent. "That way, come dinnertime, you can tell me which one you prefer and we'll have you doing that more than the other."

As to which one Blaze preferred, his first instinct was to say that he preferred working on whatever Gabe was working on, which was as stupid as any other thought he'd had that day. But he flipped open his face shield, and took off his earmuffs, and followed Gabe through the woods after turning off his chainsaw and putting on the brake and placing the chainsaw back on the picnic table.

At the wood chipper, neither Wayne nor Kurt seemed very hard at work, mostly goofing around while the chipper churned at nothing. Wayne was leaning on a large stick rather than hauling it close, and Kurt, with his gloves off, was chewing on one of his thumbnails.

"We're going to switch, guys," said Gabe. "Kurt, turn that off and I'll show Tom and Blaze how to turn it on, how to load it."

Blaze stood next to Tom as they both watched Gabe turn the crank and start the engine on the wood chipper, which made loud metallic sounds, rattling around a stray branch it was still chewing on. At the other end, a lazy stream of chips of wood floated into the dump truck.

"I don't want to switch," said Kurt, glaring. "I like doing this."

"It's important you get experience on all of these tools," said Gabe, calmly, barely looking at Kurt, pausing only briefly as he explained the parts of the chipper to Tom and Blaze, how to start and stop it, how to position the feeder. "Always," he said, "let the feeder run a bit when you're just starting, and also when you're finishing up. That way, it has time to process what might still be in there and that way you won't clog up the blades."

When Gabe turned the chipper on again, the feeder blades gnashed at each other, and the whole of the chipper seemed to shudder into the ground. He settled ear protection on his head, and demonstrated how to load the chipper, where to stand, how to wait before pushing more limbs and branches into the blades.

When he stepped back and moved over to where the controls were along the side, Blaze stepped back, too.

Unexpectedly, he felt someone shove him from behind and fell on the flat metal part of the feeder, halfway into the intake chute. Flailing, he shoved hard against the flat metal before feeling the whoosh of air from the blades as someone turned them off, and a dense weight tackled him to the ground.

Gabe was right on top of him, blocking the sun. They were chest to chest, Gabe's weight pressing him solidly to the earth as if he were desperately doing his best to keep Blaze from floating away on the silver-cold fright that filled his chest.

Blaze had known this moment would come. He'd known it all

JACKIE NORTH

along. Gabe looked as angry as Blaze had ever seen him, almost snarling, his face inches away from Blaze's.

"Damn it," Gabe muttered.

Blaze winced as Gabe shifted his weight, then stood up, hauling Blaze up behind him. Blaze's ribs ached, and when he gripped his left arm, his fingers came away with streaks of blood on them.

Blaze looked at the wood chipper, which was silent and still, and realized how close he'd come to getting parts of him chopped off. That was when his vision started to go white, like a cloud of billowing smoke had suddenly descended through the branches to surround him.

All he could see was that Kurt was laughing, silently, open-mouthed, gleeful.

"You shoved me, motherfucker." Blaze tried to pull out of Gabe's grasp to lunge at Kurt because in prison you didn't just take it when someone handed out a bucket of abuse, you fought back. If you could.

With his arm around Blaze's shoulders, not letting him move away, Gabe pulled out the small two-way radio strapped to his belt and clicked it on. At no point did he let go of Blaze, not even to grab Kurt or reprimand him. The other two, Wayne and Tom, stared at Gabe, their eyes round.

"Leland, this is Gabe. Come in." He waited a moment and then said, again, "Leland, come in, please."

The radio made a click sound.

"Leland, here," said Leland's voice. "What's up?"

"I've got a situation here. I know what I would like to do, but I'd like your feedback."

"Go ahead," said Leland.

Quickly, without being overly dramatic, Gabe explained the situation, then finished with, "I don't want Kurt on my team, not another minute. I want you to take him back to Wyoming Correctional so he can explain to the administration there why he's going to have to deal with his parole another way."

"Give me ten minutes," said Leland. "I'll come get him."

Gabe clicked the radio off, then clipped it back onto his belt. Blaze, still pressed against Gabe's side, could feel the angry energy from Gabe's scowl.

"Kurt, you're off my team."

With a sneer, Kurt flipped Gabe the bird like he couldn't give a shit, but then, as must have seemed obvious to Gabe, he'd never given a shit and didn't really want to be part of the team.

"I could just leave," said Kurt, his voice snapping into the air. "Walk up that road and never come back."

"You could," said Gabe, his voice calm, his arm around Blaze a steady, warm presence. "But you'd have a long walk ahead of you to wherever you're going. Then you'll be in violation of your parole. So think about it. Leland will take you back to Wyoming Correctional. He'll explain the situation, and you won't be in violation."

Gabe trudged them all back through the woods and past the mess tent to the first aid building. Though Blaze tried to keep his head on straight, he stumbled half the way there, then took a deep breath and made himself walk upright.

The first aid building was a tiny, white-painted wooden structure that held a metal table, a rolling chair and two tall metal cabinets full of supplies. The place could barely hold all of them, but Tom and Wayne and Kurt huddled in the doorway, watching.

"'m I okay?" asked Blaze, unable to keep his voice from shaking.

"You are," said Gabe. He was using scissors to cut off the sleeve of Blaze's blue shirt.

"Then why—" Blaze couldn't even finish the sentence. His mouth had gone dry and his heart was hammering, his head swimming.

"You got gouged on the back of your arm by a bolt, or possibly the edge of the feeder plate," said Gabe. Then he looked up. "Tom, run and get him a cold soda from the fridge in the kitchen."

"Yes, sir," said Tom. "I'm on it."

Which left Kurt and Wayne to watch from the doorway as Gabe gave up on the scissors and directed Blaze to take his long-sleeved shirt off and then his t-shirt.

His arms shaking, Blaze did as he was told, his eyesight going in and out of focus as a small breeze circled around his bare shoulders and went down his naked back.

Gabe started cleaning the underside of Blaze's left arm, then stopped and straightened up as Tom appeared at the doorway. Gabe took a can of Coke from him, opened it, and handed it to Blaze.

"Drink this," he said as Tom handed cans of soda to the team. "It's nice and cold."

Blaze drank obediently while Gabe cleaned Blaze's upper arm with something that stung but which made his arm go numb quite soon after that. Then Gabe cleaned the arm again and placed a large bandage and swathed the arm with an ace bandage.

"Can I do anything for the rest of you?" asked Gabe. "This split lip, and these ribs?"

Blaze looked down along his side, to where Gabe was pointing. He lifted his hand in the way so Gabe wouldn't touch his ribs, which were now screaming at him.

"No. I don't know," he said, barely muttering this. He didn't want to make a big deal about how his ribs had been hurting, and how they were now hurting more. This wasn't the kind of attention he ever enjoyed, less so when it was coming from Gabe.

"No?" asked Gabe, sounding surprised.

He took out a tube of something and, with gentle fingers, he stroked Blaze's ribs. Blaze's whole body reacted with a shudder, up and down, as though in memory of being stroked in the right way.

Blaze had to put the soda down or spill it, then dipped his head, trying to keep still, trying his best not to lean into that touch. But Gabe was done. He wiped his hands on a paper towel, then helped Blaze back into his t-shirt. The long-sleeved shirt was a goner, so Gabe tossed that in the trash, then cleaned up the scraps from his first aid.

"We'll get you a new shirt," said Gabe, then he stopped and turned to the door.

Blaze could hear the angry, low growl of a truck's engine. Which wasn't for him, was it? He blinked as Tom and Wayne and Kurt moved

THE COWBOY AND THE RASCAL

out of the doorway, and then Leland stepped into view, looking tall and hard-eyed, his cowboy hat nowhere to be seen.

"Kurt," said Leland, without moving a muscle. "Go get your stuff, then get in the truck. I'm taking you back."

"Fuck you," said Kurt without any fear.

"Don't make me tell you again."

There was no way Blaze would have ignored such a command and, evidently Kurt, suddenly docile, couldn't either, and marched out of the first aid hut, Leland right behind him. After a few moments, there was the sound of a truck's engine gearing up, a pair of doors slamming shut, and then the truck trundled off.

Blaze could admit only to himself that he was glad Kurt was gone. Kurt was like Blaze's brother Alex, suddenly vicious for reasons known only to himself.

It could have been worse. He could have gotten shoved into the blades, and though he tried to remind himself that he hadn't been, he was shuddering so hard, he couldn't bring the can of Coke to his mouth.

"You fellows go on and get back to the chipper," said Gabe to Wayne and Tom. "It's almost dinner time, but you can use the scoop shovels to clean up any chips that landed anywhere outside of the dump truck. I'll be right there. We'll stack any wood, then we'll cover the tools, make sure the chipper is all the way off and secured."

Suddenly, the little building was empty except for him and Gabe. Who was leaning close as he tucked the edges of the ace bandage around Blaze's bicep, his breath whispering across Blaze's neck, feeling warm where Blaze was cold.

"I shouldn't have turned my back on him," Blaze said, wincing a bit as Gabe lowered his arm. "You never do in the prison yard, you know? Some asshole is always going to want to test you, so you have to keep your back to the wall. Which, in this yard, is a chain-link fence with a little roll of barbed wire on top of it—"

Blaze paused to take a breath, almost gasping with his desperation to let Gabe know, in no uncertain terms, that he knew how to keep the enemy in his sights at all times. That he'd fucked up. That he wouldn't let it happen again, no, sir.

"You shouldn't have to worry about that here," said Gabe. "And I'm sorry I didn't see the warning signs and get Kurt in check before something bad happened."

"Leland didn't see it either," said Blaze, reaching for the can of Coke, swallowing a mouthful down, and then another, the sugar rushing into his system.

"What do you mean?" asked Gabe. He went very still, his eyes on Blaze.

"Leland had a Zoom meeting with Kurt, right?" Blaze nodded, because he already knew it was true. "Just like he did with the rest of us. Leland," he paused to emphasize the name, wanting very much to reassure Gabe that it wasn't his fault. "Leland's the one who fucked up, if anyone did."

"Hey, now," said Gabe.

"All I'm saying is, you're not a mind reader," said Blaze with a shake of his head.

"No, I'm not," said Gabe, his blue eyes sad.

He was close, but he didn't move away. Instead, he stayed near, that warm hand on Blaze's shoulder, those eyes watchful as Blaze finished the Coke.

The smell of Gabe's sweat, the scent of his anger, all of this swirled around Blaze, unsettling him, bestirring him. Swirling feelings inside of him that he didn't know what to do with.

"Thanks," he said, looking around him for a trash can.

Gabe took the empty can and placed it on the metal counter below the cabinets of supplies.

"You want to sit the rest of the afternoon out?" asked Gabe. "Or do you want to help stack wood?"

"Stack," said Blaze without even pausing to think. In Gabe's eyes, he saw approval for his choice, and a flicker of something else that darkened the blue to midnight.

"You'll need a new shirt," said Gabe.

"Why?" Surely an ex-con like himself could work in a torn and bloodied t-shirt.

"You don't want to work with wood with bare arms," said Gabe. "Or in a bloody shirt. It might attract bears."

With a nod, Gabe straightened up, though his hand remained on Blaze's shoulder for another long, warm minute.

"Go and change and meet us near the wood chipper. We'll stack our wood there and cover it with a tarp, and let it season."

Gabe started clearing away the used supplies, throwing away the cotton swabs he'd used, dark red with dried blood, and cleaned off the scissors he'd used to cut Blaze's shirt.

Standing in the open doorway, Blaze realized Gabe's broad back was to him, as if he'd not the slightest concern that Blaze would jump him unawares.

"Okay."

Maybe two years in prison had taught him never to expect kindness or to be treated decently, though he knew, deep in his heart, that being a member of the Butterworth family had already taught him that, years before.

Today, though. Today. Blaze had been treated like he mattered. Like his wounds deserved tending. Like concern and caring were simply what Gabe had inside of him in abundance. Enough to share. Enough to give to Blaze.

"Okay," he said again. "And thanks."

Gabe looked over his shoulder at Blaze, drying the scissors with a paper towel at the same time.

"For what?"

"For everything," said Blaze, and then he turned and hurried along the path to his tent, where not one, but two other brand new shirts waited for him. It was so different to live this way, and though he didn't really believe it would continue as it was, part of him wanted it to, oh, so very badly.

CHAPTER 10
GABE

A quick call to Leland in the evening told Gabe exactly what he'd been expecting. That Kurt wanted no part of playing lumberjack, as he put it, and preferred to serve out his parole in the usual way. In a halfway house, checking in with his PO every week, and taking state-scheduled drug tests, though Gabe imagined Kurt had put it more stridently.

Maybe for Kurt, the known pattern of this kind of parole made him more comfortable. And maybe, as Gabe's training had warned him, some ex-cons simply weren't interested in taking advantage of any opportunities to start a new life, even if they'd been shoved into a wholesome situation like the valley presented.

It won't matter, the instructor at Wyoming Correction had told them. *No matter how frustrating, these men are grown adults and are allowed to make mistakes. We can teach them, and demonstrate to them, and do everything that would encourage anyone else to take a different road this time, but for some men, it simply won't matter. And you have to be willing to walk away from it.*

So Gabe had come to the point where he needed to walk away from caring too much, though it was hard. His intention had always

JACKIE NORTH

been to make himself useful, to help others adjust to a different kind of life, just as he had when he'd come out of the army.

No change was stress free, even good ones. But, at that moment, as he sat in the middle of the ten-person table, with three freshly showered ex-cons huddled around him like he was the single guiding light in their existence, maybe he was making a little bit of difference.

Tom, as though freed from any reticence by the violence of the afternoon, was talking a blue streak about his girlfriend and his little baby, whom he had never seen, as she'd been born while he was behind bars.

"Joanna wouldn't bring my little girl to the prison because she didn't want her to be around all of that." Tom shrugged as if the price he'd paid with having no visits would all be worth it in the end. "But I'm going to talk to her again tonight and ask her to visit on Sunday. That's all right, isn't it, sir?" Tom looked up from his dinner.

"Gabe," said Gabe, smiling into his cup of coffee. Maybe Tom was messing with him, or maybe he honestly forgot. "Just Gabe, please."

"How about *boss*?" asked Wayne, snickering, but in the way of a man who knew he could tease the man in charge, just a little bit, which was the kind of trust Gabe knew he'd enjoy cultivating. "Can we call you that?"

"What do you guys think?" asked Gabe, putting his coffee mug down and looking at each one in turn.

All three of them, Tom, Wayne, and Blaze, looked at him with those wide *Who, me?* and *I-didn't-do-it* eyes, which he'd realized from the first were expressions they'd learned to wear in prison, to keep from being someone the guards might pick out from the crowd, simply to have someone to lay the blame on. Or maybe they simply didn't know what he was asking them.

"I prefer it if you call me Gabe," he said. "Since we're all working on the same team and doing the same work, *sir* sounds too formal." He gestured at them. "And, in my view, calling me *boss* makes it sound like we're in a chain gang, and I'm standing on the sidelines with my vicious bloodhound or something while you guys are digging ditches."

"They use German Shepherds sometimes, too," said Wayne, again breaking from his usual reticence. "But this is the furthest thing from a chain gang that I've ever been on."

"And it's not like the chain gangs you see in prison movies," said Blaze, quiet and on the side, almost like an afterthought. "You're not like a boss at all. I mean—like in movies about chain gangs." Blaze shrugged helplessly, like he was worried he'd made a mistake in saying it the way he had. "You're still the boss. Still in charge."

"That I am," said Gabe. "Okay, you can call me boss if it suits you."

"So what about Sunday visits, boss?" asked Tom, leaning forward, both hands on the table. "Or was that just fluff someone put in the agreement I signed?"

"Sunday visits are a real thing," said Gabe. "Guests can come from ten to five. They can stay for lunch or dinner, but in that case, we'd need to know so the cooks can make the right amount of food. Sound fair?"

"So how long can we take with the visit?" asked Tom.

"As long as you like," said Gabe. "Just like with showers. Just be aware of the needs of others around you."

"I can't with this guy," said Tom with a dramatic moan, pressing his palms to his eyes.

"It's the truth," said Gabe, laughing. "You basically have Sundays off, unless there's some kind of occupational emergency, just like you would on any other job. How is that a bad thing?"

"It's different," said Wayne, eying Gabe sternly, like he should already know how new and untried this would seem to an ex-con. "Just different, that's all."

"So, yeah." Gabe bit into a chunk of cornbread that he'd slathered with butter. "Tell your girlfriend to come at ten, if you like. Just let Del or Neal know if she's going to be having lunch with us."

"The whole day," said Blaze, his voice faint. "We can have the whole day off."

"It's not a prison, Blaze," said Gabe, gently. "Like I described during orientation, we'd like you to stick around for the first two weeks until you settle in. Then, after that, you can have guests come, or you can sign yourself out. You could even check out a truck, or we could arrange other transportation for you."

The response he got to a statement like that was raised eyebrows and more suspicious silence. Maybe they'd all missed that part when he'd explained it to them the first day.

"What're *you* going to do on Sunday?" asked Wayne with his usual scolding tone as though what Gabe was saying was so far out of the realm of normal, it needed to be prodded and poked at every turn.

"I'm going to go visit my friend, Jasper," said Gabe. "He's the guy you met today. We knew each other in the army. He's the one that got me my job as ranch hand." He paused, then realized nobody was saying anything. "How about you, Wayne? What are you going to do on your day off?"

"Eat breakfast. Sleep. Eat lunch. Sleep. Repeat." Wayne shrugged. "My people live in Sleepy Eye, Minnesota, and are hardly likely to come all this way just to see me. Maybe I'll go see them when my parole is over, though."

"I'm spending as much time with Joanna as I can," said Tom. His eyes were glowing.

"How about you, Blaze?" asked Gabe, looking in Blaze's direction because Blaze hadn't said a single thing, hardly, and he was looking a little white. "Are you going to call someone to come visit you? Your family, maybe?"

"They don't—" Blaze started, and then he stopped, shoulders tightening as if he meant to make his way through what he had to say by brute force alone. "They won't—" He shrugged. "They never visited me in prison, so I doubt they'll visit me here."

"Ah." From his training, Gabe knew that sometimes families needed time to adjust to having someone with a criminal past in their midst. However, from what he'd read in Blaze's file, that wasn't the issue for the Butterworth family. As to what *was* the problem, with an audience of two parolees, it wasn't the time or the place to ask. "Well, maybe now that you're out, they might think differently?"

Blaze shrugged, looking away from the table, away from the remains of their dinner, toward the end of the tent. Gabe looked where Blaze was looking, at where the sun was sparkling through the trees, making him think, oddly, of starlight.

"Well, I'm full." Gabe stood up and bussed his dishes, smiling to himself as his team followed suit. "We can build a fire again later," he said. "We can make s'mores, if you like."

"Oh, oh." Tom half bumped into Blaze as he got up and went to the landline. "Can it wait till after my phone call?"

"Sure," said Gabe. "We'll do it right as it starts to get dark."

Wiping his hands on his jeans, Gabe looked at Blaze. Out of the corner of his eye, he saw Wayne leaving the mess tent, probably headed to his tent, which he now had to himself, as if his intention was to use every free moment he had to get as much sleep as possible. As if he was catching up on all that he'd lost while in prison.

"How about you?" Gabe said to Blaze. "Why don't you give it a try and call your family. Where are they? Denver? Is it close enough that they can come for a visit?"

Blaze nodded slowly, and he wasn't smiling.

"It'll be all right," said Gabe.

He needed to stop pushing, so he headed back to the kitchen to ask whether or not they had everything they needed to make s'mores and, if not, who might be willing to run into town to get supplies. He'd be willing, if it came to that, but he was informed that they had plenty of everything.

When he came back to the mess tent, Blaze was on the phone, and Tom was seated at one of the tables. Gabe went over to him.

"I thought you were going to make a phone call," he said to Tom.

"I'm going to be on the phone for at least an hour." Tom waved in the direction of the landline, where Blaze, seated on the metal folding chair, was hunched over the phone. "So I thought I'd let him go first. He said it'd be short, anyway."

"Nicely done," said Gabe.

He touched Tom on the shoulder in a friendly way to show how much he approved of this small sacrifice, then stepped closer to Blaze, standing behind him a little way as if he, too, wanted his turn on the phone, even though he had his own cellphone. It was when he heard

Blaze's voice that he realized he was standing too close and was hearing too much that simply wasn't his place to hear.

"But I'd like it if you came," said Blaze, his voice soft, pleading. "It's only a few hours' drive to get here, and—"

Suddenly, Blaze held the phone's handset away from his ear, his whole body wincing. A tinny sounding voice, raised and loud, squawked through the receiver, and when Blaze put the handset back to his ear, his body went still.

He seemed to realize someone was behind him, for he turned, his face grave and still, a hard and bitter light in his eyes as he hung up.

"You're next, Tom," Blaze said, and then he saw it was Gabe and started in his chair.

"They'll come around," said Gabe. "Like I said, it can take time to adjust."

Blaze stood up, shoving his hands—his fists, really—in his pockets, in a way that Gabe himself sometimes did when he didn't know what to do with his hands and, sometimes, his emotions.

"Blaze—"

"Fuck off," said Blaze, startling Gabe into silence.

Blaze looked like he hurt all over, like he'd been pounded hard, and, as Blaze stalked off along the path toward his tent, Gabe went over the whole day in his mind, every interaction he'd had with Blaze.

Sure, Blaze had been rattled by getting shoved into the wood chipper like that, but anyone would be. But he'd almost been serene during dinner.

It had been when Gabe had asked each man on his team who might be visiting him on Sunday. That was when Blaze's behavior had changed. He, Gabe, had pushed Blaze into a phone call that Blaze had not, in retrospect, wanted to make. Then he'd been rejected by his family, which made Gabe's blood simmer beneath the surface of his skin.

Every man on his team deserved their second chance, which they were going to get by being in the program. They also deserved support from family and friends.

Blaze had trusted Gabe enough to make that call, so it was up to

Gabe to step up and find out what was really going on and then do his best to help Blaze. At the very least, he could lend a listening ear.

Gabe looked over his shoulder. Tom was yammering away to Joanna, his whole face a smile, hands animated, pure love shining through him. This was the woman Tom had gone to jail for in an attempt to provide baby supplies, and Gabe looked forward to meeting the woman who inspired such devotion. And maybe Wayne's relatives might eventually make the flight from Sleepy Eye, who knew.

As for now, he needed to see how he could help Blaze, so he walked along the path through the woods, thinking about the flagstones that were soon to arrive and would need to be installed, and stopped when he stood in front of tent #4.

It was important, as his training had instructed him, to give each man his space, the right to own his own territory. Equally important was to let each man know he was there to support them in their efforts.

"Knock, knock," he said as he rapped the tent pole lightly with his knuckles. "Can I come in?"

"It's fine," said Blaze's voice, thick and hard.

Gabe stepped into the shadows of the tent. The far end had the canvas rolled back, the screen zipped tight, and there was a nice breeze, the sun warm on the wooden platform.

"I didn't mean it was fine, you could come in," said Blaze with a snap. "I meant I'm fine, don't bother me."

Gabe's eyes adjusted to the slightly dim interior. Blaze was sitting on the left-side cot, fists on his thighs, hair lank in his face. One green eye staring hard at the wooden planks of the floor as if there'd be something to see there.

"If you want to talk—" Gabe began, but was shushed by Blaze's hand jerking up to stop him. "It's okay to be angry," he said, trying again.

"Please. Just stop with the counseling mumbo jumbo." Blaze looked up at him. "If that's okay to say to the boss man."

Blaze's whole body shifted on the cot, as if he were preparing himself for a blow or, at the very least, a sternly worded lecture.

Gabe wondered, quite suddenly, as if he'd never considered it before, or if he had, it had only been fleetingly, how prison could change a man. How someone as confident and outspoken as Blaze seemed to be could be turned into someone whose body reflected the feelings in the room, violent or not, mean or not, like a human barometer. Pulsing away when things got dark, but moving forward at the slightest chance that it would not get bad.

Tom and Wayne and even Kurt seemed like they were who they always had been, and maybe prison had solidified or changed that, but they really remained the same as described in their files.

Not Blaze. His file indicated that when he'd gotten arrested, he'd been doing and dealing drugs. Maybe being in prison had become a poison in his system. But not once, at least not in Gabe's presence, had Blaze behaved like someone for whom drugs were the goal. He seemed too smart for that, too alert to his surroundings, as if looking for which way to jump.

Suddenly Gabe wished he'd had more than a two-hour seminar on the drug world because if he had, he wouldn't be so puzzled now.

"Can I sit?" asked Gabe. When Blaze shrugged, Gabe sat on Tom's cot, hoping he wouldn't mind. "I'm here to listen, if you need it."

"It won't matter," said Blaze. "You won't want to hear what I have to say."

"Why wouldn't I?"

"Because nobody else believes me about what happened, even if it is the truth."

Gabe considered this as he leaned forward, elbows on his thighs, hands loosely clasped between his legs, which was the least aggressive stance he knew. "You talking about whether or not you're guilty?" asked Gabe.

During every day of their training, they had been reminded as to how many times they'd hear *I wasn't even there* or *I'm not guilty* or *It was a setup.*

Gabe believed in the law, and felt that most of the time, if you got

THE COWBOY AND THE RASCAL

arrested, it was for a good reason. Then again, he couldn't jump to conclusions; he needed to hear what Blaze had to say. That was, if Gabe could get Blaze to trust him, even for a minute.

"Blaze—"

"Look, it doesn't matter, okay?" Blaze's expression was hard as he sat up and pulled his hands into even tighter fists. "My family is shit. It's in my file, which you have no doubt read. We're carnies. We follow carnivals. We work the booths. We scam people all the time. I was taught to pick pockets at a young age. Then we started doing the driveway scam."

"I read a bit about the driveway scam," said Gabe. "But it was only a paragraph. How did it work?"

With a glance at Gabe, Blaze's words slowed down, as though to make sure he could get the idea into Gabe's obviously stupid head that way.

"You get an old person," said Blaze. "Or two old people, a couple. Doesn't matter. Old people are lonely and they are rich. You tell them you've been authorized to redo their driveway. The longer the driveway, the better. You tell them that you need a deposit and could they write a check, please? Mostly they do because we've got uniforms, and badges, and a pickup truck dressed to look like it's from a company in the area. Then we pocket the check and never come back. That's the scam."

"That's pretty mean," said Gabe. He almost wasn't worried about making that particular judgment, because Blaze seemed so upset and indignant about it.

"I didn't like it." Blaze frowned, his lips pressed together. "I couldn't stand their old faces trying to comprehend what we were asking for. It was like they didn't have anybody to check in with about it, and my dad would put the pressure on so hard, there wasn't anything they could do but write the check. We could have made thousands, but we stopped doing it."

"That's not what you got arrested for," said Gabe. "Though it's easy to see there was something in this scam that didn't sit right with you."

"Listen, I was raised to scam people from the day I was born."

JACKIE NORTH

Blaze's scowl trembled like he was holding himself back from bursting out screaming. "But yeah, the driveway scam was too much."

"You were arrested for doing drugs, possibly dealing, and for domestic violence." Gabe nodded, because the arrest record had been written quite clearly.

"I was *arrested*," said Blaze, quite firmly and slowly, "because I was getting my GED and my family didn't like it."

"Your GED?" asked Gabe, though he knew that Blaze had been studying for it while behind bars. It also occurred to him that since Blaze was twenty-four years old, the gap between him and any formal education was at least five years. Blaze had been trying to better himself, to lift himself out of the swamp of his own past, which took hard work and guts.

"I was trying to get it, but they didn't like it. And I was *arrested* because my brother Alex was doing and dealing drugs and he had a hard-on for teaching me a lesson about it. When he attacked me and tried to beat me up and the cops came? My folks said I was the guilty one. Me. Not Alex."

"You were arrested," said Gabe, feeling solemn and still at the certainty he had inside of him at that moment. "Because you weren't following the family tradition." Anger flared all over again at Blaze's plight. He knew what that felt like to be rejected by an entire family, but he stemmed his reaction, knowing that sharing his feelings wasn't what Blaze needed now.

"That's why they won't visit me." Blaze seemed to crumple, shoulders rolling forward, his hair falling in his eyes again. "They've cut me off and now I don't have nobody."

Blaze's eyes looked hot and shiny, as though he was near to tears and Gabe was horrified with himself for pushing so hard, too hard, because it was suddenly obvious to him that Blaze hadn't been completely hardened by prison, had never developed a poker face. Was struggling, more than Tom or Wayne seemed to be.

Gabe was the only one to blame for bringing Blaze to where he was, sitting on his cot, struggling to compose himself. To pretend he was rubbing the corner of his eye with a hard palm because there was something in his eye and he needed to get it out.

"That sounds rough," said Gabe, wanting to allow Blaze his privacy at the same time he wanted to help Blaze feel more settled. "I know what it's like to be alone, and I'm sorry I suggested that you call them."

"Get out," said Blaze, barking it. "*Please* get out."

Enough was enough, and Gabe knew it. Anything more he might say, however kindly intended, would only make it worse.

"All right," he said. "I'll leave you be, but I'm here if you need to talk. And don't forget, we're doing a bonfire and having s'mores at sunset."

Saying that last bit felt incredibly and foolishly optimistic. As if a bonfire could fix anything. As if s'mores could repair the crumpled heap that Blaze's family's betrayal had left him in.

Blaze's reaction to his family's betrayal, his lashing out at Gabe, hit Gabe more than Kurt's *Fuck you* ever had. Gabe wasn't pleased at how it had gone with Kurt, but it was easy to see that this wasn't the right situation for Kurt. But it was for Blaze, surely it was.

The program had only been underway for a few days and already Blaze was stripping away layers of himself for all to see. Or maybe just for Gabe to see, as Blaze didn't seem to talk like this when there were others around.

Or maybe Gabe was making things up in his own mind, being overwhelmed by the events of the day.

What if he'd not been watching Kurt at exactly that moment? What if he'd not been quick enough on his feet to slam into Blaze and send them both to the ground, out of harm's way? Blaze could have been severely wounded, or even killed, and that blood would have been on Gabe's hands.

And he did have blood on his hands, for as he looked down, opening and closing his fingers into a fist, he could see that he had Blaze's blood on him, now dried, darkened to brown-red, flaking in spots.

He needed to wash up, and he needed to get his head on straight and stop intentionally pulling Blaze into private conversations. But how was he supposed to do that when Blaze trusted him enough to nearly come apart? He didn't want Blaze coming to him like that. He wanted—

He shouldn't be wanting any closeness with Blaze at all. That would be a huge mistake, given his authority over Blaze. And the last thing he would want to put Blaze through.

He straightened his shoulders and started for the facilities. There he would wash up, and look at himself in the mirror, and give himself a good talking to. Being anything other than the most straight-laced team lead he could possibly be would only lead to disaster.

CHAPTER 11
BLAZE

Blaze absorbed the sudden silence that Gabe's departure left behind. The warmth of the sun on the canvas of the tent was going away, slowly, like a long goodbye, leaving Blaze shivering. The sunshine slicing into the tent felt like a glare, one he wanted to hide from.

Scrubbing at his eyes, he wondered how the hell, *why* the hell, he'd told Gabe all of what he had.

Nearly every prison guard Blaze had ever encountered had lain in wait for an opportunity to learn something they could use as a weapon. That Blaze missed his family and didn't think he'd ever get them back would have been a terrific addition to their arsenal. Like a fool, Blaze had handed this information to Gabe. The. Boss.

He heard voices among the trees, Tom coming this way, maybe, or Wayne walking aimlessly through the woods, chewing on his nails.

He grabbed his shower kit, the newly folded pair of towels he saw on his bed, a washcloth. A clean shirt. One of the red bandanas. Then he grabbed two tokens because, damn it, he was going to shower for a whole hour and fuck anyone who complained.

He marched through the woods to the facilities, picked a stall, stripped off his clothes, throwing them anyoldhow, and turned on the shower as hot as he could stand it. Then he stood under the stream, just stood there, and pretended he was standing in a rainstorm, wiping at his eyes even as water streamed over his face.

There was nobody guarding him. He could turn off the water, dry off, get dressed, and just *go*. Except he had nowhere to go and no one waiting for him there.

There was no pretending his family gave a shit about him, let alone that they would visit. He was as alone as he'd ever been.

Not to mention, the parole program was turning into a shitstorm, and he doubted he would make it even one more day. Not with Gabe hassling him like he had.

Voices came closer, brought by the cool wind that whispered through the trees. Tom and Wayne came into the shower area, snickering over some joke between them.

"That you, man?" asked Tom's voice.

"Yeah," said Blaze, clearing the choke in his voice as best he could.

"How many tokens have you burned through?" asked Wayne.

"I'm using two," said Blaze in hard tones, like he didn't give a damn. "Two fucking tokens."

There were murmurs of approval that vanished beneath two other showers being turned on.

They would all shower, dry off, dress, and go help build a bonfire. Then, like a troop of Boy Scouts, they would make s'mores. Like they were anyone other than the criminals they were. Like they were at summer camp with a bit of work thrown in.

It was all fake, wasn't it. Even his feelings for Gabe, stray thoughts at all the wrong times, were fake. Surely Gabe's, in return, if there were any, were fake, too.

Just like Tom had said, *I can't with this guy*, in his attempt to express how very strange living like this was in contrast to being in prison, Blaze also *could not with this guy*. Gabe could not be as nice as he seemed to be. Could not be as steady and predictable and non-violent as he'd been. No way. No way. No way.

Head slumped, Blaze went through the motions of showering, using the clean-smelling Ivory soap. On the underside of his arm, the

THE COWBOY AND THE RASCAL

skin was stinging, the bandage hanging loose. He tugged at it, ripping it off, hissing as soap flowed over the cut.

He washed himself all over, slowly, even between his toes, propping his foot up on the bottom slat of the wooden ledge. Taking his time, he washed his hair with the bright-smelling, citrus-scented shampoo *and* conditioner. Not a two-in-one shampoo and conditioner, like you got from the prison commissary, but separate bottles.

Tom and Wayne finished their showers, dried off, got dressed. He heard them putting their tokens in the slot and they left Blaze alone once more.

When he was finished, and about as clean as he possibly could be, Blaze rinsed off and turned off the water. Then, after wrapping his upper arm with the red bandana, he dried off and got dressed, as well.

Propping each foot on the bench seat in the dressing area, Blaze put on a new pair of socks and laced up his still-new Carhartt boots. As he stood up straight and gathered his things together, his feet felt oddly solid beneath him, his body much more relaxed.

It had been a long time since he'd taken a good hot shower like that. As he stood there and used the towel to dry his hair a little more, he thought he might feel a bit better than he had before. A bit more like going on with things rather than allowing himself to quit.

He wasn't like his brother. Wasn't the type to give up like Alex always seemed to do when things got too hard for him. He simply couldn't believe that the rest of the summer would turn out to be as kind-hearted and earnest as Gabe was always acting like it was.

Or maybe it was. Maybe it wouldn't turn out to be so bad.

Was he mad at Gabe, who had so kindly wrapped up his arm? Maybe not. Maybe he was just taking out his frustration on Gabe, who, in turn, had just taken Blaze's anger, as solid as a stone.

Things could change if he let them. And what if they did? What if the parole program was exactly what it was purported to be?

What if *Gabe* was exactly who he seemed to be? Just a regular guy doing his best to help some ex-cons start a new life? And what was he getting out of it? Nobody did something for nothing, not even nice guys. Maybe Blaze needed to find out what that was and capitalize on it.

Or.

Maybe he could just let it be what it was. Play it where it lay rather than skulking about coming up with a mad plan to control everything and everyone in his environment. Just let each day happen as it would.

Madness. Foolishness. But better to try doing it a different way than continuing on like he was still in prison. He was not, as Gabe had so kindly told him, his voice soft and steady, his blue eyes without a trace of a lie in them.

It's not a prison, Blaze.

If Blaze allowed himself to retreat at the first indication of a lie, he could get through the summer. He'd know the lie when he spotted it, and he could back up all the way to the wall if he had to. Only then.

For now, he was going to move forward as if the promise of a better day was based in the world, the truth, as Gabe saw it and talked about it.

Moving out into the main area, Blaze put his two wooden tokens in the slot. Then, rolling his damp towel and washcloth under his arm, he strode purposefully back to his tent. There, he laid the towels and washcloth on the railing along the side of the tent, as Tom had done, and put his toiletries on the shelf. Then he grabbed his sherpa-lined denim jacket and made his way to the fire pit.

It wasn't yet dark with twilight still long between the trees, but everybody was at the fire pit, including Del and Neal, looking a bit strange out of their cook's whites. Wayne was pawing through the box that held the supplies for s'mores, and Tom was patiently handing Gabe strips of kindling wood.

Gabe knelt by the fire, one denim-clad knee in the dirt, the other thigh bent. The sleeves of his snap-button shirt were rolled up, crisp-edged, his dark hair messy over his forehead, making him look like a mountain man or a lumberjack in one of those calendars that specialized in rugged-looking men.

When Gabe looked up, his eyes found Blaze immediately. Focusing on Blaze as though Blaze had been waited for, looked for.

There was nothing in those eyes that Blaze wanted to look away from. There was no pity, no disapproval for not being manly enough to make it two years in prison, just to break down pretty much the second he'd gotten out. No. There was just that steady kindness, the same as before. Same as always.

"Blaze," said Gabe, turning the sound of his name sound into a hearty greeting. "You're just in time to help Wayne unpack the box of goodies the cooks brought for us."

Blaze looked at Wayne, who had half of a chocolate bar stuffed in his mouth, like a kid who couldn't wait to roast that marshmallow before assembling his s'more. Both Wayne and Tom were like that. Impatient, hustling through to the good stuff. Half-laughing about it all, not with good humor, it seemed, but like they wanted to dismiss it, that it wasn't serious. That it didn't matter.

Well, it mattered. At least to Blaze. If he was going to make it through the summer on his way to some other place, a new life, he knew it mattered.

"Sure," he said, doffing his denim jacket, which he wouldn't need until the sun really went down. "We can put everything on this rock over here."

Wayne was pretty much goofing around as Blaze arranged two rows of Hershey's chocolate bars—no generic stuff for the program, it seemed. Then Blaze laid out the four wax-wrapped packets from the box of graham crackers, then set the bag of marshmallows on the rock farthest from the fire that was being built.

He'd never roasted marshmallows before, but he knew from TV that you needed something long and slender to poke through them so you could hold it over the flames.

"Let's get some sticks," he said to nobody in particular.

"Oh, we've got skewers." Del hauled himself up from his Adirondack chair and pointed to the little black pouch at the bottom of the box. He pulled it out and demonstrated the little rubber grommets on the end of each prong, how the handle telescoped for length. "And they're color coded, right here."

He pointed to where the skewer met the plastic handle. Then he handed the skewer to Blaze, and the little black bag as well.

Blaze took the skewer and hefted it in his hand, thinking it would have been a whole lot more fun to scrounge for the right-sized sticks and then to sharpen the ends with a pocketknife or something. But then, it should be remembered that this whole setup was designed to please very rich people who, while they might not mind a breeze wafting around their ankles while they showered, probably didn't want any hassle when roasting marshmallows over an open flame.

"You could get some sticks, if you want." Leaning back, still kneeling, Gabe reached into his left pocket to pull out, of all things, a shiny red Swiss Army knife. He held it out to Blaze like he wasn't at all worried that Blaze would open it just to use it on him.

As if seeing Blaze's hesitation, Gabe reached his arm out even farther. "I know you want to."

Pausing, Blaze remembered his promise to himself. He hadn't known Gabe very long at all, but everything he'd done and said so far had been exactly what it seemed to be, and not just a trick to mess with Blaze.

"Yeah, I do. Thanks." Blaze took the pocketknife and hefted it in his hand as he'd done with the skewer. Right away, it felt better. In keeping with the setting. In sync with how a marshmallow roasting session should go.

He flicked open the blade, and studied the sharpness, thinking about how in his other life, he would have been tempted to steal the knife after using it. Say he'd lost it.

But he wasn't going to, and he shoved away the memory of his mom, when the family had gone to a Denny's and she'd told Blaze to steal the salt and pepper shakers.

Oddly, at the time, Blaze had refused to take those shakers, even though they probably only cost a buck each.

Once out in the parking lot, his mother had snarled at him that he was exactly like his Uncle Shawn, as if that were the worst insult she could think of. Blaze hadn't seen Uncle Shawn in years, come to think of it, and his leaving had been quite the family scandal because Shawn, it seemed, didn't want to be in on any of their scams.

Snapping the knife shut, Blaze nodded at Gabe, and went into the trees, foraging for likely looking sticks that might hold up to being held over an open flame. Instinct led him to picking up branches that seemed fresh, rather than the dried-out ones, and he felt good when he came back to the fire pit with a small armful of sticks.

The fire was going sprightly now, casting a golden glow over everything around it.

He laid his treasure of roasting sticks at Gabe's feet and handed his knife back to him, as if it had never occurred to him to steal it.

"Ah, excellent." With both knees in the dirt, kneeling, Gabe dusted his hands together and smiled up at Blaze like he was perfect just as he was and didn't need to steal to be considered useful. He picked up a branch and got to his feet. "These are perfect. I'll show you how to peel the bark off a little ways and how to sharpen them."

While everyone else was seated in one of the Adirondack chairs, glassy-eyed and looking at the fire, Gabe grabbed the pile of sticks, pulled Blaze to one side, and sat on one of the logs on the outer ring of the fire pit. He gestured to Blaze to sit down next to him, snapped the blade out again, and demonstrated how to prep the stick for roasting.

"Like this and this," said Gabe, peeling the bark back a little way, scraping the end to a point. "See? You can make room for more than one marshmallow, too. Like this."

Blaze paid attention, rapt, enjoying the moment, fully inside of it, captured by the sight of Gabe's strong wrists scraping each stick, the bulk of his forearm, the way his muscles jumped along his thigh as he leaned forward to grab another stick.

"Now you try."

Gabe handed the knife to Blaze, handle end first, and didn't lean away when Blaze started peeling the stick, doing it like Gabe had done. Rather, he leaned forward, unafraid, just like he'd been unafraid when Kurt had asked, all snotty, whether Gabe was worried that they'd attack him when his back was turned.

"Good," said Gabe, calm as anything when he pointed out a rough spot in the bark. "You can trim that back so the marshmallow goes on easier. So it doesn't tear."

"And if it tears?" asked Blaze.

"Then you eat it," said Gabe, his hands spread as he mock-scowled at Blaze as if that was the dumbest question he'd ever heard. But it was said with tons of good nature, with a teasing tone in his voice. "They really are better roasted than raw, though."

They started roasting marshmallows even before it got fully dark, which was good because they were clumsy at it. At least Tom, Wayne, and Blaze were, having not been brought up in households that did this sort of thing. Del, Neal, and Gabe were either naturals at it or had gotten plenty of practice, and it seemed they made their motions slow on purpose so the parolees could copy them.

Not that roasting marshmallows was rocket science at all, no sir. It was just such an innocent thing to be doing, and a little hard, even still, to adapt to doing something where *nothing bad would happen*. If prison had fucked Blaze up in other ways, that one was the biggest. To suspect disaster lurked around every corner, and that every person he met was already gunning for him even before they knew him.

The joy fully came over him when he'd assembled his first s'more and chomped into it, letting the gooey, hot mess melt on his tongue. And he couldn't restrain a moan of pleasure, not even when Gabe's blue eyes sought his, as if Blaze's happiness only added to his own.

Without thinking, Blaze, licking his lip free of melted marshmallow, winked at Gabe, like he would have when a customer stepped up to the ring tossing booth with the audacious intent of actually winning the stuffed elephant. Only this wasn't a trick or a con Blaze felt himself doing. It was different. Like an invitation of a sort. Only Gabe had already joined him in the moment, the simple delight of a kid's fireside treat.

"Good, eh?" asked Gabe, and though he might have been asking the question to everyone in general, maybe he was asking the question only of Blaze. At least it felt that way.

So Blaze answered likewise, his voice low, his gaze focused on

Gabe as he licked his thumb and attempted to remove a streak of fast-cooling marshmallow from his bare forearm.

"Yeah, it's good," he said.

Twilight was coming down all around them, pushing a breeze through the tops of the trees, sinking the air into coolness in a way that made them hustle into their denim jackets. Making the fire turn from pale orange into deeper orange and black as the logs settled into coals.

"This is when we should have started," said Gabe. "Roasting, I mean. When you stick a marshmallow into high flames, it's going to burn. Next time we should be more patient and wait for coals. Coals make the best heat for melting things."

Blaze leaned forward, belly full, and poked at the coals with the end of his sticky-ended stick until he was able to get a rise out of the logs to produce a scattering of blue sparks. The jewels inside of the dark heat of the fire were like a promise of more hidden beneath, if only he was patient enough to keep searching for them.

CHAPTER 12
GABE

The next morning, Gabe was in the mess tent, ready to sit down to eat, when Blaze showed up, wearing just a t-shirt and scratching under his bicep. Absentmindedly, like he didn't know he was scratching the scab from the wood chipper wound.

"Hey," said Gabe, going over to him. "You're bleeding."

Blaze froze, his fingers curled around the underside of his bicep. On his face was an expression Gabe couldn't quite identify, but that brought to mind, once again, the idea that Blaze was still trying to figure out how he'd gotten where he was. As if being an ex-con in a parolee rehab work camp was, each and every day, still a shock to him, and he was trying to figure out how to navigate his world.

Gabe's heart went out to him. Of course, if you did the crime, you did the time. He believed that, he really did. But maybe some guys, like Blaze, had made one tiny mistake, only to be overwhelmed with what must feel like out-of-scale consequences. Either way, if Blaze needed a little extra care in tending to the aftereffects of a near-miss at the wood chipper that was absolutely not his fault, then Gabe was fully prepared to step up to the task.

"Uh," said Blaze. He dropped his arms, stepping to one side as the others piled into the mess tent. "I wrapped it in a bandana, but that fell off."

"I should have helped you," said Gabe. "As for now, let's get you cleaned up."

He took Blaze to the first aid hut, cleaned the wound, and put a new bandage around it. All the while, Blaze watched him in utter silence, as though Gabe was a puzzle he wanted to solve. The silence was a bit different for Blaze, but it was nice, as well, to exchange quiet smiles as Gabe patted the first aid tape on Blaze's bicep.

"There's plastic wrap in the kitchen," said Gabe. "You should always put it on when you take a shower, then your bandage won't fall off." With a small shrug that he hoped was disarming, he said. "Or I could wrap it for you. Come to me any time."

If that sounded like a come-on, maybe it was only to Gabe's ears. He needed to play it cool, only it seemed to be getting harder way too fast.

"Come on," he said as he threw away the used first aid supplies, and reached to switch off the light. "Let's get some breakfast."

Breakfast was a quiet affair, after which Gabe threw himself into his work, ignoring his own personal feelings and thoughts for the benefit of his team.

For the next two days, Gabe had his team cutting brush and undergrowth in the mornings. In the afternoons, they pulled out the chainsaws to cut through logs for the fire, and branches for kindling.

They worked together on each task as a team, with Gabe on the chipper, Tom on the chainsaw, and Blaze and Wayne dragging branches to the chipper and helping to feed them in. It was more efficient that way, rather than splitting up and, besides, it seemed each man stepped up to his assigned task with shoulders set, a growing sense of responsibility radiating from him.

Even Wayne, always somewhat distant and off in his own mind, volunteered when, on Thursday, Gabe asked for help driving a truck full of wood chips to be dumped.

"Sure, boss," he said. "I can drive that truck up to the ranch to dump those chips. I ain't gonna run cause this is the best parole I've ever had."

Gabe sat in the passenger seat that first time to show Wayne the way, to caution him as to where he needed to go extra slow, to watch out for guests at the ranch. Wayne was turning out to be rather dependable, which pleased Gabe even though he'd had very little to do with it.

They had driven up to the ranch at the end of the day, that first time, when Gabe felt most guests would be in the main lodge having dinner. They were met by Quint, the ranch's trail boss, behind the barn at the supply hut, where the chips were being collected, to be used for ground cover around trees, around the ranch's fire pit, or whenever they might be needed.

Gabe introduced Wayne to Quint, who gravely shook Wayne's hand. It was easy to see that Quint trusted Wayne about as far as he could throw him, and maybe not even that far. That was fine, because Gabe was in charge of Wayne and not Quint. Gabe could see the value of a man like Wayne, who could work on his own with minimal direction, even if Quint couldn't.

Quint pulled a few extra ranch hands to help speed the process of unloading the wood chips so Gabe and Wayne could get back to the valley where their own dinners were waiting.

Tom was on the landline even before the dessert was served, talking to Joanna in that same animated way, his eyes bright, that smile broad. As he sat at the table for his apple pie, he announced, once again, that she and the baby would be there on Sunday, ten o'clock sharp.

"What's the baby's name?" Gabe had asked.

"Barbara Lynn," said Tom, beaming.

At the far end of the table, Blaze was a little quiet as he tucked into his apple pie, sweat on the back of his neck, his hair in his eyes.

"Everything all right, Blaze?" Gabe asked. Yes, it was appropriate that he keep his personal thoughts to himself, but that didn't mean he couldn't reach out and check in with one of his men, did it?

"Everything's all right," said Blaze, but his voice rose as if to make it a question, which Gabe took to mean that Blaze wanted to make sure he'd not done anything to get himself in trouble, and if it wasn't anything to do with that, then he didn't want to have that particular conversation.

Which was Blaze's right, of course. You couldn't make a man confide in you, though, in Gabe's mind, Blaze had already done that. Laid his history at Gabe's feet. Not with a heart full of trust, but with a soul full of pain.

And what had Gabe done? Walked off. Pretended like the conversation hadn't happened. But at the time, his goal had been to normalize, so when he'd seen Blaze looking at the retractable skewers for roasting marshmallows with abject distaste, Gabe had understood how he felt and offered Blaze his pocketknife.

"Did you need me to wrap your arm again?" he asked. "You didn't come by last night, or did someone else help you?"

"Oh," said Blaze with a quick shrug as he licked his fork. "I didn't want to bother anyone, so I skipped the shower."

"That's not right," said Gabe aloud, even though the thought felt very private. "That cut should be wrapped." He pushed his empty dessert plate away from him, shaking his head. "After dinner, I can wrap that for you, then you can take a shower, and then I'll put on a new bandage."

"That sounds like a lot of hassle," said Blaze, looking around the table at his team mates as if daring any one of them to disagree with him.

"It's not a hassle," said Gabe. He stood up and bussed his dishes, being purposeful in each motion he made to demonstrate that he wasn't going to budge on this. "That wound needs care, especially in the first few days. You want it to heal properly, right?"

Blaze had stood up and again, he was looking at Gabe like he was trying to figure him out. Then he blinked as if he was trying a different path in his mind, and was looking to Gabe to point him in the right direction.

"I wouldn't steer you wrong, Blaze," said Gabe. "C'mon. Let me

THE COWBOY AND THE RASCAL

wrap that, and you can take a nice, hot shower. Get a new bandage on that."

"Are we going to have a bonfire again?" asked Wayne, almost tripping on Tom's heels as they bussed their places.

"I thought we'd watch a movie," said Gabe. "Something different? We've got a big projector screen, and I've got Netflix and a projector for my laptop, so what'll it be?" Then, to everyone, he said, "Your teammates will wait till after you've had your shower, right guys?"

Wayne and Tom nodded in unison.

"Can we have popcorn, too?" asked Wayne.

"Anything you like," said Gabe. "We'll meet back here in half an hour."

Gabe went to the kitchen to grab the plastic wrap, and when he came out, only Blaze was waiting for him. In the after-dinner quiet, he pushed up the sleeve of Blaze's t-shirt, gently *tsk tsking* at the back of Blaze's arm, where the scab over the cut, which was around three inches long, looked a little ragged.

"This is the new rule," he said as he wrapped Blaze's arm. "Every night after dinner, we're doing this until the cut heals. You don't want an infection and you don't want a huge scar, do you?"

"No," said Blaze. "I guess not."

"And you don't want to go without a shower just because it's a bit of a hassle, right?"

This question made Blaze smile for some reason, his mouth quirking up at one corner.

"Well?" asked Gabe as he traced the edge of the plastic wrap and tucked in a bit of it to keep it tight.

"I love showers," said Blaze with a huff of a laugh, as if he was admitting a closely guarded secret he was sure Gabe would make fun of. "It's what I missed most in prison."

"Really?" Concentrating on his hands, Gabe tucked the box for the plastic wrap closed, then realized what had just happened: Blaze had shared something personal about himself with Gabe, which deserved more than an absentminded acknowledgement. So he looked up, his attention only on Blaze. "Really?" he asked again. "I guess I've not taken the time to imagine what it must have been like. What it would feel like to long for something like a shower, which I have always taken for granted."

"That's—" Blaze paused, blinking, swallowing hard. "That's how it is for a lot of guys," he said as he curled his fingers around his arm as if to test the tightness of the plastic. "Some guys miss good food. Other guys miss seeing a blue sky without razor wire getting in the way. Me." He shrugged, dropping his hands at his sides. "I missed hot showers. Long, hot showers."

"I get that," said Gabe. "I think I'd miss that, too." With a small laugh, he shooed Blaze away. "Go take your nice, long, hot shower, and we'll wait to start the movie until you get here."

Blaze smiled at him, then, an amazing smile that made something in Gabe's chest do odd, squirrely things.

"That's the first time I've seen you smile," he said, even though, once again, he should not have said his private thoughts aloud. Searching for a way to cover this over with something more practical and not so personal, he added, "But I guess it takes a few days to adjust to being out of prison. Which they taught us in training, but I completely forgot."

Why was he babbling on like this? Except it wasn't like he'd given away some great, huge trade secret, just a little bit of information about what was going on in his head, same as what Blaze had done.

"A few days," said Blaze, and his smile widened. "And I guess I'd forgotten what it was like to *be* out of prison, to tell you the truth."

Luckily, before Gabe could utter any more heartfelt comments, with a wave, Blaze went to his shower, leaving Gabe a moment to catch his breath. After which, he went to his tent to grab his laptop, which he set up in the mess tent, along with the projector and the screen, which he checked out from the supply hut.

Tom and Wayne showed up shortly before Blaze did, and together, as a team, they picked out a movie they all would enjoy, which turned out to be *Galaxy Quest*. Then, in the kitchen, Gabe made popcorn while Tom got everyone their favorite ice cold soda.

They watched the movie together, laughing at the same moments, eating popcorn in lazy handfuls. All of which made Gabe very proud of his team's progress. Only a few days before, they'd been standing in a row, fearful of what might happen to them. And though, perhaps their trust levels weren't as high as he'd like them to be, he knew they were off to a good start.

On Friday, just before dinner, he got a text from Maddy Greenway, the guest ranch's admin, who needed him to come up to her office to sign some paperwork. Letting his team know they would stop work early, he drove the valley's one truck up the hill to the ranch and stopped by her office just before five o'clock.

"Here you go," said Maddy. She held out a clipboard. "Sign this, which will make sure your team gets paid. And Leland's been trying to reach you, but the cellphone call wasn't going through. Where was your two-way radio?"

"I'd taken it off when I was showering, then didn't put it on because I was coming up here," he said. "What's up?"

"He wanted to remind you that the horses from Blue Grass Ranch are ready to be picked up."

"I'm ready," he said to her, pleasure at the prospect of working with horses again rushing through him. "Just let me know the day."

"Next Monday," she said, smiling in response to his joy. "Get one of your team to drive you up there. Then, Quint and Brody will help you drive the horses from Blue Grass to the valley, and could you check that the strand fence is in place?" She shook her head. "And it would be helpful in future if you had your two-way on you during the day."

"I will, Maddy," he said. "Thank you for passing along Leland's messages."

He knew that around twenty horses were due to be transferred. They'd have to take them down the road in a herd, as there were too many, and it would take too long to gather up enough horse trailers and drivers to move them that way. Which was fine by Gabe, as he'd not ridden since he'd started working the parolee program.

"Heard you lost a man this week," she said, taking the clipboard back from him. "It's a shame that you're down by one, but, according to Leland, that guy was a piece of work. But anyway, you still have three to help you take care of the horses once they arrive."

In the back of his mind, he was glad and didn't have anything to complain about, having only three men to help out. Still, he'd come to the ranch originally to be a ranch hand, to work with horses, taking care of them, going on trail rides. He missed the smell of horse, the soft silky plush of their noses, their ridiculously long eyelashes, their trusting calmness. He wondered if the men on his team would feel the same way about horses as he did.

"When can I bring my team to get cowboy hats and boots?" he asked her. "I think they'll enjoy the outing, plus it'll be good for the ranch," he said, filling in the rest of the sentence with the phrase he'd heard from Leland more than once. "And could you update your records to state that Blaze, I mean, Orlando, wears a size 11 boot?"

"But of course," she said. "I'll be happy to size them. How about Saturday afternoon? That's when things get slow."

Gabe knew the first counseling session was Saturday afternoon as well, but he figured they might cut it short in favor of the new gear. "Two o'clock?" he asked her.

"I'll be here."

He left her then, pausing on the front porch of her office to smile as wide as he wanted without anyone thinking he'd gone crazy. He'd missed working with horses, but had not realized until that moment how much.

CHAPTER 13
BLAZE

Blaze's first group counseling session on Saturday, right after lunch, wasn't just a drag, it was boring. And lame, especially when it was just the four of them: Tom, Wayne, himself, and the counselor, a weedy looking young man with overly large glasses and a too-tight t-shirt in city-modern gray, who wanted them each to talk in turn. About their problems, about the issues they faced that week, about their goals.

Blaze didn't invest any energy in the counseling session because none of it was going to make any difference to Blaze, anyway. Once he was finished with his parole, he had zero places to go, and no family to welcome him with open arms, and this despite of the counselor's insistence that the road was rocky but that there were rewards at the end.

But he made himself sit still, made himself look like he was invested and paying attention, that he gave a damn, even when he didn't. He also allowed himself to linger over the quick little memory of Gabe wrapping his arm before Blaze had taken his shower on Friday night. And then, after, checking the bandage to make sure it was dry and secure. It was that kind of little nicety, so rare in his life

JACKIE NORTH

up to that point, that was helping to keep him focused on his goal of giving this whole thing a chance.

The counselor, whose name might have been Brett or Bud or something, rewarded them each with a smile as he told them that he appreciated their participation, that he'd see them the following Saturday, and that if they needed him mid-week, they were always welcome to reach out to him. Then Brett or Bud handed each of them a business card.

Blaze stood up and stuck the card in his back jeans pocket, and walked toward the mess tent because, frankly, Blaze's only reward was the fact that Gabe was waiting for them outside the mess tent.

Gabe was nodding at the counselor with what looked like tons of fake patience. The counselor nodded back and smiled before hefting his backpack over his shoulder and striding off to his city car.

The entire counseling session was wiped clean by the picture Gabe presented. He was wearing cowboy boots and a straw cowboy hat, a smile tracing his lips as he gestured for the three parolees to come close.

"We have a treat for you today," he said. "I'm going to drive you to the ranch's store, and Maddy, our admin, is going to measure you for new cowboy hats." He looked at Blaze, and his smile seemed extra warm. "And cowboy boots, just to make sure of the fit. Let's go."

At the truck, Tom got in front, but then his legs were long and besides, it gave Blaze a chance to just sit in the back and say nothing, with Gabe's profile right in his view line.

Gabe drove them up the hill along the switchback road, through the pines and up over the top of the grassy hill, breezes waving through the tall prairie grasses, past the new wood cabin sitting in the middle of nowhere, and finally to the large, round gravel parking lot of the guest ranch. Gabe parked in front of what looked like a kind of store, turned off the engine, and looked at them each in turn.

"This is the guest ranch's store, where we're going to measure you for hats and boots." Gabe paused, his eyes serious. "Part of the parole program is to help you integrate back into society, but I guess you know that and don't need me telling you to behave."

Blaze knew how to behave, knew how to fit in, but as he piled out of the truck and followed Tom and Wayne into the store, with Gabe leading the way, he felt a rush of excitement in spite of himself.

He'd not been in a store in almost two years, and while he didn't have a credit card in his wallet so he could slap it on the glass counter, maybe he could wrangle a candy bar or even some gum, just to feel the small thrill of purchasing something, something of his own. He'd have to share, wouldn't he, so maybe he could talk Gabe into allowing each of them to get a little something so they wouldn't have to share.

All the while these thoughts flew through his brain, he scanned the racks of rustic looking, ranch-branded t-shirts and tank-tops, the baseball caps with the ranch's logo on them, bandana scarves in neat squares on the shelves, plus an assortment of small tubes of toothpaste, travel toothbrushes, sewing kits, and various toiletries. Along the walls were stacks of boot boxes, with little pictures of the boots inside, and a whole section of just straw cowboy hats on pegs.

"Let's get your sizes," said a gray-haired woman, standing alongside the main counter with a small tape measure in her hand.

Dressed as she was in blue jeans and a snap-button plaid shirt with the sleeves rolled up, he didn't think much of her. But then when Gabe gave her a quick hug and just about kissed her cheek, Blaze made himself rethink who she was. Someone worthy of such a greeting, to start with. Someone who could look three ex-cons in the eye and not look like she was about to back down.

"I'm Maddy, by the way," she said, which made Blaze reevaluate who she was, even more. "Step up, one at a time, and I'll measure your heads. Gabe, can you write down the sizes?"

"I'll remember them, Maddy," said Gabe with a smile, standing close by with his hands tucked in his jeans pockets.

Maddy stood on a step stool to measure each of their heads, looking them each in the eye like she simply did not care that they were criminals and that if they messed around with her, they would miss out on getting spanking-new cowboy hats.

When she pointed to the row of straw cowboy hats on pegs along the wall, she told them their sizes, and then said, "There's nothing fancy because they are working hats, not for show, and the weave of each hat is pretty similar. The band around the crown is where there'll be a difference. Most have leather strips of various colors, some have strips of woven leather, so look for something you like, as that'll be your hat for the summer."

Blaze scanned the row of cowboy hats, looking with new eyes at the hat bands and the way the straw was woven so tightly, and wondered if he'd ever imagined being where he was, looking for a cowboy hat.

Out of the corner of his eyes, he could see Maddy and Gabe stacking long boot boxes. He could tell which stack was his, or he thought he could. He wore an 11. Tom wore 12s, and Wayne wore 10s, so his stack was the one in the middle.

It was hard to concentrate because how was he getting new cowboy boots as well as the hat? Who the hell was funding this program anyhow? But while days ago he would have been instantly suspicious of such generosity, nothing he could afford to get used to, today was a different day, right? He needed to give the situation more than two minutes before he completely disregarded it, before he turned his back on how nice it felt to be in a store, shopping for new things.

He tried on three hats, but found he liked the first hat best, a finely woven straw hat with a brim that didn't look too obnoxious or huge. It had a little brown leather band with small x's woven into the leather, and there was even a small brass buckle with a galloping horse stamped into it.

"That's a nice one," said Maddy, half of her attention on him, half of it on Tom, to whom she was handing a box. "Cavender's is a good brand. You might try on those boots I pulled down for you and see if you like how they go with the hat."

Ordinarily Blaze would resent having something picked out for him like that, after all, it'd been years since he'd had a selection like this to choose from, rather than the limit of three different off-brand shampoos and razors and so on at the prison commissary. But now, yes, he was on the edge of being overwhelmed, sweating under his armpits, his mouth a little dry, half-crazy like a kid on Christmas morning, not knowing what to do first.

Maddy pointed to one of the wooden benches and he sat down, plopping his hat on his head anyoldhow, in a hurry to try on the boots. Most were all glossy and new, but it was the brown pair with a low-gloss swirl pattern that grabbed his eye. They looked like they were already broken in, and his fingers liked the feel of those boots. When he pulled them on each foot, they slid onto his feet with perfect grace, like he'd been wearing them all along.

At Maddy's nod, he stood up, adjusted his new cowboy hat on his head and turned to look in the full-length mirror. Which was, perhaps, the first good full-length mirror he'd seen himself in for years and years. Living in a trailer or working the carnie circuit, or spending time in prison, after all, did not lend itself to pausing to take stock of one's appearance.

He looked jaunty and ready. That was the only way to describe it. His hair was dark beneath the pale, cream-colored straw, messy as though it didn't quite know what to do with itself, pressed along his jaw. His green eyes were wide, and he imagined he could see a smile in them. But it was the boots that seemed to make a difference in the way he stood, pushing up from the heels through the back of his thighs, almost stiffening them, his ass sticking out in a sassy way.

Stepping to the side, he tapped the brim of his hat as though he'd encountered someone and wanted to say *how do*, the way cowboys did in the movies. Now the smile in his reflection had moved to his face, and he thought, just for a moment, that he was happy.

From behind him, standing along the stacks of boot boxes that had been rejected, was Gabe. Gabe had his hat in his hands, held just level with his hips, and he was watching Blaze through half lowered eyes. Like he knew he wasn't supposed to be looking, didn't want to be caught looking, but was looking just the same. But at what?

He was looking at an ex-con out on parole, trying on cowboy clothes that he certainly wouldn't need when the end of summer came and his parole was up. At a parolee getting far too much enjoyment out of a simple shopping expedition. Who liked the way he looked in the mirror, long-legged and capable, but who simply had no experience around horses, save the little sleepy-eyed Shetland ponies going around and around in a circle amidst the happy giggles of very small children.

But maybe that kind of experience was enough to keep Gabe from thinking that perhaps Blaze ought not to be trusted with live animals, big ones, and should stay behind to help in the mess tent or something.

"Is this a good match?" Blaze asked Maddy, but her back was turned, and up came Gabe, reaching over Blaze's shoulder to adjust his hat, tipping the brim down a little bit, making a small, curved shade beneath the brim.

"There you go," said Gabe, softly, his voice almost a whisper, as if he was talking to himself. He cleared his throat and then added, "You tilt it different ways, depending on the weather and the amount of sunlight."

Blaze nodded, looking at Gabe's reflection in the mirror, his throat dry all over again.

This wasn't the first time Gabe had helped him, just him and not any of the others. Not in a way that implied Blaze was incompetent without Gabe's help, but as if he enjoyed doing it. Like the time he helped Blaze get a new pair of work boots, and then, on his knees, had laced them up for Blaze. And the times he'd helped Blaze wrap plastic around his arm so the cut from the chipper would heal better.

It didn't mean anything, of course. It could mean entirely nothing, naturally. But the way Gabe was suddenly not looking at him, surveying the room, studying the two other ex-cons in the room, the purposefulness of his not looking suddenly came at Blaze, full force, with the truth of it.

Either all of Blaze's friendly flirting, the pushy way he'd shoved himself into the fore of Gabe's attention, had worked, or. Or maybe it had been unnecessary from the very beginning, and Gabe, quite simply, liked Blaze. Or maybe he liked ex-cons. Liked having authority over them, and that's what turned him on. Except if that were true, wouldn't the come-hither flick of Gabe's eyes in Blaze's direction, made before moving off, have shown up a whole lot sooner?

Maybe. Maybe not. It was hard to tell because the kind of conversation Blaze might have had at a carnival did not differ wildly from the kind of conversation he would have had in prison. *D'you want to? Let's go.*

Here, in Farthingdale Valley, the conversation wouldn't be between two carnies on a ten-minute break behind the corn dog stand, or between two prisoners taking advantage of the dark corners of the laundry room when they were supposed to be looking for open jugs of bleach to be used up before more could be ordered.

No. This was flat out in the middle of an ordinary life that Blaze was being shown how to integrate himself into. He'd told himself to trust this, trust where he was. To trust Gabe, even. At the same time, the suspicion lurked that anything he said might be chalked up on a tally board and held against him later.

Gabe was going over to Tom and Wayne, each in turn, leaning close to admire their selections of hats and boots, and he was not paying any more attention to Blaze at all. Except, as Gabe urged the two men to tidy the boxes of unchosen boots so Maddy could put them away, he glanced at Blaze, then ducked his head, rubbing the back of his neck.

A flush crept up the spaces between Gabe's fingers. That and a working of his jaw.

What the hell was Blaze supposed to make of that? All his life he'd been taught to read people's signals, and he was pretty good at it, too.

Most of the signals Gabe was giving off seemed to say the obvious, that Gabe liked looking at Blaze at the very least. That Gabe might have feelings for Blaze that went beyond his duties of being team leader. That if Blaze pushed some more, he could get Gabe to be more preferential to Blaze. Except he already was. Had been almost from the very beginning.

Rocking on his heels as his body tested the balance of the cowboy boots and their stacked heels, Blaze couldn't figure out for the life of him why Gabe might actually like him. But he did. At least he seemed to.

Maybe Gabe felt sorry for Blaze and had a thing for down-and-out guys. Or maybe there was another reason, one beyond the scope of Blaze's ability to read another human being.

It couldn't be as simple as the fact that Gabe liked him. It could not be.

He was going to find out. He was.

CHAPTER 14

GABE

Sunday morning, just before 10 o'clock, Gabe and his team were lined up along the edge of the gravel parking lot, waiting as if at attention for a grand parade where a pope or a king might be passing by them. They'd all showered and shaved like they were going on a date with someone special.

Tom, especially, had showered and shaved twice, and had only been kept back from a third go-round by the fact that his girlfriend Joanna was due any minute. She was supposed to be bringing the baby, Barbara Lynn, with her, and his excitement could have generated electricity for the whole state of Wyoming.

Wayne was less enthused, but no less showered and shaved and ready, as was Blaze. Who, at the end of the line, closest to Gabe, seemed to be looking at the whole ceremony of it as just that, a ceremony for something that did not involve him, but he couldn't help but stare just the same.

Gabe was beginning to wonder if he might ask the cooks to keep the coffee warm, when he heard the crackle of rubber on the gravel of a car coming a bit too fast down the switchback slope, and then slowing. It was easy to hear the low rumble of an engine through the still morning air, the pine trees tall and barely rustling, a cape of green between the valley and the rest of the world.

When the car, a dark green Subaru wagon, appeared along the last bit of road leading up to the parking lot, Tom let out a shout, a bark of joy, and he all but raced up to the car, standing back until Joanna, at the wheel, turned off the engine.

Gabe and Wayne and Blaze looked at each other, a silent message passing through the air that they would give Tom a bit of time alone with Joanna, though they all leaned forward when Joanna got out, pretty as a picture in a flower print dress and low heels, her dark hair glistening in the sunlight.

After a pause, as if asking for permission, Tom finally hugged her, and she hugged him back, and then gestured to the back seat of the station wagon, from where she pulled a sturdy baby seat, complete with a baby inside of it.

When Joanna looked up, she was even more beautiful than Tom had described her through his eyes of love. She had creamy dark skin and darker eyes as she appraised them all.

Gabe could sense that her desire to share any of this moment, or her baby, with a bunch of ex-cons was just about non-existent, but Tom gestured toward Gabe and the team. Perhaps her sense of politeness kicked in, for she approached slowly, carrying the baby seat with two hands. She should know that neither Gabe nor Tom would let anything happen to the baby, but he couldn't blame her for being apprehensive.

"Guys," said Tom, his smile broad. "This is Joanna, and this is—" He paused, his jaw working, as though to contain a rush of feelings he didn't quite know what to do with. "This is Barbara Lynn, my daughter."

Gabe leaned forward to look at the baby, because who didn't want to look at a beautiful baby, so loved that she wore a sparkling white and pink little outfit with matching booties and a matching bonnet with tiny pink ribbons. The baby, Barbara Lynn, scowled at Gabe. But maybe that was because he was too close or too serious, or maybe it was the strength of the sun.

THE COWBOY AND THE RASCAL

"Would you like to step inside some shade, ma'am?" he asked Joanna, gesturing to the mess tent, which the cooks had helped set up with coffee and iced tea and snacks, and which was as clean as a whistle.

Joanna hesitated and then looked up at Tom.

"It's nice, I promise," said Tom. "There's a little breeze that comes through and we can sit at one of the tables and visit."

With a nod, Joanna let herself be led, carrying the baby seat close to her until she sat down. Then she placed it on the table just about in front of her, touching the baby's booted feet as though to make sure of her. Tom hopped around, getting her a glass of iced tea, which she said she preferred to coffee, and she shook her head at any cookies.

"I'm still trying to watch my sugar," she said, and while her voice was soft and sweet, there was a firmness to it at the same time.

"Joanna," said Tom as he sat beside her. "This is Gabe, our team lead, and this is Wayne and this is Blaze." He pointed to each man in turn. "We used to have a guy named Kurt, but he tried to kill Blaze in the wood chipper, so he got his ass kicked right on out of here."

Tom paused as Joanna's face looked a little pinched. And of course, now she knew which was the team lead and which were the ex-cons, and though she looked like she very much wanted to move away from Wayne and Blaze, she stayed seated.

"It was really just an accident," said Blaze, suddenly, his voice quite low and, as Gabe imagined, as non-threatening as he could make it. "I'm sure he didn't mean it. We were just horsing around, you know? And now he's doing house construction or something, working out his parole that way."

Gabe did his best not to make an objection to this, because nobody knew what Kurt was up to, though he imagined if he asked Leland, he could find out. But why had Blaze lied like that, seeing as he had no real idea what Kurt was up to? In spite of that, the lie seemed to come to him as easily as breathing, and perhaps Blaze had been doing his best to keep Joanna from worrying about Tom.

"What do you mean, working out his parole doing construction?" asked Joanna, her dark eyebrows lowering.

"Well, it's—" Blaze paused, as if coming up with another layer to the lie. "You can do it another way, is all. Kurt didn't like doing lumberjack stuff, so now he's got a parole officer, and an apartment, and stuff. Checks in every week, gets his paperwork signed. Though I imagine it's all digital now. Isn't that how it works, Wayne?"

Wayne nodded as if preparing himself to pick up the baton of the conversation, like he and Blaze had practiced it for weeks.

"That's right, ma'am," said Wayne. "I've done it that way myself, but this is the best parole I've ever served, so I won't be jumping ship anytime soon."

"Oh." Joanna looked at them each in turn, then she settled her shoulders, and placed her hand, quite gently, on Tom's shoulder. "Tom, why don't you get these folks something to drink, and then I can take Barbara Lynn out of the seat, as she's starting to want to move a little."

Tom leaped to do as she asked, and Gabe enjoyed his glass of freshly brewed iced tea while he watched Joanna hold her baby and fuss with the lace of her bonnet. Then he enjoyed watching easy-going Tom become just about unglued as Joanna offered to let him hold his daughter for the first time.

All three of them leaned in to watch the domesticity, Tom's strong arms steadfastly cradling his six-month-old baby girl as if it was an energy they could absorb, as if the innocence of the baby, safe in her father's arms, could be stamped into their collective memories, freezing the moment in its purity, forever. Then Gabe realized that if they all stared any harder, they were going to be gatecrashers at a very private party.

"Hey, fellows," he said to Wayne and Blaze. "Those horses are coming tomorrow, so why don't we walk the fence line before dinner to make sure everything's all set for their arrival."

Wayne and Blaze both looked at him like he'd just broken them out of a very powerful spell.

"I've signed myself up for a nap," said Wayne. "You said we got the day off and that sounds too much like work to me."

"That's true," said Gabe, thinking all of this over. They did have the day off and weren't in any way obligated to help out at all, not even to entertain Gabe with the idea that any inch of the fence line needed a single moment of their attention. "You take that nap and we'll see you at dinner. How about you, Blaze?"

He turned his attention as casually as he could to Blaze who was, as Gabe could plainly see, already wearing his new cowboy boots, polished to shine, a glowingly soft brown—not quite a cowboy, but ready, poised as if waiting for an adventure to begin.

All Blaze needed was to put on his new straw cowboy hat and he'd create an outline that'd be damn difficult for Gabe to ignore. And Blaze was already pretty un-ignorable.

"Sure, boss," said Blaze, his voice as soft as when he'd been speaking to Joanna. "I'll get my new hat."

"I'll get mine," said Gabe. "Meet you on the other side of those trees, by the fire pit."

They could have walked together to get their hats, stopping first at Gabe's tent and then Blaze's, but then Gabe wouldn't have a handful of minutes to himself to pull himself together and ask what the hell he thought he was doing. It was nothing to spend time with one of his team, or at least it hadn't been. What was the difference now that set his heart to racing?

He knew the answer to that and if he couldn't admit it to himself, he'd be lying, just as Blaze had been lying to Joanna.

Layer by layer, yard by yard, his attention had gone to Blaze from the very beginning. Now, since he'd seen the image of Blaze looking at himself in the mirror the day before, it was as if he'd just discovered a new version of himself. He could hardly look away, not even when Blaze had caught him looking.

Blaze hadn't seemed overly annoyed at that moment, but Gabe had felt hot all over, nerves jumping, the back of his neck laced with sweat.

How was he supposed to do right by his team if he played favorites? He didn't in his assignment of jobs, of that he'd been most careful. But, as he waited by the fire pit, his hat in his hand, his fingers sweaty on the brim, he now was able to spend time with Blaze alone.

Under the shining sun, afternoon strong, bold as brass, there wasn't much he would do about it, except look. And then look some more. And maybe discover whether what he'd been imagining in his mind's eye was even the least bit true.

"Here I am, boss."

Gabe turned to see Blaze running up to him, hat in place, casting his eyes in shadows that made Gabe want to pull him close and find out what secrets those eyes hid. Blaze had pulled out his shirttails and unbuttoned a few of the bottom so his shirttails furled behind him, and the strong draw of his neck pushed at his white cotton t-shirt.

It was a hot day, growing hotter, so Blaze was folding up his shirtsleeves, lumpy rolls that made Gabe want to push away Blaze's hands and redo the folds himself. Within a heartbeat, he was unable to stop from doing that very thing.

"Here," he said, trying to be gruff, as if that would cover the intimacy he'd just created by tugging on Blaze's wrist and pulling him close. Quickly, he unfolded the length of both of Blaze's sleeves.

Blaze, like a small obedient child, stood patiently as Gabe did this. His mouth quirked into a bit of a smile, less flirty and more knowing, as if he realized what Gabe was doing and why Gabe couldn't help himself.

Ignoring this, Gabe folded the sleeve all the way up, as far as it would go, then folded the end of each sleeve over again, leaving a neat edge to the fold that would be hard pressed to come undone. Then, thinking about it, Gabe shook his head.

"It's going to be sunny," he said. "Better to have them down and avoid sunburn."

With a bark of a laugh, Blaze started unfolding his sleeves, and got to one before Gabe did the other, not buttoning the cuffs, letting them linger about his wrists as though diabolically encouraging Gabe to stare even more than he already was.

"Let's head out along the lake," said Gabe, settling his hat on his head.

He tried to imagine why he thought this would be a good idea. They'd be alone together in the bright sunshine, walking through the high grasses while looking at the fence line, which was just waiting for horses to be put inside of it.

This kind of task in this setting was just about his favorite combination. It only needed horses coming up to the fence with bright eyes, those ridiculously long eyelashes, their soft noses in his palm. Now add Blaze, his new boots making his legs long and coltish, that straw hat low over his brow, green eyes looking at Gabe as though for direction or, perhaps, invitation.

Gabe shook his head and began to lead the way. They had to go about a quarter mile along the lake, on a path that led them beside the edge of a large open field of tall prairie grass, which might have been about two acres, but which seemed swallowed by the large blue sky overhead. Then they got to the wire gate of the twenty or so acres that had been set aside for the horses.

Gabe stopped to test the hook on the gate, and to test the generator for the electricity along the fence line, turning it on and then off again.

"I had no idea this was all out here," said Blaze, following behind Gabe along the barely there path between the fence and the lake.

"It's kind of a last-minute fence," said Gabe. He didn't have to look over his shoulder to see if Blaze was behind him because he could *feel* him back there, hear the crunch of his boots on the new grass. "We got an opportunity to have first crack at some fine horses that have come up on the market. So we have this, and each week or so, we'll get a new bunch, sort through them, and decide where they'll go. Either our ranch, or someone else's. Maybe a petting zoo, or a nice youngster who is ready for a horse of their own."

"Petting zoo?" asked Blaze, a laugh in his voice. "That sounds like it'd be pretty terrible for a horse."

"Every horse will find a good home," said Gabe. "Even the older ones."

As they trudged, Gabe looked out over the surface of Half Moon Lake, where it widened till it reached the slope on the other side, so still in the afternoon that the reflection of pine trees and the gray edge of Guipago Ridge could be seen reflected on its glassy surface.

The three-tiered strand fence had been solidly built by a team of ranch hands who knew what they were doing, so he wasn't worried about it, but it never hurt to be sure. With the rush of horses that would be coming in and out of the pasture over the coming summer, it was best to have something solid in place.

"Why don't they build it out of wood?" asked Blaze, seemingly close, as though he was looking over Gabe's shoulder as he paused to test one of the main poles dug into the ground. "And how come there are water tanks instead of letting the horses just drink out of the lake? It's right there."

"The strands are white," said Gabe. "Horses can see them against the tall grass. They've got wire inside the tubes of cloth, so if a horse brushes up, they get a small shock, which encourages them to stay back. If you get a horse running into a wooden fence, they could injure themselves. Of course, no fence is perfect, but this kind is better for horses."

"Oh," said Blaze, his voice wide with astonishment, as if a whole new world had opened up for him. "And the tanks?"

Gabe stopped, propped his straw hat back on his head, and looked out over the glassy blue water of the lake, taking in a deep breath, enjoying the moment of stillness that settled all around him.

He waited until Blaze was by his side and thought about his own dream of having a bit of land like this to raise cattle, and plant a garden, maybe raise some chickens. That might not be somebody else's idea of heaven, but it was his. Also, his was the long road he'd chosen to get there, which currently involved standing next to an ex-criminal who he was, by virtue of his position of authority, not supposed to feel drawn to. Right?

"Horses like to graze in packs, to find fresh grass and water each day." Gabe gestured to the lake, to the rocky shoreline that he knew, toward the south end of the lake, way beyond where the pasture turned into a lovely slough with tall cattails in the fall, and flocks of birds and ducks making it their home. "They'd trample all of this shoreline by just being horses, when the goal is, at some point, to build more tents down this way. To create an open area where folks can more easily look at the stars at night, there being no trees to block the sky."

Gabe gulped in a breath and made himself stop talking. He could see Leland's dream landscape just as easily as he could see his own, and there was something about untouched land that made him want to touch it, not to destroy, but to encourage and protect.

His own land would be good for cattle use, and he'd make sure any Russian thistle blight was removed. He'd plant Timothy hay for his cattle, where the land could support it, and he'd—

"Boss?"

Jerked out of his own reverie, Gabe found Blaze looking at him, wide-eyed, a bit of sweat on his cheek, dust along his chin. A smile on his face, a crooked one, as if he was on the verge of teasing Gabe for his dreams, but then would ask because he wanted to find out more.

Only in Gabe's mind, surely.

"Let's head down to the slough," Gabe said. "We can catch a nice view of the lake from there."

"Slew?" asked Blaze, following close behind once more.

"It's spelled s-l-o-u-g-h," said Gabe. "Pronounced slew."

The slough was hidden amidst clumps of sweet-smelling willow bushes and tall green grasses. Beyond the slough, Half Moon Lake turned back into Horse Creek, burbling its low meandering way south across the high prairie. But here, it was a wet humid area, with birds swooping across the tops of the grasses, the low earth smell of damp mud, and the sounds of bugs in the grasses.

"We can't cross, as there's no bridge," said Gabe. "At least not yet. The plan is to build a wooden bridge across at the spot where it will interfere the least with the slough and the habitat it creates for birds."

"Who will build it?"

"One of the teams," said Gabe. "Some parolees, I think, and maybe we can get advice from the Corps of Engineers as to the best way to go about it. Leland does have aspirations." Shaking his head, Gabe looked up where he could see bits of blue lake through the willows. "But I've yet to see a man say no to him when he's got his sights set on a project. Even one as big as this one."

"You like him." Blaze came up to stand beside Gabe and pushed his straw hat back from his head in the way Gabe had done.

"I like him and respect him," said Gabe, not thinking about the words, but merely how Leland Tate fit into his worldview. "But for me, the two go hand in hand."

"Oh."

They walked up as far as they could to the edge of the slough and then had to turn back to follow, once more, the path between the blue lake and the fence line. The sun hadn't quite begun to set, it was far too early for that, but it was slanting in the sky, with puffy clouds going long as the wind began to stir the tops of the tall green grasses.

Gabe didn't have a watch, and he'd left his cellphone back in his tent, but that didn't matter because no time would have been long enough, forever enough, to allow him to capture the day and the time he'd spent with Blaze and keep it close.

CHAPTER 15
BLAZE

When Blaze arrived at breakfast, showered and shaved, excited about the mid-morning arrival of horses, Tom just about peed all over everything.

"I'm not much good with horses," he said, and it was obvious to see by the way he was dressed that he was not prepared, not one bit, to help Gabe in this. Tom was wearing regular work-in-the woods clothes, with nary a cowboy boot in sight. "I won't work the chipper by myself, but I can sure take your map and flag all those roots we're going to want to dig up."

"That's fine," said Gabe, in his typical laid-back way as he dug into his pancakes, cutting a careful square with his fork. "I appreciate your willingness to carry on."

There was nothing and nobody that was going to keep Blaze from getting into that truck with Gabe. Not with him looking the way he did as he stood up and grabbed his straw cowboy hat from the end of the table.

In his cowboy boots, Gabe was ten feet tall, thighs dense beneath his denim blue jeans, his smile genuine, coming from inside of him as he placed that hat on his head. He tilted it and then tapped it with his finger as though he were sending a special signal for Blaze to join in his joy.

Sure, Gabe was a genial guy, typically even-tempered and steady, but this morning, there was a light coming from him, and Blaze could only put it down to the morning's activity, where they were going to drive up north of the ranch and drop Gabe off so he could help guide around twenty head of horses to the lower pasture in the valley.

"One of you fellows want to drive?" Gabe asked, jingling the truck keys in his pocket.

Both Blaze and Wayne shook their heads, and Blaze quite emphatically because he had no idea where they were going and, besides, it would be nice to just sit and relax and enjoy the view. Plus, he'd make sure to sit wherever was nearest to Gabe.

They waved Tom off and hustled to the truck in the gravel parking lot. Luck was with him because Wayne seemed quite content to sit in the back of the four-door truck. This left Blaze the spacious front seat, with full view of where they were going, and plenty of opportunity to gaze at Gabe out of the corner of his eyes.

With his shirtsleeves rolled up, properly tucked the way he liked them to be, Gabe drove them up the pine-scented switchbacks, over the high-grassed, windswept hillside, past the little wood cabin, and along the dirt road to the gate.

Blaze happily got out to man the gate, then hopped back in, holding his hat on his head with one hand as he pulled the door shut. He nodded to Gabe that they could keep going, settling back in his seat as the truck rolled along Highway 211, north to lands that were so new to him that Blaze had taken his hat off so he could press his nose to the glass.

"You can roll the window down, if you like," said Gabe, and Blaze turned to see Gabe smiling at him. "It's a fine day for it."

Blaze tucked his hat near his feet so it wouldn't get blown away, and pressed the button to roll down the window. But then Wayne's complaints from the back made him roll it up again. They were going too fast, the grasses a blur, but inside the truck's cabin, Gabe had the station on soft country music, and Blaze decided this was fine, just fine with him.

At Chugwater, they went beneath the freeway bridge, and Gabe took a left and headed west along a dirt road that went across the open countryside. Early summer green grasses were blowing in the wind, bending as though brushed by an unseen and very large hand, this way and that. They crossed several wooden bridges that went over silky, flat, blue and brown rivers, and then they were in the rumpled and stony hills.

"How far is this place?" asked Blaze, wishing he had a cellphone so he could check the map and see where they were.

"It's about fifty miles," said Gabe. "But when we drive the horses from Blue Grass Ranch, we'll cut along the ridge, and then join up with the 211 and drive the horses down that. Our route will save us around thirty miles."

Before mid-morning, they had reached Blue Grass Ranch, a tidy place with a few outbuildings, and several pastures, rich with green grasses, like those on the top of the hill at Farthingdale Valley. Blaze nodded, feeling wise because he knew the kind of fence they were using and why they were using it.

Two horse trailers were lined up next to a pasture with a bunch of horses in it. Standing next to the trailers were two real-life cowboys with straw cowboy hats on their heads, leather gloves in their hands, and leather chaps around their thighs. The men waved at Gabe as he parked the truck and got out.

Blaze looked back at Wayne, and Wayne shrugged.

"Should we get out?" asked Blaze. "We're just going to drive the truck back, right?"

"I don't know." Wayne looked a little glum, though Blaze couldn't figure out why.

Blaze got out, shutting the truck door carefully, as if a loud noise might spook cowboys and horses alike.

By the time he got over to the nearest trailer, Gabe was putting on leather chaps, bending to attach a clip-ring from behind his thigh up along his hip, and then behind one knee, and Blaze froze.

The chaps came up to the tops of Gabe's thighs, the leather contrasting against the blue denim, cupping his buttocks, flaring with the slightest fringe. One of the other cowboys, a gruff looking man with short hair cropped close, handed Gabe a pair of leather gloves, and it was then that Blaze realized his jaw was hanging open.

This was Gabe, as he'd never seen him. It wasn't just the close fit of those chaps, nor the lazy grin showing his sharp white teeth as he put on sunglasses. It was everything from the easy slope of his shoulders to the relaxed way he chatted with the two other cowboys. One of them brought him a pale-colored horse, and he stepped up into the stirrup and swung his leg over and settled in the saddle like a cowboy in the movies.

Gabe gestured Blaze close and, shutting his mouth, Blaze walked up to Gabe on horseback pretending like he did it every day and not like, as most certainly was true, he was stepping into the shadow of a ten foot giant.

"Blaze, this is Quint and Brody. They're going to help me drive the horses down to the pasture in the valley."

"Hi." Blaze lifted his hand to wave, but could find no easy patter to send back in the direction of the two men, who nodded and tapped their hat brims with their gloved hands.

"We're going to head out," said Gabe. "We'll meet you at the gate at around three or so. Can you have it open for us, with the power off?"

"Sure thing, Gabe," said Blaze, lifting up on his toes. He looked past Gabe to the pasture, beyond the horse trailers. Two men had gotten out of those trucks and were just about to open the gate. "Can we watch?"

"Yes, you can," said Gabe. "But head out as soon as you can, go back the way we came in, and when you park the truck, park it just at the end of the cutoff, where that little gully is. Put the truck in front of the gully. That way, we won't have to worry about the horses taking a wrong turn."

"You'll need a bit of fence there, I'm thinking," said Quint, his voice low and serious.

"Yeah, I think so, too, but that'll have to wait for another day."

Gabe settled in his saddle, lifted the reins, and whistled between his teeth. When the two cowboys opened the gate to the pasture, he said to Blaze, "Better get in the truck or in the truck bed. These horses have been pastured a while and are eager to stretch their legs."

Blaze scrambled into the truck bed, and Wayne leaned out of the window to watch as the horses came out of the pasture. Their hooves stirred up dust, manes flying, their eyes wide at their new freedom. A low energy grew, and then doubled again and just as the horses surrounded the truck, flicking their tails, tossing their heads.

Quint and Brody, now on horseback, guided them away, past the horse trailers and off into open country. Following up in the rear was Gabe, whistling through his teeth, using a circle of rope to slap against his thigh as he helped to keep the horses together rather than letting them sprawl as they seemed to want to.

Dust settled around them, and the two cowboys left behind got into their respective trucks and drove off, slowly trundling down the dirt road toward Chugwater. They nodded at Blaze and Wayne as they went by, but didn't stop to chat.

From his open window, Wayne was sneezing as Blaze got in the driver's seat, and got the engine running. He waited until Wayne was in the passenger seat, his eyes watering, snot running from his nose, his face red.

"What's the matter with you?" asked Blaze.

"Boss man's going to kill me," said Wayne, wiping his nose on his shirt sleeve, following this with two hard sneezes. "I'm allergic. I was when I was a kid and I thought it had gone away. But if I can't work with horses on account of it, is he going to get rid of me?"

"He didn't with Tom," said Blaze, as he drove away from the now-empty pastures, leaving the faintest of dust clouds behind him as he sped up on the dirt road.

"He *likes* Tom, that's why." Wayne slumped into a gloomy heap.

"He does, that's for sure." Blaze kept driving, keeping the country music low, enjoying the feel of being behind the wheel, being trusted not to run off with the truck, being his own man beneath the bright blue May sky with not a cloud in sight. "I'm sure he'll understand. Besides, you do everything else he asks you, so I'm sure it'll be okay."

Gabe didn't seem the kind of guy to get rid of Wayne just because he was allergic to horses, any more than he was the kind of guy to keep a guy like Kurt on his team any longer than he had to. That sense of fairness had been an alien concept to Blaze, at least before he'd met Gabe.

He found himself thinking of what Gabe would say when he came back to the valley and found the truck parked in the exact right space, the gate wide open, the power off—everything just so, like he wanted it to be. He would turn to Blaze, his eyes full of admiration, and he would say something encouraging, like *Well done*, or *Great job*. Words that Blaze was not used to hearing, but that he wanted to hear.

He made the turn from Chugwater onto Highway 211 proper and hummed under his breath as he guided the truck along the road, delight bubbling up from beneath his breastbone. This was part of what he'd missed while in prison, this sense of freedom and the unsurpassed, seemingly limitless horizon that spread all around him.

Beside him in the passenger seat, Wayne was seemingly recovered from his sneezing fit, chewing on a hangnail, but still glum. He'd not cheered up any by the time Blaze slowed down going through the town of Farthing, and followed the no-name dirt road that went alongside the edge of the entire valley.

There was supposed to be a track that went into the valley where the pasture was. Gabe had explained to Blaze how to get there from the dirt road, but on his own, he wasn't sure.

"Is this the way?" he asked himself and Wayne at the same time.

"I guess." Wayne shrugged. "You can try."

Trying might lead them to a spot where they couldn't turn around or back out, but to go back the way they came, through Farthingdale Ranch and down the switchbacks, would take more time than Blaze wanted to take. He wanted the truck to be in place and the gate open well before Gabe and Quint and Brody arrived with the herd of horses.

Taking in a sharp breath, Blaze drove between the break in the

THE COWBOY AND THE RASCAL

trees, tires crunching on old grasses from when other trucks had passed this way. To the right, the land swept down, like it was in a hurry, but along the left, closer to the trees, the way seemed flat and easy to navigate. It was, but by the time Blaze had parked in front of what looked like it could be a gully or a ravine that might be dangerous for horses who were new to their surroundings, he was sweating beneath his armpits.

"Let's get some lunch," he said, looking at the pasture in front of them, at the wide green valley that seemed so much more familiar to him now. More like home. More like a place where he belonged. "Then we'll come back and check to make sure everything is in place."

"Why bother?" asked Wayne. He was already getting out of the truck, slamming the door behind him. "You guys checked the other day, and it's not like the water tanks are going to get up and walk away."

Blaze didn't holler after Wayne, as he might have done in his other life, in prison or at the carnival. Wayne wasn't into horses, was allergic to them. Tom, as well, wasn't interested. Which left Blaze and Blaze alone to work with Gabe.

It made his heart rush, as though hurtling down a headlong slope for which there were no brakes, only a sense of anticipation, and a kind of new horizon, empty of anything but full of hope, that spread out before him.

He shook his head, made sure the truck was in park, and left the keys in the ignition. He'd have lunch, and he'd have a quick shower, maybe find an old cloth to run over his boots to get rid of the dust. He'd be ready, so ready, for when Gabe returned.

CHAPTER 16
GABE

Gabe was finally able to pull down the bandana that covered his mouth as the herd of horses reached Highway 211. The two-lane blacktop road was easier to navigate the horses along, but more difficult as well, since there were cars that drove past them. Granted, there hadn't been that many cars since Highway 211 wasn't highly trafficked, but still. Some of the horses were shod, some weren't, but all needed to be kept on the verge between the road and the stretch of barbed wire.

They headed south, Quint out front, Brody along the road, and Gabe behind, where the dust was. He didn't mind, not one bit. He'd missed this, the sense of teamwork, of working with guys who weren't going to question orders, or who hadn't committed petty crimes in the past. Maybe he should do more of this, connect with the guys he used to work with last season just so he could retain his sense of balance, of what the real world was like.

"Hup, hup," he said, urging his horse to speed up a little to make sure the stragglers knew they were last in line and needed to move along with the rest of the herd.

His thighs hurt, the insides especially, reminding him how long it had been since he'd ridden like this. A bit of his neck he was sure was sunburned, and the skin along his neck itched with dust and sweat. He couldn't be happier.

They were about a mile out from the cutoff that would take them into the valley and the horses, perhaps sensing water, or that they had been granted some preternatural advice that their twenty-mile journey was at an end, all started to trot.

He saw Quint look back at Brody and shake his head, which Gabe read as the signal to get them to slow down.

"Woah, now, woah," he said, gently, but loud enough for the horses to hear. They'd all been in pastures with limited shelter, going to the wild in their minds. Some shook their heads as though he were speaking a foreign language.

They were hale and healthy looking enough even after their wintering in Wyoming, but they all needed grooming and lush pastures. New horseshoes, courtesy of Jasper. And maybe a visit from the local vet, depending on what Gabe found when he went over each horse. Maybe he could teach Blaze to help him with that.

"Hup, hup," he said again, watching where Quint took the no-name dirt road along the edge of the valley.

They were almost at the end of their journey, and in spite of the skill of each man, the horses hurried up into a canter, heads high, manes and tails flaring behind them like flags. They might have been fully wild for all the attention they paid to Quint's calls, or Brody's low *shhh-shhh-shhh* sounds.

"Damn it," Gabe said under his breath, and urged his mount to a canter to keep up, at least.

Quint would guide the horses into the valley just fine, and Brody would keep the stragglers in line. All Gabe had to do was keep the tail end of the herd as tight as he could so they would all go through the gate—hopefully open—and they could finally pull up and settle the herd, and make sure they knew where their feed and water was. Then they could close the gate, turn on the generator to power the fence, and go get some well-earned dinner.

Would Quint and Brody want to eat with a trio of parolees? He didn't know but he would ask, first, however—

As he held his horse to a trot, he saw the truck parked in front of the gully, a flash of silver against the green pine trees. The truck was parked exactly as he would have done it himself.

Blaze stood at the end of the truck, one foot on the bumper, one hand on the tailgate, ready to swing inside the truck bed, if he had to. Wayne was nowhere to be seen, but at this point, that was fine. He'd been a help earlier, for all his lack of enthusiasm.

Blaze waved, which startled a few of the horses at the tail end, but Gabe clicked and urged his horse forward, keeping those few horses focused on the herd ahead of them, till at last all the horses rushed through the gate. They milled about in the field, snorting, trotting along the fence line.

Gabe wheeled his horse, thinking to dismount and close the gate and the rest of it, but Blaze was already rushing to do this very task, dark hair flying about his face, a grin as wide as could be. He fumbled with the hook mechanism, but then secured it, focused, concentrating. Then he turned the generator on, a low hum amidst the tall grasses, and Gabe could finally draw a really deep breath.

"Good job," he called over to Blaze, feeling warm inside when Blaze did an *aw-shucks* kick at the dust and shrugged like it was no big deal.

Within the pasture, the horses were a little jumpy, unsure of where they were, hooves clicking against bits of stone, some wandering further out to investigate the grasses, some clumping by the metal watering troughs, drinking their fill.

Gabe went over to where Quint and Brody, still astride, were looking over the herd. He knew they were searching for any horse that seemed to be by itself, or not interested in its surroundings, perhaps limping, all signs that a vet needed to be called in right away, sooner rather than later.

"All of them need new shoes," said Quint. "It'll take Jasper all week, four days, at least."

"Shall we bring them up to the forge?" asked Gabe, thinking ahead to logistics and the priority of tasks already underway, such as clearing underbrush, marking stumps for removal. "Or have him come down here?"

"That's up to him, I'd say," said Quint, all business, his eyes hard and focused on the horses. "He might work more efficiently at his own forge, and I know he'd appreciate it if the horses were brushed down before they came to him."

"I'll give him a call," said Gabe, mentally agreeing. "And set up a schedule."

"Let's have the vet out anyway," said Brody. "There's nothing amiss with this little herd, but it wouldn't hurt."

"Agreed," said Quint, leaning forward in his saddle.

Blaze was waiting outside the fence, perhaps rightly thinking that at some point he'd need to turn off the fence to let the riders out, and then turn it on again. He was alert, looking at Gabe, almost on his toes, in anticipation of the request. Gabe made himself focus on the question of dinner.

"You fellows want to join us for dinner?" he asked, looping the leather reins loosely in his hand.

Brody and Quint looked at each other. In Brody's eyes was *maybe*, and in Quint's eyes was *hell, no*.

Gabe added, "It'd do them a world of good, at this point, to interact with someone besides me." Still no answer, so he tried again. "The grub is really good, and we eat in a mess tent, with a view of the pine trees where the breeze comes through, so it's just like eating out of doors. It's nice."

Brody shrugged and slouched down when Quint gave a silent nod, and Brody followed suit, nodding with a smile.

"We'll ride back, get cleaned up, and then come back to the valley," said Quint.

"I'll have Blaze drive the truck up so he can carry me back," said Gabe, not hiding his smile. "Thanks, I appreciate this."

Logistics for the evening solved, Gabe rode over to the gate, and nodded at Blaze, who turned off the power, and opened the gate for them to ride through, as easily as if he'd practiced at it for weeks. Then he reconnected the fence, and turned it on, turning to watch as

THE COWBOY AND THE RASCAL

Quint and Brody rode directly through the camp, on their way to the ranch.

"I've invited them to dinner, and so they're going to clean up," said Gabe, before Blaze could voice the question that was clear on his face. "If you could follow me in the truck and bring me back down so I could shower as well, I'd appreciate it."

It seemed natural to pose this as a question rather than an order, and if anyone had told Gabe a week ago that was how it would go, he wouldn't have believed him.

The responding pleasure on Blaze's face at the small errand had Gabe wondering whether it was the idea of having company for dinner or spending ten minutes in the truck with him that had created the pleasure. He didn't know. The only way to go was forward, doing the best he could.

"Where's Wayne?" he asked as he rode up the slope, going slow, as they made their way to the truck.

"Uh." Blaze stopped, his hand on the door handle of the truck. "I think he's with Tom. They're marking stumps."

Blaze looked like he wanted to say more, but wasn't going to let himself.

"I'll just follow you up the switchbacks, right?" asked Blaze. He opened the door, pausing, as though waiting for Gabe's nod.

When Blaze was in the truck, Gabe started off at a steady walk. Going through camp on horseback gave him a sense of pleasure to see the orderliness of it, the expansion of cleared areas between the trees, how it was coming along. The horse, a sweet mare, wanted to canter a bit, so he let her and then made her walk up the switchbacks, which were too steep for more speed than that.

At the top of the hill where the pine trees cleared to open grassland, windy with an evening breeze, he heard the truck growling low behind him. Now he could let the mare canter, though he walked her through the guest ranch, all the way up to the barn.

Quint and Brody had already groomed their horses and stabled them, so Gabe hurried, pleased to hear the truck pull up, even more pleased to see Blaze, a little wide-eyed, coming into the barn amidst the end-of-day bustle where the ranch hands and cowboys and guests were all doing the same thing—grooming, brushing, and getting ready to settle down to their dinners.

Blaze came up to the mare, already tied to a post, just as Gabe was lifting the saddle from her back.

"Anything I can do?" asked Blaze, though it was obvious by the way he looked at the mare that he had very little experience around horses.

"Give her nose a pet and say hello first," said Gabe, reaching behind him for a body brush. "Then you help me with this. You ever groom a horse before?"

Shaking his head, Blaze came closer, reaching out a tentative hand to the mare's nose, pulling it back when she huffed at him.

"Take this," said Gabe. He handed Blaze the body brush and grabbed a hoof pick. "Just start brushing her in the direction of her coat. Go slow. Be gentle. She's not going to hurt you."

Working this close with Blaze, enfolded in the scents of the barn, of warm horse and cool, crisp hay, was gratifying in a way he'd not expected. Typically, when he worked in the barn, he was a bit off by himself, and maybe the other ranch hands considered him a loner. But as Blaze brushed the horse while Gabe tended to the mare's hooves, they were building a small world that contained just the two of them.

He showed Blaze how to comb out a mane and a tail with long, slow strokes, gently, not pulling any more than he had to. How to wipe traces of sweat away with a chamois cloth. How to oil hooves.

"We'll put her in her halter and then take her to the holding pasture," said Gabe. "There's water and hay there for her, and later someone will decide whether she goes in the barn, or to the outer pastures."

"Got it."

Gabe turned his head as he latched the gate shut behind the mare and watched her, in her green halter, amble off to the rest of the horses, who were chomping down on hay. Blaze's eyes were on Gabe, his attention focused, rising on his toes in that way he had, as if in anticipation of something quite special.

But there was nothing special, only the traces of cleaning up after a horse just inside the wide open double doors of the barn. Only ranch hands rushing around to tend to final tasks before they were let go for their dinners. Only the dust rising in the slight breeze outside the barn. Only this.

"Everything all right?" asked Gabe. He wasn't as uncertain of Blaze's state as he pretended to be. It was only that he knew, really, that the energy between him and Blaze was an undefined spark, looking for a place to alight. Sometimes unexpected sparks could be dangerous. Other times, they could light up the darkest night.

"Yeah." Blaze shook his head at the cloth Gabe offered him to wipe his hands, then, perhaps rethinking it, took the cloth, wiped his hands, and gave it back to Gabe. "I'm just not used to—" He paused. "In prison, people don't work like this, all happy and shit. So many together, I mean. All at once."

Gabe could not imagine what it would be like to work among grumpy criminals who only longed to be free so they could go where they wanted, but he could see in Blaze's eyes that it was an adjustment. So he said, "Let's go back to the valley, get cleaned up, and have some dinner. Sound good?"

Blaze nodded, and tried to give the keys to Gabe as they walked toward the truck, but Gabe shook his head.

"I could use the break," Gabe said, climbing into the passenger seat.

He watched the pleasure move across Blaze's face as he got behind the wheel and started the truck up.

If all ex-cons could be so easily repatriated by a bit of trust, then Gabe knew he could handle a world of parolees. As it was, there was something about Blaze that made him unique in this. Or maybe the sense of ease came from the chemistry between him and Blaze.

Gabe didn't quite put his booted feet up on the dash, but had it been an older truck, one he owned himself, then he would have, as he allowed his gaze to travel over to Blaze as often as it wanted.

CHAPTER 17
BLAZE

Blaze had never showered and shaved so fast in his life, except maybe in prison, but certainly not since coming to the valley, where he could linger under the spray of deliciously hot water, spending all of his tokens. Tonight, though, he rushed through his ablutions, jittery inside, drops of water still on his skin as he pulled on a clean snap-button shirt, and used the edge of his towel to wipe off his cowboy boots before striding out of the shower and straight to his tent where he dumped his things before racing to the mess tent.

There, his buoyant joy collapsed into empty steam as he took in the long table where they usually ate. Those two cowboys, Quint and Brody, were in attendance, and taking all of Gabe's attention as they sat across from him. Tom and Wayne were sitting on either side of Gabe, and though they didn't exactly look enchanted as Quint glared at them, they were taking up space that Blaze wanted.

He couldn't walk up to them and demand that they move. It would cause a scene and not the right kind. Blaze felt his chest tighten as he walked up to the table, and it didn't matter that his boots were shiny or that his shave had been perfect, without a nick, or maybe even that he smelled nice. He was locked out from the precious circle around Gabe and his handsome shoulders and his easygoing smile.

JACKIE NORTH

Dubious, he sat next to Quint, right next to that mountain of a man who smelled like smoke and engine oil and who barely grunted a hello in Blaze's direction. But at least Blaze had a direct eyeline to Gabe, whose smile at Blaze was warm, his eyes sleepy with pleasure.

Blaze opened his mouth. What he wanted to say was how amazing Gabe had looked on horseback, how dusty and manly and utterly edible. But not only would Gabe not be receptive to that kind of babbling overflow of Blaze's feelings, nobody else sitting at the table would care, that or they would be horrified. And just when had Blaze decided he gave a damn about what anybody thought of him?

It'd been forever since anybody had given a damn about him, and he knew that.

"That was fun today," said Blaze, trying it out, a medium tone, a happy, upbeat attitude. "Are we going to do it again?"

"It's possible," said Quint, leaning back when the cooks came out with T-Bone steaks and green beans cooked with butter and garlic. Then he leaned forward and began slicing into his steak without saying anything else.

Across the table, Gabe, a bit more restrained, smiled to himself and then looked up.

"I had a good time, that's for sure," Gabe said in a general way. Then he focused his attention first on Wayne and then on Blaze, perhaps lingering on Blaze for a minute. "And I sure did appreciate the help I got from Wayne and Blaze. And Tom showed me how many stumps he marked with flags this afternoon, which will give us a good direction to follow when we bring the stump digger in."

"You gonna have to rent that digger?" asked Quint, and it was all Blaze could do not to stir in irritation, bump Quint with his elbow and glower. It was all well and good to talk shop, but what he really wanted—

Was just to be with Gabe. All by himself. Just him and Gabe.

"We will," said Gabe. "I don't know how to use one, so maybe we hire a guy who does? Save us all a headache."

Nobody said anything about the time that Kurt had pushed Blaze into the wood chipper, but then, maybe they didn't have to. There was a grapevine in prison, so there must be one up at the ranch as well. Everybody must have heard that Blaze had come that close to losing parts of his body because of Kurt.

"As to your question, Blaze," said Gabe, drawing everyone's attention as he looked at Blaze as if he was the only other person at the table. "We'll be getting small herds of horses throughout the summer, so we'll have plenty of days like this one where I'll need help getting out to the drive and getting picked up from the ranch afterward."

It could be that Gabe was looking at Blaze like he felt Blaze would be the only one he wanted to do this for him. Or maybe not.

Gabe didn't seem the type to play favorites, so he was just answering Blaze's question, and surely meant nothing by it. Blaze needed to make his heart stop pounding with want and needed to focus on making it through this summer program intact. Then he needed to figure out what he'd do once he got his walking papers.

"I'll also be doing an orientation about horses and horse care after dinner," said Gabe as he tucked into his meal. "For my team."

Everyone at the table nodded, as if that was the most sensible course of action. All except for Wayne, who was looking at Blaze, wide eyed, and Blaze knew he was debating whether now was the time to bring up the fact that he was allergic.

Blaze shrugged and tipped his head at Quint, who seemed the kind of guy to think someone was weak simply because they were allergic. Wayne shrugged back, but it wasn't till after dinner, when Quint and Brody left them to go back to the ranch, that Blaze jabbed Wayne with his elbow.

"He's gonna understand," said Blaze as they trailed after Gabe to the pasture, where just beyond, in the growing shadows, the lake, furled by a small invisible breeze, winked silver and blue amidst the green pines.

"You think?" asked Wayne, but they'd arrived, and Blaze just jabbed him again.

"I think."

Wayne needed to spill his guts, and it was occurring to Blaze, in a delicious, heady way, that if Wayne and Tom were both off horse duty, he'd have a chance to have Gabe to himself for chunks of hours at a time. That way, even if he didn't dare say anything, he could stare at Gabe and call it work.

At the pasture, Gabe gestured to the fence line, explaining, once again, how it worked. Then he unhooked it without turning off the generator, explaining how you could do it this way, if you were careful not to touch the cloth-covered wires. They followed him through and waited while he re-hooked the gate, then he talked about the feed troughs, and the water tanks, and about the need to build a small shelter for the horses, if they felt like being in the shade.

"There are trees about, but they are at the far end of the pasture. This is where the food and water are, so the horses are likely going to want to be here rather than out there."

Blaze knew all of this, and he was tired of Wayne's face looking all pinched.

"Wayne has something to tell you," he announced. "Don't you, Wayne."

With a shrug and a nod, Wayne finally blurted it out. "I'm allergic to horses," he said. "I can't get within feet of 'em or I start sneezing and my eyeballs explode."

"Why didn't you tell me this before?" Gabe seemed genuinely puzzled, his dark brows furrowed, but, being the kind of guy he was, patient and kind, he didn't look mad. "And it's not in your file, so—"

"Was allergic when I was a kid," said Wayne, accompanying this with another shrug. "I thought I'd grown out of it. Sorry."

He didn't look terribly sorry, and Blaze tried to make up for this by looking extra sorrowful and sad, even though, on the inside, he was shouting, bubbles of joy moving up inside of him. Wayne's loss. His gain.

"Well, you're off the hook then," said Gabe, a little laugh as he tried to make a joke of it. "You can work with Tom."

"Thank you." With a nod, Wayne made his way back toward his tent, head down, hands in his pockets, seeming to shuffle through the grasses along the path, but he was hurrying and Blaze knew he must be glad to get that part over.

THE COWBOY AND THE RASCAL

"Just you and me, then," said Blaze, doing his best not to sound too pleased about it, but utterly failing. Utterly failing to keep from smiling, as well, though perhaps Gabe only thought that Blaze was trying to be upbeat and cheerful, a team player. "Show me what you got."

He did not mean that to come out sounding like it had, creatively suggestive, come-hither-inducing, but somehow, the words lingered in the air in just that way. Gabe blinked and looked toward the ridge of mountains, then pressed his hands together, then cupped one hand on his hip as if he didn't quite know what to do with it.

"I'll show you what I know," said Gabe, as if he didn't know very much and it wouldn't take very long and that Blaze shouldn't be prepared to be very well schooled in the art of horsemanship.

It turned out, as Blaze figured it would, that Gabe knew about horses. In fact, he knew a lot, and it seemed he was pleased to have Blaze as his only pupil, however inept he was, and unused to being around horses.

They spent the evening going over the basics, the parts of a horse, how to use the body brush, the chamois cloth, the hoof pick, all of it. How to judge how much hay to give a horse by counting out the flakes. How to walk up to a horse, how to walk away. How to move slow, and to always be watching.

"They've all been broken to ride," said Gabe. "But that's the outdated way to say it, *broke*. We say, these days, that they've been *started*, they've been whispered into agreeing to work with us." He smiled as a larger horse moved forward and bumped Gabe's elbow gently with its muzzle. "This one knows where his eats and treats come from, that's for sure." With a soft pet to the horse's neck, he gently pushed it away. "One daily chore we're going to have to do until the horses are settled elsewhere is to clean the manure and make sure overflow from the water troughs is draining away properly."

The words settled over Blaze's shoulders like a reassuring cloak. Frankly, he didn't care what he had to do. He'd even shovel horseshit and carry it away in a wheelbarrow. As long as Gabe was his teacher, as long as he didn't have to share Gabe with anyone. If that made him selfish, so what?

They quit around sunset, and on Tuesday, while Tom and Wayne were away in the woods, chopping down trees, Gabe and Blaze spent the morning feeding and watering the horses, checking the fence line, and Blaze even got to be in on the cellphone conversation between Gabe and Jasper, the guest ranch's blacksmith. Who appreciated the consideration of having the horses brought to his forge, rather than him having to set up a makeshift forge.

"You want to trailer 'em up here or walk 'em up?" asked Jasper over the cellphone's speaker. "It's easier to lead four than to trailer four, eh?"

Gabe looked at Blaze as if for confirmation, though surely he knew the answer all on his own, and Blaze nodded, feeling wise.

"Depends on the horse," said Gabe. "I'll teach Blaze how to do both, trailer and lead."

"What about the other two?" asked Jasper, his voice a little tinny through the speaker. "Don't you have three on your team?"

"One's allergic and one's not interested."

"I'm interested," said Blaze, though he knew the truth of it was that it wouldn't have mattered if Gabe was in charge of pulling weeds, as long as Blaze got to work with that blue-eyed, broad shouldered, strong and silent man.

"Will you be ready for us tomorrow? Wednesday?"

"Sure will," said Jasper. "Mornings are best. I can take four tomorrow, starting at nine."

"You got it."

Gabe clicked the cellphone off, then moved it back into his pocket.

"I'm all in," said Blaze as if Gabe had asked him a question about it, and wasn't sure about Blaze. "I won't ghost you, I swear."

"I know you won't," said Gabe, responding as solemnly as if Blaze had sworn a vow. "We'll get breakfast tomorrow. Tom and Wayne will be on lumberjack duty, then you and I will groom four before walking them up to the forge. Sound good?"

Blaze mouthed the word *forge*, not sure what it was or, without the internet, how to look it up.

"It's Jasper's workshop, is all," said Gabe. "It's where he shoes

THE COWBOY AND THE RASCAL

horses and makes horseshoe nail jewelry and the like. It's just a workshop, really, but he likes to call it a forge."

Jasper could call it anything he wanted, for all Blaze cared, but he kept his smile small, so as not to overwhelm.

"So let's catch a few and start brushing them down." Gabe looked at Blaze, and again his joy blazed from his eyes. "And I'll bet you're wondering how we catch those without halters, aren't you?"

"Yes," said Blaze, and then he watched, amazed, as Gabe pulled a long rope tie from around one of the open bales of hay, and walked up to a horse with the tie coiled in his hand. The horse didn't shy from Gabe's hand and seemed quite content to have that tie around his neck as Gabe guided him to the edge of the pasture, turned him around, and then let him go. Then he caught another horse in the same way and held out the tie for Blaze to try.

Normally, Blaze would have backed up, hands up, palms out, objecting to a task he had no experienced in. But with Gabe waiting patiently, tie held out, he could hardly say no. Plus, if there was anything Blaze was good at, it was copying someone else's motions, expressions, body posture, all as part of the ruse while telling them a story, or getting them to slap down ten dollars to pay for three darts that would most assuredly miss each and every tough-skinned balloons tacked to the thinly painted particle board.

"Sure," said Blaze. He reached for the bright yellow tie, his fingers touching Gabe's, the moment stretching until it snapped and fell apart. "I can do this."

If Gabe was near, he could probably do anything, including catching horses without halters.

CHAPTER 18

BLAZE

When the landline rang right after lunch on Wednesday, Tom leaped to answer it, shoving Blaze to one side as he got up from the table and lunged at the phone. His eyes were bright as he greeted the caller on the other line, as if he'd been expecting that call. That he already knew what the conversation would bring.

They all could hear every single word Tom was saying, so it was obvious, at least to Blaze, what Tom was about to tell them.

"That was Joanna," said Tom as he slammed the receiver down, smiling at them because he knew that none of them would be surprised by the information. "Her dad has agreed to hire me in his contracting firm in Cheyenne, so I'm going to be finishing my parole while working for him. Oh, and Joanna and I are getting married the day after tomorrow."

"Congratulations," said Gabe, though Blaze thought he looked a little disappointed to be losing yet another man from his team. "When are they coming to pick you up?"

"Today?" The question in the single word seemed to freeze Tom where he stood, as if he imagined that Gabe would put up some kind of barrier to his leaving, a bunch of red tape, something. "By dinnertime? Or sooner? Like, now?"

"That's fast," said Gabe, nodding as he rubbed his chin with his hands. "What can we do to help you get ready? Help you pack? Do I need to sign any forms?"

Wayne seemed thrilled and pounded on Tom's back, and the cooks even came out to congratulate him. But Blaze, unexpectedly shocked, watched all this in a kind of sound fog where mouths moved, where the tones were dampened beyond his hearing. As if there was cotton wool in his ears, blocking off not just sound, but feeling, leaving him cold all over.

Tom's leaving would leave behind more Gabe for Blaze, but it would also mean that Blaze would be alone in the tent at night, and as the panic rose in his chest, he barely heard the rest of the conversation. Barely heard himself adding to the chorus of congratulations and happy wishes for all the best.

There was no way this was turning out like it was. No way he was going to have to sleep alone in that tent. Darkened by shadows, it would be the perfect trap, the perfect corner to back him into. And though he knew that there wasn't a pair of convicts just waiting for lights out before they sprung, in his mind there was.

"Everything all right, Blaze?" asked Gabe, standing too near, not a bulwark this time, but a wall, tall, ten feet tall, cement, impenetrable.

"Sure." Blaze shrugged and made a face as if Tom's leaving had nothing to do with him and his own private and untamable fears that had burst up from below, an open-mouthed *thing* ready to swallow him whole.

He trudged with the others to tent #4 and made motions with his hands that he hoped could be mistaken for actually helping Tom pack.

Someone, one of the cooks, perhaps, had gone to the store room and brought back a large cardboard box and an old green duffle bag, and into those went all of Tom's stuff. It was when Tom picked up the cardboard box, and Gabe slung the strap of the duffle over one shoulder, that Blaze knew there was no stopping any of this.

He barely heard the dull sound of his own booted footsteps in the

THE COWBOY AND THE RASCAL

grass as he helped walk Tom to the parking lot. There, Gabe was making small talk with Tom, finding out what his plan was, what kind of work he was going to do, not at all concerned that no work was getting done. That they were all basically lollygagging as they waited for Joanna to show up.

Within the hour, a shiny, new-looking red Lincoln town car drove down the switchbacks and into the parking lot. Joanna got out, holding Barbara Lynn in her arms while her dad, a tall man who wore a three-piece suit, introduced himself as Glen Baxter and took the time to shake everyone's hand.

"My son-in-law to be spoke very well of you, Mr. Holloway," said Glen.

"Gabe, please," said Gabe, shaking Glen's hand. "We're sorry to see Tom go. He's a hard worker."

They helped Tom put his things in the enormous trunk of the town car and said their last goodbyes. Then Tom helped Joanna put the baby in her car seat while Glen warmed the engine. The sound of doors slamming echoed in the small clearing, sending reverberating thuds into Blaze's heart as Glen drove off in a small cloud of dust.

Which left Wayne and Gabe and Blaze standing in the clearing that served as the parking lot, waving goodbye at the taillights of the car like they were extras in an old black and white movie about the demise of a small town.

When the car was truly out of sight, the smell of exhaust fading, the scent of pine trees growing, the cooks headed back to the mess tent.

"I guess we better get back to work," said Gabe. "Blaze and I will take care of the horses, and Wayne, will you be able to finish up mapping those stumps? Then tomorrow, I can get someone from the ranch to help you, as I hate to think of you working alone with those sharp tools."

"I'm good, boss," said Wayne. "I don't mind being alone. Makes a nice change from prison. Just a ton of silence and me."

"Fair enough." Now Gabe turned those blue eyes to look at Blaze, and Blaze suddenly couldn't come up with enough song and dance to keep Gabe from asking again if everything was all right. Because it wasn't, only it wasn't anything he could put into words that would make any sense to anybody.

Time flew forward, as hard as Blaze scrabbled to make it stop or at least slow down. When his chores were done, and he'd managed to at least pretend to eat dinner, Blaze was at liberty to enjoy his evening.

He could borrow a book from the little library in the mess tent. He could take an hour-long shower. He could take another one. He could grab a snack from the mess tent, if he wanted, and read in his bed, or Tom's bed, if he wanted to, to save himself from having to sleep in a litter of Cheez-It crumbs.

Instead of doing any of this, he went to his tent, sat on his cot, and stared at Tom's cot, at the rumpled bedclothes, the empty shelf, the odd single shoelace beneath the bed. It was odd because nobody wore sneakers around the valley, though Tom might have had a pair he'd brought with him and lost the lace while packing.

Thinking about all these details, unimportant and dismissible, was better than doing what he was really doing, which was watching the shadows grow long and then longer, black fingers, inky and sharp, reaching through the trees to his tent. Twilight became deep blue and then purple, and then, finally, without any attention to Blaze's desire to stop time and the sunset, night entered the tent.

Shaking, Blaze stood up and, without letting himself think, made his way along the path out of the clump of trees, and around to Wayne's tent. Wayne was reading by his flashlight, or maybe he'd been jerking off and reading at the same time, because at Blaze's approach, the flashlight went off.

"What do you want?" asked Wayne, his voice hard, the sheets rustling.

"Can I sleep with you?" asked Blaze. "I mean, in Kurt's old cot?"

"Hell, no." Wayne didn't offer any excuse, but he was adjusting the sheets again in the dark. "You've got two cots, so if you don't like yours, sleep in Tom's. Now, go away, 'cause there ain't no way I'm giving up this roomy tent just to do your stupid ass a favor."

Wayne liked to work alone. He'd said that more than once. And after prison crowding, to Wayne, a tent to himself was the perfect setup. But it left Blaze standing at the opening of Wayne's tent, his skin prickly with worry, an untamable pounding in his head, brain crawling to get away from itself.

"Fine," he said, but it wasn't fine, though there was nothing else to do but stumble back to his own tent. There, he sat on the edge of his cot, his head in his hands, the light overhead casting very stark shadows over the memories that climbed over him.

His last night in jail, after the guards had shown up, he'd been hunkered on the floor, his naked back against the wall, knees bent to his chest, his nose bleeding, one eye swelling up hard enough to block his vision. His ribs pounded with hurt, skin peeled back from his knuckles.

You're fine, the guards who had stopped the assault had said. *Nothing happened, you're fine. Get up and clean up and get to bed. You've got a big day ahead of you tomorrow.*

Maybe that was what had made it even worse than it actually had been. That the two guards who'd stopped it hadn't cared what had almost happened to Blaze.

Sure, they'd been alerted by Blaze's muffled curses, the banging of the metal bed against the wall, Blaze's stuff thundering to the floor from his little metal shelf, maybe a combination of all three. But even with his boxers torn and the scratches on the other prisoners' faces, after they checked that he wasn't bleeding from any orifice, they didn't treat it as anything other than a rough game of gimme-your-commissary-tokens.

The two prisoners who'd made their way into Blaze's cell hadn't said anything, just denied all wrongdoing, and Blaze, pushing himself up along that wall as he pulled up his boxers, wasn't about to say anything either.

You're fine. Nothing happened.

Which was just about as bad as, *Officer, this is all Blaze's fault. He's such a bad influence on my son Alex, and he's the one that caused this fight. These drugs are his. This gun is his. Alex has done nothing wrong.*

Or was it worse? The guards owed him no loyalty, and his fellow

JACKIE NORTH

prisoners certainly did not have any affection for him. But his family? Now it was all mixing together, and Blaze struggled hard to shove it all into the back of his brain so he could at least try to get to sleep.

He never got as far as actually putting his head on his pillow, but remained upright on the edge of his cot, where he met daylight, grateful but exhausted, his eyes burning, his limbs so heavy, he could barely stand up.

But he did stand up and went through the motions of shaving, not looking in the mirror at the wild, burned look in his eyes. After which he stumbled to breakfast and ate what he could as he avoided Gabe's concerned look his way.

"Everything all right, Blaze?" asked Gabe as they finished with breakfast and went to the pasture to feed and water the horses. "Already missing Tom?"

This last was asked with a little laugh because, of course, Gabe, or any man, would find it funny that Blaze might be missing his tent mate. There was no malice in the humor, he knew that, but he had to clamp his jaw tight over any reply.

Toward the middle of the day, when the sun was high in the blue sky, spreading golden light over everything, it was easier to pretend that he *was* okay. That he wouldn't be freaking out come nightfall over memories of what *almost* happened to him. But being alone at night made it feel as if it could happen to him. Which made absolutely no sense at all because those two guys were still in prison, and nobody in the valley had it in for Blaze. There was only Wayne, and Gabe, and the two cooks. Not an aggressive bone among them.

After lunch that day, when he'd gotten his second wind and his body felt like it could keep going, he was on chainsaw duty. Which was fine. He could wear the face protection, clamp on the noise-canceling earmuffs, and just work without having to pretend he wasn't the least bit interested in conversation or human connection, not even Gabe's.

The less attention Gabe paid to him, the better. That way, Blaze could just soldier on until dark in the hopes that he could ignore the memories crowding in the back of his brain and just get some damn sleep.

Blaze kept his focus on the work that was in front of him. That was the best way to get through this. Except, as he buzzed through the trunk of a dead tree, he'd not checked to see which way it might fall, or even paused when he saw that Wayne and Gabe were standing in the path of that fall.

As he clipped through the last bit of bark along the base of the trunk, he lifted the chainsaw away, reaching to turn it off as he watched the tree tumble through the air. And though his mouth opened in warning, not a single sound came out. Without knowing how else to warn them, he ran the chainsaw faster, and shoved it into the time-hardened tree stump, where it made an awful clattering and snapped the chain.

Wayne and Gabe looked up just in time and skittered out of the way as the tree crashed to the ground, and when Blaze turned off the broken chainsaw, an unearthly silence filled the air.

This was it. Gabe was going to yell at him, fire him, send him elsewhere to finish his parole a different way. The prospect of this loss made him shake all over as he dropped the chainsaw to the ground and whipped off his eye protection, his earmuffs, flinging them away into the undergrowth.

"Holy *shit*," said Wayne, loud enough to scare birds from branches.

Gabe touched Wayne's shoulder as if making sure of him, then came around the fallen tree to where Blaze was. On his face was nothing but concern, though he looked a little white, and a bit of sweat had plastered his hair to his temples.

"Are you okay?" Gabe asked when he was close enough not to have to shout. In fact, his voice was low and steady as it always was, and as he came right up to Blaze, his hand reached out, not to strike, but to touch. As if Gabe wanted to be sure of him, too.

"I fucked up," said Blaze, blurting this out to get it over with. "I didn't check the felling path. You both could've gotten hurt. Killed."

"We're fine," said Gabe. He took off his leather gloves and tucked them into his belt. Then he curled his fingers around Blaze's arm, quite gently.

"I broke the chainsaw," said Blaze, desperate to be understood. "They're expensive. I know that."

"They are," agreed Gabe. "But when you broke it, you did that to warn us. Besides, you're worth more than any chainsaw."

Blaze shook his head because this idea was ridiculous, and Gabe ought to know that.

"You are," said Gabe. "More importantly, tell me what you learned right now."

"What?" asked Blaze, feeling totally stupid, even more so as Wayne came up to join them, slapping his leather gloves in the palm of his hand, grinning like he was enjoying Blaze squirming under Gabe's scrutiny like he was.

"Sure, we had a near miss." Gesturing at the tree, Gabe seemed almost too calm for a guy who just about got his brains smashed in. "But this is how we learn. You won't forget to check the felling path next time, will you." It was not a question. Then Gabe added, "You don't look like you got any sleep last night. Did you?"

If Wayne looked disappointed that Blaze wasn't going to get hauled across the coals, Blaze actually *felt* disappointed. He should have gotten yelled at. It might have helped focus him if he'd gotten yelled at. Most of all, was this guy for real? He'd almost gotten killed by Blaze's carelessness, and his first concern, well, maybe his second concern, was whether or not Blaze had gotten any sleep.

"You didn't, did you." Gabe moved a bit closer, as if he wanted to make sure Wayne didn't overhear him or see the gentle expression in his eyes.

It was so like Gabe to simply see that something was wrong and follow his concern by a desire to do something about it. But what could Gabe do? Hold Blaze while he slept?

The thought was ridiculous but oddly comforting, but it gave Blaze enough energy to shrug a bit and smile in what he hoped was a self-derisive way.

"I didn't," he said, disassembling with the absolute truth, which he followed with a lie. "I'll catch up tonight, though," he said. "Thanks for not yelling."

"Like I said," said Gabe. "This is how we learn. And I'm not here to penalize you for not being an expert lumberjack. I'm here to help you build new skills, like how to trust yourself, your team, me."

Gabe's gentle grasp on Blaze's arm turned warm, almost a caress.

"Why don't we take a break," Gabe said. "We can get some iced tea and update the map. That way, we can streamline our efforts, rather than just using brute force to get through this project. Sound good?"

"Sure," said Blaze, casting a glance at Wayne. Who, true to his nature, did a little happy dance at the prospect of not working. "Iced tea sounds good."

He could have told the truth just then. Could have done as Gabe had asked, and trusted Gabe with what was really going on. Only that would mean opening up all the parts of himself that he'd shut off two years ago when his family had betrayed him.

He wasn't ready for that kind of vulnerability, or at least he didn't think he was. When Gabe found out what a fucking coward Blaze was, he wouldn't be concerned anymore. He'd be disgusted and turn away, and that Blaze knew he couldn't bear.

CHAPTER 19
BLAZE

Blaze managed to get through the rest of the day, squinting through the blur his vision had become. He did his best to appear cheerful as they looked at the map and updated it with a red grease pencil. He did his best to eat his dinner and sit in the mess tent to watch the movie Wayne had picked out, which was, oddly, *My Cousin Vinny*.

Gabe made popcorn that Blaze could barely eat, though he did his best to pretend he was eating it, avoiding scrutiny with as much energy as he could muster.

When the movie was over, the popcorn bucket empty, Blaze said something that might have resembled *Goodnight, everybody*, and stumbled to his tent. There he turned on the light, sat on his cot, and did his best to prepare for the endless wait until dawn.

He didn't know what time it was when his body told him he needed to pee. Boldly, he stepped into the woods and somehow managed to make his way to the facilities. There he peed, washed his hands beneath the glare of the light.

The problem started when he turned off that light because now everything was in pitch darkness, so dark that he didn't know how to get back to his tent. And he'd stupidly not brought his flashlight with him.

Turning to the left, which felt like the right way, he bumped into a tree, pushed off it, and found himself tangled in another tree's branches.

By the time he managed to untangle himself, he was in a small clearing surrounded by darkness all around, and by silver shots of starlight amidst dark branches with absolutely no idea how to get back to his own tent. But he had to try. It was either that or stand in the darkness all night waiting for something to eat him. With his luck, it would be a very angry bear.

Moving forward, he stumbled across the uneven ground, arms in front of him, fingers curled, reaching for whatever might be in front of him. Which was, of course, more branches that reached right back, grabbed him, and wouldn't let go.

Tussling with them like he might an invisible many-tentacled beast, he tried to yank himself free, but fell to the ground, clawing the air, wincing as something smacked him in the face.

In the night, something cracked, a stick of wood, or maybe it had been a shotgun. Blaze went still, hugging his knees to his chest, eyes wide, seeking what was out there. Not that he could stop whatever was coming for him, but maybe he could beg a little bit—

A flash of light crossed his eyes. The crunching sound came closer, more regular now. More like footsteps and not the scary slow drag of some unnamed, unknown beast with fangs.

"Blaze, is that you?"

Gabe's voice. Solid and steady in the darkness, soothing, something for his ragged brain to grab onto.

"Uh," was all he could manage, his teeth were clicking together so hard.

"Did you get lost?" The steps and the light came closer until Blaze could look up and see Gabe's face half-limned by the flashlight.

"No," he said, but of course, it was obvious that he had.

"Let me help you up."

Blaze sensed that Gabe was holding out his hand, and he took it,

THE COWBOY AND THE RASCAL

mind going blank as Gabe pulled him to his feet with one steady pull. Up close, with the flashlight pointed at the ground, shining between them, Blaze took his first full breath since he'd heard the news Tom was leaving.

"No flashlight?" asked Gabe, not moving back, not letting go of Blaze's hand.

"No," said Blaze, soaking up Gabe's warmth. "Forgot it."

"Well, let me take you back to your tent, then."

"*No.*"

Blaze couldn't help it that the word came out a half-shout, barked into the stillness of the night that, as his voice died away, became louder with the wind in the trees, the far away whinny of a horse, the burble of the river along the edge of the main part of camp. Crickets. Maybe an owl, somewhere, in the branches, waiting for a mouse.

"I can't go back there."

Panting, Blaze took a breath and tried to reverse that to make it seem that everything was okay so Gabe wouldn't worry. An impulse to divert and deny, even though he very much enjoyed the sense that Gabe was worried, because in his old life, nobody ever worried about him.

"Why not?" Gabe took a step closer and tilted his head closer to Blaze's head, like they were about to share secrets.

"I can't."

Blaze snapped his jaw shut, but the words came anyway, spilling out of him, about that night and the two prisoners two cells down who'd decided he'd been next on their roster.

How the two guards had come just in time to save him from being raped, but that it didn't seem to matter in the end because he had been just as scared as if he *had* been raped.

And how that fear was back in him now, anxiety following him in the dark, especially in the dark, and how only now was it coming to the surface because Tom wasn't there.

Tom had never stood guard, had never known about any of this, but now that he was gone, there was nothing between Blaze and his fears.

"This wasn't in the file," said Gabe when Blaze finally shut up. Then he seemed to shake himself. "I mean, I read the file, so I know why you were all banged up when you arrived, but why didn't you tell the guards about this when they were there?"

There was no way that Gabe could understand how prison worked. How if you squealed on another inmate, you'd find yourself getting a shiv shoved between your ribs at the most inopportune moment.

If Blaze had blabbed about the almost-rape aspect of the attack, it wouldn't have mattered that in less than twenty-four hours he'd be leaving prison for a summer spent digging post holes for future rich visitors. He wouldn't have made it till then.

"There was no point," he said, horrified when his voice wobbled on each and every word.

"No point," said Gabe with a sigh, and maybe Blaze imagined it, but Gabe's shoulders sagged as though he was attempting to take the weight of Blaze's problems on his own shoulders. And sure, Gabe had broad shoulders, but that didn't mean he deserved to get stuck with everything Blaze had been dragging behind him since he left prison, and even before that.

"Doesn't matter," he said, but his voice was still shaking, his teeth clicking together, feeling that if Gabe let go of his hand, he would have grabbed onto it all the harder.

"It does matter." Gabe seemed quite sure about this and when he finally did let go of Blaze's hand, his arm went around Blaze's shoulder for a good warm squeeze before he finally dropped his arm. "Come back with me to my tent, then. I've got a second cot, and if you don't mind that I snore—"

Blaze heard himself gasp, gratitude lacing his breath, the pounding in his heart settling below a hard pound to something less defined, and nodded as Gabe pointed the flashlight through the trees to where, now, Blaze could easily see the clump of trees, inside of which was his tent. Which had been right there all along.

"Let's grab some things for you, okay?"

Again, Blaze nodded and followed Gabe, going in when Gabe went

THE COWBOY AND THE RASCAL

with him. He grabbed his sleep sweats, a t-shirt, his little toiletry bag, knowing that he was about to run out of his little tube of prison-issued toothpaste, which he'd been using instead of the name brand toothpaste the valley had given him, saving it for best, saving it for later, saving it—

"C'mon," said Gabe, his voice softer now as he waited until Blaze had left the tent, then zipped it shut. "That'll keep out the bugs."

Then he led the way along the path between the clumps of trees to the bank of tents that would one day be occupied by the valley's more permanent summer staff, but which currently only housed Gabe.

"This is me."

Gabe unzipped the screen on his tent, then clicked off the flashlight as he turned on the overhead light. The tent was much like tent #4, though it had a power strip with a laptop plugged in and a charger for Gabe's cellphone. It felt a little bigger than Blaze's tent, better equipped, with a more luxurious feel to it.

"You're living large," said Blaze, trying for normal as he followed Gabe into his tent.

"It might be a bit much," said Gabe. "But while future guests come here for what I call adult summer camp and want to stay comfortable, while roughing it, future staff won't be expected to." Gabe tucked his flashlight on the second shelf on the shelf between the beds, then made quote marks in the air. "With yoga, arts and crafts, archery, birdwatching, canoeing, fly-fishing, a little bit of nature walking, even horse rides, the whole thing reeks of summer camp for grownups."

He turned, and Blaze was sorry that he'd not made it more than a foot inside to show how relaxed he was, how easy it was for him to adjust to sleeping in Gabe's tent.

All of his wishes and desires were *not* about to come true, but tell his heart that, the warmth rising in his belly, overcoming with some tenacious power his earlier anxiety. There was such a mix running through him that he just about wanted to barf.

"You can have this cot." Gabe bent to move some books from the cot to the shelf, and a small pile of folded laundry that looked like underwear and socks. When Gabe straightened up, his arms full of that laundry, all Blaze could do was blink.

"The light's a little bright in here sometimes," Gabe said. "I'll light the lantern."

Blaze had no idea what he meant, but he went to sit down on the now empty cot, feeling the luxurious thickness beneath his thighs, even though it was probably the same kind of cot and setup as Blaze had in his own tent.

He watched Gabe pull down a green lantern-looking thing from an overhead hook in a beam across the highest point of the ceiling. Then Gabe turned a knob, pumped a lever a bunch of times, then stuck the end of a red stick lighter into one of the slots near the bottom.

When a small yellow and orange flame exploded inside the glass, Blaze almost jumped out of his skin, but Gabe quickly turned one of the knobs, and the flame turned into a soft yellow glow, accompanied by a gentle and continuous low hiss. Gabe hung the lantern from the hook again and looked down at where Blaze was looking up at him.

"I like the way it smells," he said, as if Blaze had asked him to explain himself. "I like the sound as background while I'm reading."

Blaze looked at the lantern, which said *Coleman* on the side in red letters, thinking that he'd just uncovered another layer of Gabe-ness, though there was obviously more beneath that.

He wasn't like anybody Blaze had ever met. Back at the carnival, most everyone Blaze knew was nice on the surface, and conniving below the surface, always on the lookout to screw the other guy over. Two layers, max.

Gabe had so many, all of them kind and decent, all Blaze wanted to do was dive into them.

"Now let me tend to those scratches," said Gabe. He pulled out a little plastic box, snapped it open, and laid it on the bed beside Blaze. Of course, Gabe would have a mini first aid kit in his own tent. Of *course*.

"I'm all right," said Blaze, but he did not pull back when Gabe touched his fingers to Blaze's chin, and dabbed at his cheek with a square of alcohol soaked gauze, patted his temple with it, along with other various spots that he examined with narrowed eyes.

The alcohol stung, but Gabe's fingers were gentle, his manner unhurried, as if it bothered him not one whit that his bedtime ritual had been disturbed by finding in the forest a guy who was too stupid to bring his flashlight with him.

"Did you take a shower?" Blaze asked, unable to stop himself, because the little cotton robe Gabe was wearing had opened to reveal a loose white cotton tank top and a pair of enormous blue boxers that seemed to go halfway down Gabe's thighs, almost to his knees. Short pajama bottoms, then.

"Yeah, I like to last thing at night." Straightening up, Gabe threw the used gauze in a little plastic trash can at the end of the bed, then he returned the plastic box beneath the bed. Everything with a place, everything in its place. Except for Blaze.

"I can go back to my own tent now," he said, not quite whispering but not quite saying it out loud.

"There's no need," said Gabe and if Blaze heard *please, stay, I'd like you to*, it was only a voice in his own head, fitful dreaming that he could not seem to stop doing. "You seem pretty shook up and I don't mind the company. Might be nice, in fact. You'll help keep the bears away."

"Are you afraid of bears?" asked Blaze, surprised.

Gabe laughed, a low chuckle, and went to zip the screen shut on the tent, then came back to sit on his cot. The tent wasn't so big that Gabe was very far away, no matter what he was doing, but Blaze liked it when they were sitting on the two cots, just about knee-to-knee.

"Not really," he said. "I mean, not realistically. We're too far out of the mountains and it's their time to be up at higher altitudes, foraging. And they'd only be little black bears, anyway." He winked at Blaze and then reached for one of the books from his shelf. He didn't have very many, and seemed to be able to pick out the one he wanted without even looking, an old-looking medium sized paperback with a mostly gray cover.

"*Scary Stories to Tell in the Dark?*" asked Blaze.

"You guys wanted ghost stories, but I didn't know any, so I got a book." Gabe waved the book in Blaze's direction, smiling, proud of himself. "Want me to read you one?"

Blaze had never felt less like reading, let alone listening to a ghost story, so he shook his head, though he had never felt grateful for such a simple gesture.

"Got a Firefox book. Could read to you about spinning and weaving." Gabe stood up to take off his robe, an unguarded trusting gesture that made everything in Blaze's body relax.

"Yeah," said Blaze.

The simple word floated in the air for a minute before Blaze realized how close attention Gabe had been paying to him, and how he settled into his bunk, long legs, those blue cotton boxers, the soft-edged paperback book in his hands. How he waited for Blaze to change into his sweats and, barefooted, climb into bed.

When Blaze was settled, Gabe cleared his throat and began to read.

The words themselves didn't matter. The rhythm and tone of Gabe's voice did, deep and soft, warm whiskey, a slow, even cadence.

Those words vanished beneath Gabe's voice, and un-wove and wove again, into a blanket that settled over Blaze like the tenderest touch. A weight coming down, protective, curling around him.

At one point, he tried to blink his eyes open, to stay awake, but why, why, why when Gabe was on duty, watching over him. Protecting him.

Sleep, when he met it, was a blessing he'd not been prepared for.

CHAPTER 20
GABE

The first thing Gabe became aware of upon waking up was the energy of another body in the cot across from his. When he did open his eyes and cast them that way, he wondered what he'd been thinking last night, tender feelings pushing up inside of him. Any of which were surely outside the scope of his responsibilities as team lead.

Blaze was a fully grown man, of course, and not all that innocent, but to come upon him in the darkness of the woods, crouched down with his back against a pine tree, had pressed every single one of Gabe's buttons, impossible to resist.

Now, Blaze was curled under the bedclothes, a sheet and woven cotton blanket, his hair a dark shock on the white pillow, fingers grasping the pillowslip. A soft rise and fall of his ribs as he lay on his side.

Gabe didn't want to wake him, wanted to look some more and drink his fill. Wanted to imagine what it might be like if they'd met before Blaze had spent two years inside prison walls.

They could have met, would have met, at a county fair. There would have been a cotton candy scent in the air, sawdust, the racket of the Tilt-a-Whirl, and it would not have been Gabe's scene at all. Too much shouting. Too many people and machines. Too much hustle, barkers calling for folks to lay down a ten-spot for a chance to win an enormous purple octopus. No, not his scene at all.

Would he have stopped to talk to Blaze at one of those booths? Or would Blaze have been operating one of the rides? Standing tall in a colorful vest, his hands on the gears, ready to help Gabe get into a seat on a Ferris wheel, keeping a watchful eye as Gabe rose in the sky?

Fanciful notions, all of them. He wouldn't have given Blaze the time of day had he happened to meet him at a county fair. Or at a grocery store, for that matter. Gabe would have turned away from the sly grin, the messy hair, the flirty patter.

He would not have been interested, not one little bit. But now, now that the semi-wild wilderness of the valley had broken through a bit of Blaze's reserve, right through the armor that Blaze had pulled around him in prison, now Gabe was interested and quite unsure what to do with the tender feelings inside of him at the thought of what Blaze had gone through.

"Hey."

Gabe focused on the now, drawing himself out of the drowse of early morning, to the crisp green of Blaze's eyes, the hand through that dark hair, the closeness between them, silky soft and unassuming.

"Hey," said Gabe.

Right away, the single exchange of greetings started Gabe's mind to working, a desperate attempt to focus on the day's tasks and projects, an imaginary list furled to its full length. Horses. Those stumps. The delivery of the wood chips that needed to happen that day, or they'd run out of room in the dump truck.

Blaze sat up, the top sheet slithering around his hips. Gabe looked away as Blaze adjusted himself in his sweatpants, sunlight pouring through the end of the tent, through the screen, gold strands, dust motes in the air. The canvas of the tent starting to warm, the breeze full of rushing damp from the night before.

"Shall we get some breakfast?" asked Gabe. He sat up, as well, and rubbed at his eyes, and wondered again at the simple pleasure of it all.

When he'd started this job, this was not the picture that had risen in his mind, nor the feeling.

"Yeah," said Blaze. He stood up, stripped, and stepped into his blue jeans and pulled on a t-shirt, not turning or shielding himself, and Gabe imagined he must have learned this lack of modesty while in prison. Not that Gabe stared, no. He concentrated on getting dressed himself, on making his bed, the latter of which drew Blaze's attention to him.

"What?" asked Gabe as he finished, turning to look at Blaze, who was scowling slightly at him.

"Do you do that every day?" Blaze asked. "I mean, we had to in prison, but I didn't know people did that in real life."

"I picked up the habit in the army," Gabe said. "It makes it nice to look forward to, getting into a bed that's been made."

It was mundane, all of this, talking about making beds, thinking of the schedule for the day. When what he really wanted was to follow impulses that should never see the light of day. That he should never give in to.

"Ready?" asked Gabe, lacing up his work boots, then grabbing his toiletry bag.

Silently, Blaze followed him along the path to the facilities, then back to his tent to drop off his things before heading to the mess tent. Wayne was already there, nose-deep in a mug of coffee, looking content at his solitary state, but giving them a nod as they sat down.

"What's on for today, boss?" asked Wayne, thankfully not asking why Gabe and Blaze seemed attached at the hip. They were, though Gabe couldn't actually find any reason to complain about that.

"Well," said Gabe, tucking into some amazing eggs and bacon. "Four horses need to be taken up to the forge; Blaze and I can do that if you, Wayne, will finish marking stumps. This afternoon, we can run some logs through the wood chipper and I thought—" Gabe paused because while he really didn't want to be seen to play favorites, it was already a done deal. "We really need to haul those chips up to Chugwater and Whiting. There are two landscape companies there who would greatly appreciate it."

"Count me in," said Blaze, sitting up in his seat.

Wayne shook his head. "Does that mean I get the afternoon off while you're gone?"

"You sure do," said Gabe. "You are at your leisure."

This seemed to satisfy Wayne, who liked being on his own.

With breakfast over, Gabe and Blaze went down to the pasture, doled out flakes of hay, checked the water tanks, and used Gabe's rope trick to grab the four closest horses and halter them.

Between the two of them, they quickly groomed the horses, and Gabe took some pleasure in how Blaze followed his lead, copied his motions, learning fast, showing very little fear of the horses as some novices might.

"You seem pretty good with them," said Gabe as they clipped leads onto the four horses. Taking two each, they led the horses out of the pasture and up the road.

"Ponies," said Blaze with a little laugh that lit up his face, even in the shadow of the pine trees. "Lots of ponies. A kid's ride, you know? Where they have five or six little Shetland ponies all roped to a ring that went slowly around, and the kids don't know any difference, right? They get to ride, and the parents take pictures."

Taking care of a kid's ride like that didn't make a man good at horsemanship, so maybe Blaze had, among his carney talents, a streak of cowboy running through him. But rather than dig for more of Blaze's past, Gabe held himself back as they walked in companionable silence. The switchback was on the steep side, but they took it slow, and it was only a mile or so beyond that to Jasper's forge, anyway. A good, healthy walk.

At the forge, Jasper and Ellis, his assistant, got right to work. Gabe and Blaze said yes to two bottles of water and a seat in the shade, their attention focused on the bellows that Ellis pumped, old fashioned leather ones that had to be worked by hand, and the sparks that flew from Jasper's hammer as he shaped each shoe to fit each hoof.

In short order, he and Blaze were leading the horses back to the pasture and giving them extra flakes of hay for behaving so well. Then they had lunch and were in the woods at the chipper before the afternoon grew hot.

With Wayne manning the chipper, Blaze handed him the large branches and sticks that Gabe drew over. They were going to need to empty the truck, then use it to haul the wood chipper deeper into the woods. The work might take them all summer, which was not a bad way to earn some money and get that loan for his ranch.

It was around three in the afternoon when he and Blaze clambered in the truck. With Gabe driving, they went through the cutoff to the no-name road to Farthing, and beyond to Highway 211 on the way to Chugwater.

The dump truck was on the old side, and the seats had little cracks, a dusty plastic smell coming from the vents. But if the engine strained going up hills, it was hauling over ten thousand pounds of damp chips, which would make a mighty fine mulch for many gardens.

Best of all, they silently agreed to drive with the windows down, which they had to crank open by hand. Gabe shut off the A/C vents, which smelled, and then he could enjoy the scenery and the air and the sight of Blaze settling back into the cracked plastic seat, his arm on the open passenger window.

The smile on Blaze's face made him look more like he was a regular working man, not an ex-con, not someone who'd spent two years in prison. But someone Gabe would like to get to know.

"We'll head up to Whiting first," said Gabe, shifting the gears down as they went up the first big hill as the road headed east, shadows behind them. "Then come down to Chugwater." He looked over at Blaze as the dump truck hopped over some bumps on the road. "You ever drive one of these?" he asked. "Want to learn?"

Maybe teaching an ex-con how to drive an H-box stick shift on a beater dump truck hadn't exactly been on the syllabus for the summer, but it had been a skill Gabe had learned in the army and had come in handy more than once. Plus, if a man could drive a dump truck like this one, he could drive anything.

"Sure," said Blaze. Wind whipped through his dark hair, flipping around his ears, sliding over his green eyes.

His relaxed posture, back curved into the slightly lumpy seat, told Gabe that this was, perhaps, as relaxed as Blaze had been since his arrival, maybe even since his arrest. But until last night, Blaze hadn't been very forthcoming about his time in prison, for which Gabe didn't blame him.

"I'll give you a driving lesson on the way back from Chugwater, when the truck is empty." Gabe nodded, satisfied with this idea, the road, straight as an arrow, allowing him to rest one wrist on the steering wheel, basically driving with two fingers on one hand.

Highway 211 was dirt and gravel in some places, faded blacktop in others, making for a smooth ride sometimes, a bumpy one other times. Still, the air was sweet, and the grasses along the side of the road swept past, hypnotic and soothing.

Going along I-25 was not as soothing, as the dump truck seemed to hit its max speed at sixty, and other cars and trucks were annoyed, going around, honking. By the time they reached Whiting Gravel and Landscape, Gabe vowed to take the back road next time.

Two attendants directed them to the area where they could dump the chips, and Gabe went slowly, using the mechanism to raise the truckbed and allow the door to swing open, knowing Blaze was watching. He dumped about half the wood chips, then lowered the truckbed, ground the gears a little bit before heading out of the yard, and smiled at Blaze as they endured the bumps in the road, and shared a sigh when the road turned to blacktop.

"We're going to miss dinner in the valley," said Gabe, as he looked at the old-fashioned analog clock on the dashboard. "I should have thought of that, but maybe we can grab a burger in Chugwater on the way back."

He was thinking of the Stampede Saloon, which made amazing chili burgers, and when Blaze nodded at him, mouth curving in a pleased smile, Gabe was happy enough to take I-25 south and endure the rude honks.

Along the way, he called Del and let him know they'd be absent for the meal, and if he could let Wayne know, as well. That determined, Gabe settled into the drive, turning on the radio to soft rock 'n roll, which took him back to his army days when he'd been a quartermaster and in charge of stuff like this, his own man, just doing his job.

In Chugwater, he drove to the Lone Tree Feed and Grain, just at the edge of town, beyond the Stampede Saloon. There, they made quick work of dumping the rest of the wood chips, and Gabe breathed a sigh as he pulled the truck into the wide, flat parking lot of the restaurant, parking at the edge so he'd be in nobody's way.

"Hungry?" he asked, putting the truck in first, and thumping the parking brake with his foot.

"Yeah."

Had anyone been looking at them as they entered the Stampede Saloon, just as twilight was falling, they might have thought the two of them were co-workers, maybe even friends. Certainly not that one of them was a parolee, still adjusting to life on the outside.

Blaze sat across from Gabe at one of the round tables near the back, amidst branding irons, dusty cowboy boots, and rust-edged wagon wheels pinned to the rough wood-paneled walls.

The tablecloths were oiled red and white check, pure homeyness that the restaurant's customers adored, and as Gabe looked blankly at the menu, having memorized it long ago, he told himself they weren't on a date. No, they were not.

"These chili burgers look good," said Blaze.

"They're known for it," said Gabe, lifting his chin at the waitress so she would know they were ready to order. "But you can get anything you want. It's on me."

Blaze's dark eyebrows rose a fraction, but if the idea of them being on a date, too, crossed his mind, he didn't say anything. Just told the waitress what he wanted to eat and drink.

"You want extra jalapeños on those cheese fries, hon?" asked the waitress, whose name tag read Linda.

"Yes, please," said Blaze, and when Linda left, he leaned forward, smiling broadly at Gabe, and whispered loudly, "This is my first time in a restaurant in two years."

Low-level grief hung below those words. Blaze had spent two years behind cement walls and razor wire. Existed two years on another man's schedule. Two years without the freedom to get a chili burger, if he wanted one.

"I'll bet it's still an adjustment, even after almost two weeks," said Gabe, leaning back when Linda brought them their two iced teas and a small bowl of quartered lemons, so freshly cut he could smell the citrus in the air. "Maybe for you it was like it was for me when I got out of the army. Or maybe it's not."

His voice went up in a question at the end of those words, inviting Blaze to open up and tell him anything he wanted to tell him. But maybe that might feel too vulnerable, and certainly Blaze didn't respond, but merely squished a lemon quarter between his fingers, then dumped it in his tall plastic glass.

"It's not been so bad," said Blaze with a shrug.

Which Gabe knew could not be true, not possibly. But he couldn't keep digging and force Blaze to talk to him about how he really felt. That'd be cruel, unnecessary.

The sun was setting as they walked out of the restaurant after they finished dinner, and Gabe worried at the cheese stain on his shirt for a minute before reaching into his pocket for his keys.

"Here," he said. "It's a straight shot home, so you shouldn't have any trouble."

He was only a little nervous as he climbed into the passenger seat, buckling in as Blaze did the same. Then he walked Blaze through the steps, clutch, ignition, first gear.

The dump truck was parked so that Blaze didn't have to back up, and though the engine shuddered a bit as Blaze tried to put it into second too soon, their departure from the parking lot, and down the road to go under the bridge toward Farthing, went without a hitch.

Beneath the low burr of the engine as the truck wended its way homeward, Gabe knew he needed to fish or cut bait. He needed to stop having thoughts about Blaze, or he needed to stop torturing himself and do something about those thoughts. Only he didn't know whether he should, because he was obligated to look out for Blaze, not have feelings for him.

He was supposed to function as Blaze's team lead, that and nothing more. And this in spite of the fact that his heart was full because Blaze had trusted him. That kind of trust was a treasure beyond price.

Besides, how did someone go about telling a parolee that more would be better? That the connection between them could become a bridge that might never collapse beneath them?

CHAPTER 21

BLAZE

Blaze's palms were sweating on the steering wheel, but he kept his foot light on the gas pedal. Driving so slowly, he never felt out of control, even though the dump truck felt as though he was steering an enormous elephant. In the passenger seat, on the other side of the huge stick shift, Gabe seemed relaxed, so Blaze must be doing something right.

"We're about fifteen minutes out," said Gabe. "But just past this hill, pull over."

"Pull over?" In an overexcited motion, Blaze turned the steering wheel to the right side of the road, bumping over several deep ruts, but finally coming to a stop in a cloud of dust that he could see in the headlights.

"Yeah." Gabe undid his seatbelt and leaned forward.

The engine was still running, the dashboard lights casting up an icy green glow that lit up Gabe's face, his smile. For a moment they looked at each other as the engine coughed, cooling down, and the low sound of the wind across the grasses grew.

"Turn the engine off, and the headlights," said Gabe. "Come look at the stars."

Eagerly, Blaze did as he was told, undoing his seatbelt, clambering out, and, leaving the keys in the ignition, threw himself out of the truck's cab, landing hard.

He could see the top of Gabe's head—a dark shape, a shadow—and followed, going to stand where Gabe was. Then Gabe reached out and, with warm fingers, pushed Blaze's chin up to look at the stars.

"Maybe you could see these in prison," said Gabe, softly. "But maybe they look better from out here."

They did. There was no barrier to the night filled with stars, save the soft edges of low hills along one side of the road, and the foothills and mountain range in front of them, but miles away. All the rest was a crisp, dark blue, the stars looking almost fake, so silver and hard pointed. There weren't any clouds blocking those stars, no light pollution from anywhere, no haze.

"Wow," said Blaze, but it seemed such a lame response in the face of all this brilliance, added to which was Gabe standing so close.

All of Blaze's flirty patter, any running commentary he'd been planning to make, faded away, absorbed by the darkness, into nothingness. Leaving the stillness of night, the wind in the grasses, maybe the faraway hush-edged rush of a shallow river nearby. And his heart, beating all out of proportion to the fact that he was just standing there. Inches away from Gabe.

Gabe moved close, seemed to cough low in his throat, then his shoulder pressed to Blaze's.

"This is nice," Gabe said, half-low, as if to himself. "Just to be in the midst of all this and look up."

Another layer of Gabe peeled back, revealing a cowboy with a poet's heart, a child's sense of wonder. Wonder that Blaze had lost long ago, if indeed he'd ever had any. Wonder. Innocence. Awe.

"It is nice," he said in return, returning the press, ducking his head to touch his temple to Gabe's shoulder.

Quickly he withdrew. Gabe could interpret that how he wanted and respond how he wanted, and never in his life had Blaze felt so scared, so daring at the same time. Gabe wouldn't want someone like him, his edges torn, his background littered with yesterday's sawdust, a soundtrack of lies.

"We should get back."

The words came low, almost soundless beneath the faint wind, and Blaze felt his heart brittle inside of his chest.

"Okay," he said, because there was no fighting it when a man said no.

He couldn't make Gabe want him the way he wanted Gabe, but as Gabe got in the driver's seat, and Blaze pulled himself into the passenger seat, he ran over what had just happened between him and Gabe. Advance, retreat. Advance again, retreat again.

Why would a man do that? Because he was scared. Because he had hard limits and wouldn't cross them for someone like Blaze. Because, perhaps, and most importantly, he had a sense of honor that wouldn't allow him, as Blaze's team leader, to step down from that, to use Blaze like that.

Blaze held his tongue all the way back to the valley, the window open, hanging onto the handhold above the window, holding on till his fingers ached. All of him ached now, with wanting what he couldn't have, what had been so close. Telling his body to be still, just be still.

And then there was the question as to where he was going to sleep that night. Again in the tent with Gabe? Or on his own, sitting up in the dark until sunrise?

When Gabe parked the dump truck once more beneath the dark, dense shadows of the trees, he turned off the engine and, before it had even begun to cool, he slid out of the truck.

Blaze was on his heels, and he would not have accused Gabe of running, no, but he had to hurry to keep up, telling himself the only reason he was going with Gabe to Gabe's tent was to get his stuff. After that, Blaze's mind was a blank.

Gabe stepped into his tent and pulled the chain for the overhead light. The tent was flooded with bright edges and crisp shadows, and Blaze longed for the Coleman lantern to be lit. For the soft yellow glow to surround them the way it had before.

Gabe's back was to him. Hands on hips, staring at his little bookshelf as if it stored all the answers he needed.

Blaze held his breath and moved close. Close enough to put his hands on Gabe's hips, over Gabe's hands, to tuck himself along Gabe's back. Gabe whirled around, dislodging Blaze's hands, but making their bodies even closer, almost hip to hip.

Gabe opened his mouth, but Blaze placed his palm gently over that mouth.

"Wait," he said. "You bought me dinner."

Gabe's deep blue eyes acknowledged that this was so, and he didn't grab Blaze's hand and pull it away. Blaze could feel Gabe's soft breath on his skin.

"You touched my face and made me look up at the stars."

Gabe, nodding, was still focused entirely on Blaze.

"And then," Blaze couldn't stop the bark of a laugh from surfacing. "You let me drive the *truck*—all of which is just about a marriage proposal to an ex-con like me."

Gabe laughed, a low quick laugh, but when Blaze drew his hand away, Gabe didn't pull away or stop Blaze from moving closer. Didn't seem worried that Blaze's hand was on his hip, curving around denim-clad bone, that he was trapped between his cot and the bookshelf. That he either had to give in and let Blaze do what he wanted to do, or shove Blaze aside and flee.

The first touch of their lips was Blaze's choice, pure and simple and, eyes half narrowed, he took Gabe's face in his palms and kissed him fully. Then he paused, lessening the touch, but waiting. He needed a *yes* and maybe even a *yes, please,* before he went on, for if anyone knew what it was like to not want what was coming, it was Blaze.

Gabe lifted his chin. A greeting, an admission, a *yes, please,* in Blaze's mind. He kissed Gabe again and then again, slowly, letting it linger, the touch of their lips, the exchange of breath and warmth.

"Yeah?" Blaze asked, wanting it confirmed out loud.

"Yeah." Gabe's voice was whisky warm, the taste of him edged with sharp sparks, luscious together, leaving Blaze wanting more.

The tent was not enormous, the cot where Gabe slept, a long, single mattress. Blaze stepped forward and Gabe stepped back,

THE COWBOY AND THE RASCAL

pulling Blaze with him as he sat down, Blaze straddling his hips, feeling the heat between them, the hard center of Gabe pushing up into him. He was dizzy, almost tipping forward, and Gabe caught him, holding him fast, burying his face against Blaze's chest.

"It's been a while," said Gabe, muffled.

"It's like riding a bike," said Blaze, very assured of this. Then he barked a laugh. "Or in your case, a horse."

He felt Gabe's chuckle move through him, a warm buzz, those arms tight around his waist as Gabe leaned back on his bed and now Blaze could be fully on top of him, a knee on either side as he bent down, hands by Gabe's face as Gabe scraped Blaze's hair back, tucking it behind each ear.

"I've been wanting to do that for a long time," said Gabe, his expression tender, his blue eyes half lidded. Then he gripped Blaze's hair and tugged him close, ever so gently.

Blaze closed his eyes and let himself be tugged and kissed and held, Gabe's arms strong around his back, holding him.

If Gabe had unlatched the gates, giving permission, then Blaze flung those gates wide, opening his eyes to scrabble with Gabe's snap-button shirt, pop, pop, pop, opening that shirt, revealing the old fashioned t-shirt beneath, what every cowboy wore, Blaze guessed.

He yanked that up, dragging it from the waist of Gabe's blue jeans and belt, pulling till he could lean down and mouth the warm skin of Gabe's belly, trailing sucking kisses behind as he went, scooting down till he was at the buckle of that belt, his hands on it, fingers at the ready.

"You don't have to do that."

Blaze looked up as Gabe reached down to touch Blaze's chin.

"But I want to," said Blaze, determined. "That's why we're here. It'll be fun, you'll see."

Though he could see the flicker in Gabe's eyes that fun in the bedroom wasn't exactly his style, Blaze made a mental note and kept going, undoing the button and the zipper, peeling back cloth till he got to skin, running a sweep of his closed lips down the dark track of hair. Tugging at the elastic waistband of what were, of course, tighty-whities. Bleach clean and almost brand new. Of course.

This was something Blaze loved doing, all the way down to the bone. In prison, he'd exchanged a few blow jobs, a bit of give and take, something to pass the time. But not in a long while had he kissed soft pink skin and not braced himself for a quick suck and swallow, no. This time, he wanted to go slow, to inhale Gabe's scent, to linger in the warmth of him, stroking Gabe's length, letting out a long breath as his body relaxed while Blaze hovered over Gabe and let the moment sink into him.

"You really don't—" said Gabe, as if, perhaps, taking Blaze's pause for hesitation.

"Hush, you," said Blaze with a half growl. "Let a man linger why don'tcha."

Gabe's head fell back on the pillow as if he'd been defeated by hours of Blaze's arguments and points of logical reasoning. Then Blaze did what he'd been wanting to do for a while now, he tugged on the elastic band of those briefs and kissed the rosy, damp head of Gabe's cock, then pulled even more, framing that cock in his hands, leaving long kisses, licks with his tongue. Tangling a finger in a dark curl of hair. Tasting the warmth of Gabe's body, stroking him, bringing him to full hardness, all the while, Gabe sighed, his belly trembling.

Blaze was trembling too, with holding himself so still, with the answering pulse in his own groin, the heat of desire, the sound of his licking in his ears. Gabe's ragged breaths. The creak of the metal frame of the cot beneath both of their weights.

He tugged now, to get those briefs down over Gabe's hips to his thighs, which meant pulling thick blue denim down, which meant getting off the cot, urging Gabe to rise, his warm hands on the cool curve of Gabe's buttocks, more trembling, a sigh.

"C'mon now," whispered Blaze beneath his breath as he scooted to kneel beside the bed between Gabe's parted thighs, raising himself up, whispering more kisses, suckling now, tasting Gabe, licking his lips as the taste of him grew in his mouth.

Gabe responded, surging into Blaze's mouth, hot and slick, as Blaze drew him in, renouncing all things evil, it seemed, as the goodness of it swirled around him.

Gabe's head was thrown back, his expression in the bald overhead light, vulnerable and open. Eyebrows raised over closed eyes, a tender curve to his mouth. Faint sounds in the back of his throat. Sweat on the length of his throat.

There was no wind, yet it was cool in the tent, the air sweet from where it had come across the lake and raced through the pines. The chorus of crickets and maybe even frogs talked to themselves in the night, all the way down in the slough.

If the world ended, then Blaze knew he could take this with him, this scent, this feeling, the trust that Gabe had given him with open hands, open arms. So Blaze gave it back as best he could, opening his throat and taking Gabe down, sucking soft and then hard, and then again, dipping his fingers to move between Gabe's strong thighs, a wicked pleasure given, layered with sweet.

He could taste Gabe's pleasure building, and mentally sighed as he swallowed the pulses from Gabe's cock, strong, hearty pulses, wild with the pounding of Gabe's sturdy heart. When the pulses slowed, Blaze soothed Gabe with both hands, long strokes, rising up more to lay a tender kiss just below Gabe's belly button, and another on the soft skin inside the curve of his hip.

"Yeah?" asked Blaze, settling back on his heels, looking up at Gabe as he sat up, arms behind him, sweat on his brow, his dark hair a mess over his forehead.

"Yeah," said Gabe. His blue eyes were almost black as he reached out and, again, tucked Blaze's hair behind his ear. "You have—your hair. Usually the guys I've been with—"

But Blaze shook his head.

"We're not talking about them now," he said, soft, curving his fingers around Gabe's hip. "Because I'm not like them at all."

"No, you're not," said Gabe. "And that's a fact."

But he didn't seem concerned that Blaze was different, and maybe he didn't care, not really, that Blaze was an ex-con, and in fact was

JACKIE NORTH

innocent of the charges against him. But all ex-cons said that, didn't they, and now was certainly not the time to convince Gabe otherwise.

"Come up here," said Gabe.

"Light the lantern," said Blaze as he stood up, his throat going tight for reasons he didn't understand.

Certainly he could hardly say out loud, *Light the lantern so I can see you bathed in gold.* Gabe might laugh, and become distracted rather than doing what he was doing, shucking his briefs and jeans all the way so he could stand up and pull out the lantern. Pump the gauge. Pull out the nightstick and set the mantle alight with a flash of flame that settled into a soft yellow glow.

Blaze reached and pulled the chain to turn off the overhead light, and now the tent was how he wanted it. A cave hidden amongst the trees, a protection against the darkness, lit from within, a place that only he and Gabe knew.

Gabe stood before him, shirt rumpled, his pupils huge and dark, jawline limned with yellow light. He reached for Blaze and pulled him close.

Blaze went, thinking, and perhaps he'd thought this before, that if he'd known this had been waiting for him all this while, he'd have been better behaved. Left home as soon as he could, sought out the ranch, gone to Gabe and begged on his knees.

But Gabe didn't make him beg or wait. He kissed Blaze, fingers in his hair, strength surging beneath the gentleness that swept Blaze's breath from his body.

With his other hand, Gabe undid the snap and zipper on Blaze's jeans, and cupped Blaze's hard cock for a moment on the outside of his briefs. Then he slipped that hand, warm, strong-fingered, inside, and stroked Blaze, slowness growing to urgency. And just at the moment where he seemed he would go to his knees and take Blaze in his mouth, returning the favor, Blaze stopped him, slinging his arm around Gabe's neck.

"Just like this," he said, rasping in Gabe's ear, a hard kiss to the line of Gabe's jaw. "Fast as you can, sweet Jesus, please, please please."

Gabe did exactly that, with hard strokes, meant to arouse, maybe even abuse, rather than to soothe or be tender. His grip was tight and at one point, he licked his own palm, a broad stroke of his tongue right in front of Blaze's eyes, then, once slick, returned, stroking between Blaze's thighs, tucked into his briefs, constrained, almost awkward in the most perfect way. Pulling with a twist of his wrist, trailing his fingers along Blaze's length, a swirl of fingertips along the top of Blaze's cock.

And always fast, fast the way Blaze wanted it, almost punishing, but never cruel. Pushing Blaze right to the edge and then, with the sweetest of taps at the base of his cock, he sent Blaze's brain rocking to the back of his skull as he came in Gabe's warm hand.

Trembling, Blaze slumped in Gabe's arms. Gabe, who stood as still and solid as a rock, held him, and waited while Blaze's breath slowed. And all the while, the lantern glowed, soft and bright and steady.

CHAPTER 22
GABE

Saturday had gotten off to a late start, though nothing had ever been more pleasant than to wake up with Blaze in his arms, the metal cot beneath them creaking as Gabe turned to look at Blaze and tuck that dark hair behind his ear.

Then Blaze's green eyes had opened, that quirky flirty grin forming. Beardgrowth and morning stubble had accompanied their kisses, Blaze's soft sighs as Gabe had scooted down and taken Blaze's morning hardness into his mouth, a quick pleasure given that he didn't want returned now. Later, yes, surely, later, and he could promise himself this while he tasted the bitter salt on his tongue, and kissed Blaze's belly, and smiled at the panting breaths from the direction of the pillow.

Then came a horse's whinny and the smell of fresh coffee in the air, and it was all go from that moment on. No time for words between them, promises or explanations or defenses, none of it. As they worked as a team, Gabe's mind was spinning with what he was supposed to do with how he felt when his cellphone rang. He answered it, thinking it was the prison's parole board, calling to remind him of their non-fraternization rule that he'd simply and quite blithely ignored.

"Leland here," said Leland on the other end of the line.

"Hey, Leland," said Gabe as he gestured to Wayne and Blaze that the morning's work was done, and that they could meet him in the mess tent for lunch. "What's up?"

"Do we need a meeting?" asked Leland, quite without preamble. "I thought I had it on my schedule that we were supposed to meet this morning, even if only by cellphone. Did I miss it?"

"No, I missed it," said Gabe, wincing as he walked away from the mess tent because he had a feeling he was about to get hollered at and he didn't want witnesses. "I'm sorry. I just got caught up with everything that needed doing."

"So, is your team suffering from being down not just one man, but two?"

"There's been a little bit of adjustment there, but no suffering," he said. "Turns out Wayne is allergic to horses, but he's been doing all right on his own with clearing undergrowth, mapping stumps, and so on."

"So, a hard worker."

"Hard," said Gabe, agreeing wholeheartedly. "Blaze is too. He's willing to jump in and take up the slack at whatever task."

"Quint and Brody spoke well of their dinner with you," said Leland, now, and while he didn't seem like he was seeking praise, Gabe was happy to give it.

"Your theory is working," said Gabe. "Give a man good food to eat, a comfortable place to sleep, and decent work to do and—"

"I've never seen it fail yet," said Leland, and if he was pleased with himself, Gabe couldn't blame him. "Well, except with Kurt, who seemed like he'd be a good fit, but that'll teach me to tighten my vetting process."

"I've still got a good team, even if it is only two men," said Gabe, and he could see that Blaze was standing at the opening of the mess tent, as if waiting. As if he wasn't going to eat his lunch until Gabe could.

"We'll have some new parolees sometime next week," said Leland. "I'm having Royce take them on. He'll have them fine tuning some of the landscaping closer to the lake, surveying the outer reaches, and he can help you with the horses."

"Sure thing." Gabe nodded. Royce came from a ranching family up in Montana where they raised expensive horses and grew lush alfalfa hay, though Gabe could never understand, if Royce had all that, what he was doing so far south working on a guest ranch. "And we'll have eight horses ready to process, if Quint or someone wants to come by and help me look them over."

"I'll have him call you."

"Sounds good," said Gabe. He lifted his chin, though at this distance he didn't imagine that Blaze could see it. "The boys are waiting on me for lunch," he said. "Talk to you later."

He tucked the cellphone in his back pocket, then hurried to the mess tent. There, the cooks had put out their usual spread, more than that, even, perhaps a bit out of desperation to prove their worth even though they only had three people to cook for.

"We're getting more parolees next week," said Gabe to everyone in general as he sat down. "Leland will have the actual numbers soon."

Now that they were sitting at the table, Blaze and Wayne on one side, himself alone on the other, the question that had been safely tucked away during his and Blaze's rush out of his tent, the scurry to feed and water the horses, and to help Wayne at the chipper, now seemed to loom upwards.

What was he supposed to do now that he and Blaze had shared what they had, touches to bare skin, kisses, the taste of Blaze's spend on his tongue? Such trust from Blaze could not have been given easily, and Gabe did not want to squander that trust.

Just as he was about to dive into what looked like an amazing plate of spaghetti bolognese and toasted garlic bread, his cellphone rang again, and when he pulled it out, it was Quint.

"I'll be down after lunch with some saddles and bridles," said Quint. The sounds behind his voice, people talking and laughing, told Gabe that maybe Quint was in the dining hall at the guest ranch, just about to sit down and eat but taking care of business first. "Will that work? Can we put one of your boys up in the saddle to see how they move?"

Gabe knew that Quint meant he wanted to see how the horses moved with someone astride who might not know what they were doing. A well-trained horse, experienced and steady, could handle an untrained rider, where a poorly trained horse could not.

"I'll bring a lunge line," added Quint, as if he could hear Gabe's resistance due to the fact that it sounded like Quint was willing to use Gabe's parolees as crash test dummies, that he thought ex-cons were disposable. "I've been informed they can't ride, but I'm not expecting them to. I just need the weight up in the saddle. Real weight."

"That'll work," said Gabe. "I've only got one man that you can use. The other one's allergic to horses."

He heard Quint's *tsk tsk* sound, derisive and quick, but that was Quint. Good at what he did, but judgmental of weakness, and that included allergies. At the same time, Quint was an amazing horseman and even if he sometimes rubbed Gabe the wrong way with his taciturn manner and fierce air, he was very patient with questions, even from greenhorns.

Gabe hung up. Wayne rolled his eyes and smirked, as if he knew Quint's opinion but didn't give a rat's ass about it, and Blaze was looking at him, his green eyes wide, a contented air sifting around him, settling on his shoulders.

"Quint's coming to help me review the horses, the eight that are ready, to see about them. Whether they can be sold or donated and to who." Blaze's expression turned expectant, eyebrows rising. "We need an inexperienced rider so we can get the mettle of the horse. What say you, Blaze?"

"I can't ride," said Blaze. "I mean, I *can't* ride."

"I know, but you'd be on a lunge line, wouldn't have to steer or anything. Just get up there."

There was a sense of panic in Blaze's eyes, but then he shrugged. "Okay," he said, and there was nothing after that. No demands, no *You ought to treat me like I'm special.* Nothing like that.

Making Gabe wonder all over again how a guy like that had gotten

THE COWBOY AND THE RASCAL

mixed up in dealing drugs. Maybe the all-prisoners-insist-they-are-innocent was true in this case. Maybe Gabe ought to read Blaze's file again. Or maybe Gabe could concentrate on getting Blaze to tell him his own story, one not filtered through the prison system.

"My hat'll come into good use, at least," said Blaze as he wiped his mouth free of garlic bread crumbs with the back of his hand. "And my new boots."

"Can I come watch?" asked Wayne.

"Anything to get out of work," said Blaze, jabbing Wayne with his elbow.

"Hey," said Wayne, jabbing him back. "I get more done in four hours by myself than I ever got done working with a team."

"You can come watch," said Gabe. "There's always something that can be learned."

When they finished lunch, they grabbed their straw cowboy hats and pulled on cowboy boots and headed down to the pasture to halter the eight horses that Quint would look over.

Gabe turned off the power to the fence and lightly tied each horse's lead to the top wire. They needed a shelter for the horses, and they needed a few hitching posts, so Gabe put that on his mental list of things that needed doing, feeling a little out of kilter that what was supposed to be a side project was turning into a full-time gig. Or maybe it would balance itself out when a fresh van of parolees arrived the following week.

Quint soon drove up in one of the ranch's silver trucks. Quickly, he got out and went to the back of the truck, where he pulled out two beat-up looking saddles and hung them along the edge of the truck bed, hooking a bridle over each saddle horn.

"Hey, Gabe," he said with a short wave, tugging on leather gloves, settling his hat on his head. "Which ones? Oh, I can see already. Thank you."

Without seemingly any effort at all, Quint picked up one of the saddles, and nodded at Wayne, who unhooked the gate for him, holding it open for Gabe, who carried the other saddle. Blaze trailed behind, maybe a little uncertain as to how all of this was going to go down. Wayne re-hooked the gate as Quint and Gabe saddled the two horses and replaced halters with bridles.

With his gloved hand holding onto the bridle of the closest horse, Quint turned to Blaze, and Gabe readied himself to step in, in case Quint's sense of superiority got flung around too hard.

"Blaze has volunteered to ride on the lunge line," said Gabe.

"You ever ride?" asked Quint.

Blaze shook his head no.

"Doesn't matter," said Quint. "You're the weight in the saddle, and don't need to do any more than sit there. I'll help you up, and Gabe will guide the horse through its paces. Walk, trot, maybe lope, if we can manage it. This is just to see how they go. We'll be taking notes, as well. You're going to help us determine what kind of life this horse needs. Needs and *deserves*."

Maybe Quint was making an unspoken comment about ex-cons getting what they deserved, or maybe, as was more probably true, Quint was hyper focused, as he usually was, on the horse's needs over its rider's.

"Up you get," said Quint, motioning to the stirrup, holding it still.

With a bit of a scramble, Blaze hauled himself into the saddle, sitting straight and still while Quint adjusted the length of the stirrup on either side. The horse, an older mare with large liquid brown eyes, stood still with only a faint flick of her tail, a shift from a fore hoof on one side to a hind hoof on the other as she adjusted to Blaze's weight on her back.

"You're all set," said Quint. "Take it away, Gabe."

"She's a good girl," said Gabe, coming closer to pat the mare's neck gently. "What a good girl." Then to Blaze, he said, "Hang onto the saddle horn if you like, or you can hold the reins, but loosely."

When he nodded at Wayne, Wayne handed him what looked like a long lunge whip, but which was actually a training flag, never meant to be used on a horse, only near it.

"Hup, hup," Gabe said as he let out the long lunge line Quint had attached to the mare's halter.

The mare, as Gabe could see, was quite experienced and knew

how to move out to the end of the lunge line and to go in a circle, to slowly turn, at a walk when he signaled with the flag, and then to trot, and again turn the other way, so all in all a peaceful ride.

"She's older," said Quint, as Gabe pulled the mare to a stop, coiling the lungeline in his gloved hands to bring her closer. "But she's got a lot of work left in her, so what do you think, Gabe?"

"Good contender for beginning riders on the ranch," said Gabe, without hesitation. He looked up at Blaze, who sat with his hands on his thighs, a thoughtful expression on his face. "What about you, Blaze? Did it feel safe?"

"Yeah," said Blaze. "But, I don't know, did she want to go faster?"

"She sure did," said Quint. "But she was following Gabe's orders to the letter."

They saddled up the rest of the horses one by one. Blaze got on two horses, average looking, average height, both of which would make good additions to the guest ranch, which tended to have more inexperienced riders than experienced.

Four of the horses, Gabe and Quint earmarked to sell to beginning riders in the area. The last horse, a thin gelding with a scraggly mane, didn't even make it as far as being saddled up. He threw up his head, hand shy, eyes rolling as he tried to jerk his head out of Gabe's grasp.

"Oh, sweet one," said Gabe to the horse, as if he were alone and didn't have an audience of three astonished men to hear him speaking to the horse as if it was a baby. "Who did this to you?"

"I expect he's getting picked on by other horses," said Quint. "You guys don't have stalls to separate them into, but if we build that—"

"We might as well build a barn," said Gabe, petting the horse quite gently with his bare hand, having taken the glove off and stuffed it in his pocket. "Maybe it'll come to that, even if we take it down before the next season starts. What do you reckon, Quint?"

Gabe was asking about the destination of the horse, what they should do with it.

"He needs somewhere quiet where he can graze and not get picked on," said Quint. "With someone who'll make sure he gets his fair share. Someone who'll groom that mane of his back into being pretty again."

"Mrs. Tate sometimes takes horses in," said Gabe. "Maybe we could ask her."

They helped Quint haul his gear back to the truck, and even though all Gabe wanted to do after he watched Quint drive off was to pull Blaze to one side so they could share a quiet word together about what was to happen next, he knew the horses needed taking care of. Then he needed a shower, hopefully before dinner, but maybe Blaze did as well, so maybe that was when—

"Boss," said Wayne with a cavalier wave. "I'm going to take a shower."

"Sounds good," said Gabe, and then Blaze was standing in front of him, almost blocking his way. Gabe could easily have gone around, of course, but he didn't want to and was grateful for the excuse of watching Wayne walk away, leaving them alone.

"Shall we groom?" asked Gabe, for the horses still needed caring for, even after their short ride. Still, he now had time alone with Blaze and hadn't the faintest idea what to say.

"Sure."

Gabe grabbed a bucket and put some grooming supplies into it from where they'd been stored beneath a canvas tarp.

"We need a shed for all this gear," said Gabe as he took the halter off the smallest gelding, the one with the raggedy mane, and looped the lead through one of his belt loops. Then he handed Blaze a body brush and between them, they brushed the horse down.

The gelding seemed particularly fond of the way Blaze smelled, snuffing amidst his pockets as if he might find a lump of sugar or something he might like.

"I guess we could build a shelter of sorts, as well," he said to Blaze over the horse's back, hoping for a response. "Do you know carpentry?"

Blaze shook his head no, then paused, his hands resting the brush on the horse's narrow withers. "Bet I could learn, though," he said. "I know how to drive a dump truck now, so I can learn anything."

There was a tease in those eyes, a flicker of silver in green, a toss of dark hair, and Gabe, drawn in, leaned close, as if to whisper a secret, and was rewarded by a kiss of soft lips.

"Let's hurry this up," said Blaze. "Then we can go off on our own."

Gabe didn't gasp, but his indrawn breath almost choked him. "Sure," he said, wishing they were done. Wishing they had something to stand on rather than an uncertain future, with a separation at the end of summer the only sure thing. "Sure."

They had their own little bubble, but for how long? Next week, Royce would show up to fill his role as team lead, along with an unknown number of parolees. The bubble couldn't last if they were surrounded by other people, intruders into the small dream that had taken root in Gabe's heart, keeping him warm inside. Which raised the question, should they even be doing this, him and Blaze?

CHAPTER 23
BLAZE

Blaze could feel Gabe's withdrawal as they sat at dinner. The three of them, Wayne and him on one side, Gabe on the other, were silent like a very small family who had run out of conversation. At the Butterworth trailer, conversation, the lack of silence, anyway, had never been a problem because one of them always had something to say, and Blaze had typically joined in just to keep up, sometimes having to shout to be heard.

In the group counseling session earlier that afternoon, as Blaze and Wayne sat around a table in the mess tent, Bob or Ted or whatever the counselor's name was, had tried to encourage the two of them to talk about how they processed their feelings. About how to communicate those feelings. How to let the feelings move through your body without stopping them, and other happy crappy stuff like that.

Blaze had done his best to stumble through the exercise so as not to piss the counselor off, but he'd fallen into silence, just the same. A silence much like this one, where the only sounds were faraway-seeming chatter of the two cooks in the kitchen hut in back of the tent, the clank of silverware on white china, the faraway rush of the wind in the trees, bird call.

"What will happen to the little horse?" asked Blaze, a sense of desperation filling him to fill the silence.

"Dog food factory, I'll bet," said Wayne with a grunt, polishing a dark smear of A-1 sauce from his plate with a bit of bread.

"No, that won't happen." Gabe wiped his mouth with a paper napkin, then folded it on his plate. Maybe he wasn't meeting Blaze's gaze on purpose, or maybe he was just focused on setting Wayne straight. Either way, he wasn't looking at Blaze at *all*.

"Leland's policy on this project is a home for every horse. Even the skinny ones. Mrs. Tate, that's his mom, has a pasture out back of her house that's five, maybe ten, acres. We'll take the little horse there. That'll give him time to fatten up, then we can decide where he'll go."

Leland Tate hadn't seemed like a guy who had any gentleness in his heart, but Gabe certainly seemed devoted to him, as did Quint, so maybe his kindness was just hidden from Blaze. Just like Gabe was hiding his gaze now, as if mortified over what he and Blaze had been up to. Not because he was a shy virgin, but because he was a responsible man who might have issues with taking advantage of a parolee in his care.

Except he hadn't taken advantage, not one bit. Blaze had thrown himself at Gabe and Gabe had caught him, responded in kind, kiss for kiss, with that stomach-tingling hair tug, and the soft-voiced statement, *I've been wanting to do that for a long time.*

A man without feelings wouldn't have said anything like that. A man without feelings would have shoved Blaze to his knees and made Blaze take him in his mouth, made him swallow. Gabe had done none of those things. Instead, his touch had been tender, his eyes soft, and he'd lit that lantern when Blaze had asked him to.

Who did that? Somebody who cared, right?

Except he didn't know what he was doing any more than Gabe did, evidently. There were no indicators anywhere around to tell Blaze what to do next. Except follow his gut, as he usually did.

Gabe stood up, taking his plate and cutlery to the end of the buffet line, and then he strode past the table where Wayne and Blaze still sat, quickly walking out of the mess tent.

THE COWBOY AND THE RASCAL

Wayne looked at Blaze, his eyebrows going up. Wayne wasn't a fool, but whether he was on to what had happened between Blaze and the boss man was another question altogether.

"He seem pissed to you?" asked Wayne. "Maybe he's going to turn into a chain gang kind of boss."

"No," Blaze said with a scoff.

He stood up, grabbing his plate, almost stumbling as he walked to the buffet line to leave his dishes. His legs were shaky, the insides of his thighs alight with fiery tenderness, rubbed raw by even the slightest movement of the cloth of his jeans moving over skin.

Maybe he'd take a long shower. Maybe he'd ask Gabe to open the first aid hut so he could get some Tylenol, maybe some kind of muscle ointment. Maybe—

"You all right?"

Wayne appeared at his shoulder.

"What?"

"You're just standing there, staring. And you smell like horse, and that's making my eyes water. Go rinse off, will you?"

Blaze ignored Wayne, not responding as he marched off, or tried to. The more he moved, the better he felt, but his legs were as weak as overcooked spaghetti, and he just hoped he'd be ready for work in the morning because he didn't want to let Gabe down. More than that, he wanted to find Gabe and make sure that what had happened between them wasn't a fluke.

Gabe didn't seem like the kind of guy who'd use another guy and then toss him aside. But, again, maybe his conscience was eating at him and he didn't know what to do any more than Blaze did.

If Blaze were in prison and at loose ends, he might head to the break room, or, if there was a movie on, he'd go watch that. Somebody might have a poker game, and he could join in, playing for pennies or the cigarettes he kept winning but never smoked.

Behind Blaze, Wayne was on the landline phone talking to someone he knew in Sleepy Eye. Ahead of Blaze were the woods in the growing twilight, paths tromped in the grass leading off in the direction of the lake, or the pasture, or the facilities.

The paths were starting to look untidy and ragged, though Blaze imagined that, at some point, the plan was to neaten them up while still letting them look rustic. To make you feel like if you took one of those paths, you'd be headed on the adventure of your life. Which still didn't tell him which way Gabe had gone.

He tried to imagine it, as if he were Gabe. Steady. Handsome. Quiet. A lot on his mind, the responsibility of two parolees, the care of a herd of horses, the day-to-day operation of clearing wood and brush. Now it was after dinner. The sky was clear, the air soft. Where would Gabe go?

Blaze turned and followed the trodden path to the lake, which, as he advanced through the trees, blossomed before him, a flat, blue glassy plate reflecting the evening sky in streaks of pink and white. And there, just near where the picnic benches were, still unpainted and smelling like new pine, was Gabe.

He sat on the picnic table farthest from Blaze, his feet on the bench, elbows on his knees. Without his cowboy hat, without that sense of purpose that seemed to drive him every day, his shoulders slumped, he seemed a little lost, at least to Blaze.

Would he want Blaze interrupting his stillness? Blaze decided to risk it, his heart speeding up as he walked to the picnic table and sat down next to Gabe, his feet on the bench, elbows on his knees, as casually as if he'd been invited to echo Gabe, to be his shadow.

Gabe's gaze flicked over to him, then returned to the lake, smooth and still, its splendor stretching out for a good long way, turning into the woods, the last tail part of it hidden from view like a secret waiting to be discovered. Which, Blaze supposed, was the whole point of the place. To create pleasant, non-threatening discoveries around every corner, every bend of the trail, every inch of shoreline.

"Gabe."

A small sound of acknowledgment that Blaze had spoken was all he got from Gabe.

Blaze whooshed out a breath. In the Butterworth family, the conversation, mostly shouted, or at the very least carried on in raised voices, would already have been half over.

For this quiet man, the way forward was more subdued and Blaze knew he had to be careful if he wanted—if he wanted what? Well, maybe to find answers, to pin this down, which was the least-like-him action he could possibly take.

Besides, it was up to Gabe, right? It had to be because Gabe was the man in charge, and Blaze was just a dumb ex-con who barely had any rights. Which was easier to believe than anything else at that moment.

"Gabe."

Gabe looked at him fully now, his hands clasped gently between his knees, his shoulders rolled forward, his eyes moving to the lake and then back to Blaze again.

"All day," said Gabe.

The pause after those words went on long enough that Blaze thought to touch Gabe's knee, to get his attention then, but he didn't need to, as Gabe took a breath. Licked his lips. And seemed to try again.

"All day I've been thinking about it," he said. "And my favorite part? Waking up this morning. Not alone."

"But," said Blaze, knowing there must be a *but* in there somewhere, though the idea of Gabe being so alone that waking up with someone like Blaze was his favorite part? Impossible. Unlikely. Outrageous.

"No buts," said Gabe. He smiled to himself as he rubbed his jaw, then settled his hands on his knees again. "I don't know what to do, but I know I liked it." His body shifted until he was half turned, fully focused on Blaze. "This morning. Last night. You."

"But—"

"I've been thinking," said Gabe.

"I can see that," said Blaze, feeling a smile on his face, a lift in his heart.

Now Gabe laughed, a low laugh, and he turned his gaze back to the lake.

"As you must be aware, we are where we are." He gestured at the stunning sky, turning to pink, reflected in the lake, ruffled now to cats' paws as the sun began to set. "I have a responsibility to you. To

Wayne. To Leland. This place. I don't want to mess that up, and I don't think you'd want me to either."

Blaze nodded slowly and made himself not hold his breath. And figured that Gabe hadn't said as many words all at one time to another person, perhaps not in years.

"But," said Gabe, now, pausing to laugh, his smile lighting his face, his eyes very blue as he once again looked at Blaze. "Nobody knows what the next morning will bring, but we have now. We have this summer. And if we can be cognizant—"

Gabe paused, looking at Blaze, and he nodded. He'd been studying for his GED. He knew what the word meant.

"And aware that we have responsibilities, to ourselves, and to the job we've agreed to do—"

"That you're my boss—"

"That when we're *working*," Gabe said, slowing down to emphasize the word. "During that time, I'm the team lead, directing the work. And when we're not—" Gabe paused again, straightening up.

Blaze could see that yes, Gabe had been thinking about this all day, coming to his decision with slow, decided care. Care that Blaze didn't think he was worthy of, but maybe it seemed like Gabe did.

"Then we can have sex in your tent," said Blaze, smiling when Gabe barked a laugh in response. "Or maybe in the shower, if you prefer, and while I've never actually had a fantasy of having sex in the woods, I suppose I can be up for that as well." He smiled, tucking his chin to his chest, wondering at his own bravery to admit what he was about to admit. "Or maybe sometimes, we can just, you know, be together. Like we were. When you lit the lantern. Being in that glow."

He shook his head, his face flushing because who had time for such fanciful ideas? What guy was going to want to keep a Coleman lantern at the ready simply because Blaze was afraid of the dark?

"I have a large kerosene allowance," said Gabe, smiling as though at his own attempt at humor. "And there's a whole box of light sticks in the supply hut."

As if those were the most important things, though, the way Gabe dipped his chin, in an echo of the way Blaze had done, and looked over at Blaze, almost shyly, told its own, quite different story. But where would that story take them? That was the question. But never mind, they had the summer, at least. Gabe had just said they had.

Gabe was waiting, and Blaze knew he was doing what he felt needed doing, which was waiting for a signal from Blaze. Because Gabe was the team lead and Blaze was the parolee, Gabe was giving, no, *shoving*, the power of choice, all of it, right into Blaze's lap.

"Well," said Blaze, straightening up, his hands on his thighs, feeling brighter than he had all day. "Like I said before, I could use a shower. And then." He looked down as he stroked the inside of those thighs. "I have never ridden a horse, and my thighs feel like they've been pounded with a hammer, and just what am I going to do about that?"

"I can take care of that," said Gabe, quite quietly, his voice low, leaning closer as if he meant to impart a secret. "Shower first, then salve. Which I can get from the first aid hut. Which I can put on you." He paused. "If you like."

The answer to that would never be *no, thanks*, but would always be *yes, please*.

CHAPTER 24
GABE

In the wooden shower stall farthest from the entrance, water sprayed over them both, rainwater style, a mist falling all around, a breeze at their ankles. Gabe had his hands in Blaze's hair, using his own shampoo, letting his fingers linger in the dark strands.

"Don't get it in my eyes," said Blaze, and Gabe knew he was pretending to whine, laughing at the same time, his eyes closed, suds streaming across his face.

"Too late," said Gabe. "Let me fix it."

He sluiced water across Blaze's forehead, gently tipping his head back, wiping Blaze's dark eyebrows, kissing his damp cheeks. When Blaze opened his eyes, green and bright, Gabe finished rinsing his hair, then eased conditioner into it, massaging Blaze's head all the while, fantastically slow. They must have gone through two tokens, still yet to be put in the slot, but the hot water had yet to run out.

"You can kiss me now," said Blaze, his dark lashes half-lowered, a tease in the words.

"Yes, sir," said Gabe, teasing right back, kissing Blaze's wet mouth, sighing into the kiss, flicking his tongue against Blaze's tongue, warm amidst the warm shower.

Two weeks ago, he could not have predicted that this pleasure would be his. Now it was, for however brief a time. But he could not linger on any sad thoughts, for Blaze, water from his hair dripping down his chest, sank to his knees. Gabe's mouth fell open, a little in shock, a little in anticipation.

He gauged the shower, moving forward so the spray would be mostly on him, and Blaze wouldn't drown, and then closed his eyes as Blaze's warm mouth slid over his cock, wetness all around, warm suction, Blaze's hands digging into his thighs.

Shudders ran through him, his breath coming shorter and shorter as the strokes of Blaze's mouth grew longer, paced and slow until Gabe, gasping, had to brace his arm along the wooden wall of the shower. He pressed hard, trying to still himself but failing, warm pulses swallowed with hard suction, and if Blaze hadn't stood up and held him, he would have fallen over, weak knees collapsing beneath him.

"Got you," said Blaze.

"Yeah." Warmth filled Gabe's chest, a sense of contentment, of rightness. The feel of Blaze's sleek chest beneath his palms, the thunder of the shower overhead, Blaze's breath in his ear as he kissed his cheek.

After the shower, he dried Blaze off very slowly, starting with his hair, brushing kisses as he went down Blaze's body with a towel. With the full intention of returning the favor, on his knees, he was surprised when Blaze tugged at his hands, pulling him to his feet.

"Not here," said Blaze with a shake of his head, to which Gabe responded by kissing him and then kissing him again.

"In the tent, then," he said, picturing it in his head already, Blaze laid out in the glow of the Coleman lantern.

Back in Gabe's tent, before he could light the lantern and even as Blaze sank to the bed, sitting at his side, hip to hip, Gabe's cellphone rang. Glancing over, he could see it was Leland, so he had to answer it. With a touch to Blaze's mouth, one finger to that softness, he picked up the cellphone and clicked it on.

"Hey, Leland," said Gabe, tilting his head into the kiss on his cheek from Blaze. "What can I help you with?"

"We're at the two week mark on Monday," he said. "And I believe a night out for you and your team was promised."

"Oh, yeah." Gabe had forgotten the team outing to John Henton's tavern, completely.

Two weeks ago, such an outing with four parolees and himself would have seemed an impossibility. But now, with only two team members, and two weeks' worth of working with Wayne and Blaze on a daily basis, he could now see the effect of Leland's plan: good food, comfortable beds, reasonable work, leisure time—all of it had come together to create an atmosphere where trust could be built.

Even Wayne, whether on his own or with Gabe, could be trusted with taking a task to completion. Sure, he wasn't more social than he had been to begin with, but at least now, he would say where he was going, usually to get extra sleep. As for Blaze—

"Do I need to reserve a table at the tavern for Sunday evening?" asked Leland, only half joking, as he wasn't much of a beer drinker and didn't spend much time there.

"Maybe not," said Gabe. "But it'd be nice. Little card on it that says *Reserved for Gabe's Team.*"

"I will make it happen," said Leland. "I know I put a lot on your shoulders, but you've done a great job."

"But we haven't actually finished any project that we've started."

"Let me let you in on a little secret," said Leland. "It doesn't matter if, by the end of the season, the work doesn't get done. What matters is that the work is *being* done, and it's providing these guys with not only good food and a place to sleep, it's providing them with purpose. We get tax dollars for hiring them, so we gain, too. At the end of the summer, I could hire a whole slew of contractors to come in and finish inside of a month. And I will probably have to, so we can make inspection standards. But in the meantime, we're making a difference and those guys don't have to struggle as much as they adjust back into the real world. Don't you agree?"

The valley was Leland's passion project, but after last season, when he'd brought the guest ranch back from the brink of financial disaster, the owner, Bill Wainwright, was more than willing to let Leland do pretty much whatever he thought best. Including this humanitarian way of rehabilitating small-time criminals. Which Leland, yes, tended to preach about to an overwhelmingly zealous degree, as though trying to convince a world of unbelievers, even though everybody already agreed with him and was on the same page from day one. Including Gabe.

"Again," said Leland, his voice utterly serious. "You were the man I needed at the front of this project, and you've done an outstanding job. I'm going to want you to meet with Royce so you can brief him."

"He's had the training, right?" asked Gabe.

"He's at training right now, staying at the Holiday Inn in Torrington. He'll be back at the ranch on Monday, so if you could spare some time for him then, I'd appreciate it."

"Will do, Leland," said Gabe.

With gratitude, Gabe hung up the cellphone and placed it on the shelf between the beds, and turned his attention to something far more fulfilling, far more deserving.

"Are you warm enough?" he asked, reaching for the light stick and the lantern.

"Yeah." Blaze's voice was low, his eyes half-lidded as he sprawled on the cot, arms above his head, the bedsheet swirling around his hips and thighs. "And I'm ready. For you, I'm always ready."

Gabe lit the Coleman lantern and turned it on low, which draped a golden glow over the tent. Then, burying himself in Blaze's arms, Gabe sank onto the cot and closed his eyes.

He simply held on for a moment, absorbing Blaze's warmth, the murmur of his heart, the scent of him, salt and warm, surrounding him. He kissed that sweet mouth and swept Blaze's hair behind his ear, and knew he never wanted morning to come.

But morning did come, bringing with it warm sunshine, and a late breakfast of sausage and eggs, and the report Gabe forgot he was supposed to write. He grabbed his laptop and came back to the mess tent, where the cooks had laid out snacks, crackers and cheese, and cold iced tea.

As he wrote his report, at the other end of the table, he recalled how, on Saturday, though the visiting counselor had done his best to hold his team's attention, both Blaze and Wayne had looked unenthused, and Blaze's elbows had been on the table, and he hadn't even pretended to smile.

Gabe added a note to his report that maybe the counseling sessions were unnecessary. Each team lead could get extra training and stand in as counselors when needed, rather than forcing the parolees to sit through an hour, maybe an hour and a half of over-forced sharing. Leland could make a decision about that, at any rate, so Gabe finished his report and sent it off with a hard slam on the Send button.

Now done with paperwork, Gabe pulled his very small, but very effective, team into a different meeting.

"Help yourselves to iced tea," he said as he gestured them closer.

Blaze pulled the cheese and crackers closer, and Wayne even jumped up to pour Gabe a glass of iced tea.

"Here you go, boss," he said. "But we are all out of lemons," he added, which seemed to crack him up for some reason.

"What's up?" asked Blaze, looking like he wanted to scoot closer to Gabe on the bench seat but was holding himself back.

"We've done so well, these first two weeks of the program, that Leland is treating us to a night out. At the local tavern in Farthing. So." Gabe paused, smiling, seeing their faces, enjoying the moment. "You guys have the day off, and this afternoon you'll need to spiff up and get ready to go to town tonight."

"Does that include free beer?" asked Wayne.

"Yes, it does," said Gabe and though he wanted to include a lecture about the consequences of over-drinking, as one might be apt to do when offered free libations, he restrained himself.

By now, the men on his team had heard what he had to say about taking responsibility for what they were doing, whether it was being cognizant of how much hot water they were using, and thinking of the other fellow, or demonstrating common manners by bussing their own plate and silverware. So either they'd caught on, or they never would, and one more lecture wouldn't make a difference.

There was no real work the rest of that day, but considering new parolees were due to arrive in the next day or so, Gabe updated his map, made a list of outstanding projects, and basically caught up with paperwork while Blaze and Wayne lollygagged in the mess tent, playing cards and arguing over who was cheating and who was not. Then Gabe finished up and gave the signal that it was time to get ready for their outing.

Since they were all taking showers at the same time, Gabe could not, as he very much wanted to, share a stall with Blaze. But he could listen to the chatter over the top of the wooden walls between Wayne and Blaze, and join in with a comment of his own, and be well pleased with himself that the first two weeks had gone well.

So instead of having dinner in the mess tent, once dressed, they met in the parking lot and Gabe drove them to the tavern, telling them who used to own the cabin as they drove by it, and pointing out Iron Mountain, to the west.

"The tavern is named after John Henton, you see," he told them. "Because that's his cabin."

It wasn't very far, only a mile or so to the gate of the ranch and then a mile after that into town. Farthing wasn't a big place, and as it was early for the normal Sunday night crowd, it was easy to find a parking spot along Second Street.

"You guys go in," said Gabe as he pulled up and parked the truck.

"We'll wait," said Blaze, and so it was as a team that they entered the John Henton's tavern.

Gabe remembered when the place was called the Rusty Nail, when the owner was good enough at what he did, but had a reputation for coming down hard on his staff. There'd been some accusations of actual abuse, but what mattered in the end was that the guy, Gabe didn't know his name, had gotten arrested and the bar had been bought by the cook at the guest ranch and a friend of his from back East.

Now the place had a real western flair to it, with wagon wheels and cattle brands, much like the Stampede Saloon in Chugwater, but with a higher-end feel to it. The food was a bit citified for Gabe's taste, what with salads including fresh figs with honey-balsamic vinegar drizzled over it, and onion rings made with only organic onions. But the beer was top notch, all local brews, so it was with great pleasure that Gabe told the hostess that they needed a table for three.

"You're Gabe, right?" asked the hostess. "Maddy called. You actually have a reserved table in toward the back, and some of your party is already here."

"Thank you," he said as they followed her amidst the circular tables to one of the coveted bench tables along the back wall.

There, to his surprise, sat Jasper and his partner, Ellis. He'd not seen Jasper in a while, so he bent to hug him, and was hugged right back, with Ellis looking on in his typical silent way.

"Did you see?" asked Jasper. He pointed to a small folded card where someone had written *Reserved - Farthingdale Valley* in black Sharpie. "I had no idea you were one of the elite."

"I'm not," said Gabe. "But my team is. Jasper, you've met is Blaze, and this is Wayne. Guys, this is my friend Jasper and his partner, Ellis."

The booth was large so they could all fit in, and while Gabe would have liked to sit next to Blaze, it was almost as good to sit opposite him so he could watch the expressions as Blaze experienced his first night out in almost two years.

Gabe didn't know what it would be like to be told what to do twenty-four seven, the way Blaze and Wayne had, and he never wanted to. Still, he could enjoy their joy as the two parolees looked over their menus and discussed beer types and whether lobster mac and cheese was better than plain old mac and cheese.

"I'm getting the lobster, for sure." Blaze folded his menu away as the waitress came up and took their orders, then he looked at Gabe as she went away. "You can have a bite of mine," he said. "I'll share."

When Blaze said this, his smile was low and flirty, perhaps without Blaze realizing it, but Gabe's heart sped up just the same. He wished that after having shared a bed that this outing could have been a more private affair. Where they could look at each other and say what they wanted and share bites off their plates without drawing any attention whatsoever.

Because already, as their food was ordered and delivered, Jasper was looking at Gabe with appraising eyes, even nudging his shoulder when the beers came, as though it was an accident. Gabe knew Jasper fairly well and knew it wasn't an accident. Gabe didn't say anything in response to that look, just joined in the general chatter, the sounds of appreciation when those onion rings arrived.

It wasn't until they'd ordered dessert that Jasper nudged Gabe with his knee.

"Need to use the facilities," he said, and Gabe obligingly stepped out of the booth, only to find Jasper's strong hand on his sleeve, drawing him away from the booth and along the wall.

"What?" asked Gabe.

"That's what I'd like to ask," said Jasper, but there was no malice in his voice, only friendly curiosity in his eyes. "You and Blaze." He made a gesture with his hands as if to encompass all that was between them.

"Um."

"I've seen you looking at each other all night. Like you two are in your own world, so be honest. What's going on there?"

With a sigh that felt as though his chest was collapsing, Gabe didn't hold back the truth. "I shouldn't have done it. It shouldn't be happening, but it was. It *has*," he said, emphasizing the last word, visions of Blaze's face, limned in the light of a kerosene lamp, the memory of the soft feel of Blaze's mouth on his.

"Oh, I see." Jasper stepped back so they'd be more out of the way, on the edge of the area where the pool tables were. "And you think that's a problem?"

"I know it is," said Gabe. "It's so good—but it's not right, Jasper. I'm in charge. I can't be taking advantage like this. And yet—"

"Are you forcing him?" asked Jasper, keeping his voice low. "Intimidating him, threatening him?"

"No, of course not."

"I've had these same conversations with myself," said Jasper. "Same scenario, right? But I love Ellis, loved him almost from the moment I met him. I had the same questions as you have now, but my heart was in the right place, and he knew that from knowing me. And I'll bet your Blaze knows it as well."

"I know this," said Gabe, and he did. But having witnesses to what seemed a very private, convoluted relationship only made it bare and stark in the light of reality.

"You don't," said Jasper. "Or you wouldn't be getting all twisted up about it."

Gabe chewed on the inside of his cheek, looking out over the happy Sunday night throng, wishing it were more straightforward than it felt.

He knew Jasper, knew the man did not enter relationships lightly, knew that he would never take advantage of another human being, let alone one that, at one point, he'd had had power over. He'd managed, in spite of everything, to navigate a fairly tricky path to where he was now, happy as could be, with Ellis, a one-time ex-con and parolee who was now his partner.

"What should I do?" Gabe asked. "I told him I wanted to be with him, at least until the end of summer, and then we'd have to see. Only now, I don't know how even that much is possible."

"Follow your heart," said Jasper. He tapped Gabe's breastbone quite lightly. "I think you're good for each other. He seems pretty well adjusted, even after spending time behind bars. As for you, I've never seen you smile quite so often as I've seen tonight. So don't throw this away because of someone else's rules, or society's idea of what a relationship is. Know what you have, and give it all you got."

A surge of hope rose within his chest. Jasper almost never gave advice; he guided by example. His relationship with Ellis was a very good example, perhaps the best, of how it could be. All Gabe could do was try, with all of his heart, and he was going to do that. Right now. With Blaze.

He nodded at Jasper and turned to go back to the booth. Maybe he couldn't kiss Blaze in front of this Sunday night crowd, but he needed to stop acting like a teenager about to get busted for dating a guy from the wrong side of the tracks. He was long past that. Long past.

CHAPTER 25
BLAZE

When Gabe and Jasper left at the same time, it was obvious that it wasn't merely to go to the restroom, or at least it seemed that way to Blaze, who was suddenly left alone with Wayne, who was cocking an eyebrow at him. And then there was Ellis, who was studiously attending to his pecan pie that the waitress had just delivered, and ignoring Blaze with everything he had.

"Are you guys fucking or what?" asked Wayne, who had absolutely zero restraint.

"What?" asked Blaze, dragging up everything he could to keep his face neutral.

"Don't give me that," said Wayne. "I saw where you were coming from this morning, and it wasn't your tent."

"What, you're a tracker now?"

"Don't have to be," said Wayne, his smile triumphant and a little mean. "Went to have a piss, and the shower was running. Was still running when I came back to brush my teeth so I looked. There were two pairs of feet."

"We were trying to be discreet," said Blaze, giving in, looking over at Ellis, who drank his coffee with one elbow on the table, nonchalant, like he was in a coffee shop staring out of the window at the rain.

"You suck at it." Wayne nudged him with his elbow. "I don't give a fuck," he said. "But you're just so coy, like a virgin or something. You're fucking the boss. Who cares."

"There are rules about this, right?" Blaze didn't know, but there had to be something about this, even on a ranch like this one. In prison, if a guard and an inmate were caught fooling around, the guard got demoted or fired or fined, and the inmate got written up and transferred. "Anyway, it's none of your business."

"Like I said, I don't give a fuck."

Half in desperation, half in confusion, Blaze looked at Ellis, who, silently, looked back at him. He gave a little shrug as if to say *I don't give a fuck, either*, which was funny because Blaze couldn't recall whether Ellis had said a single word all evening.

Still, the message was pretty clear that Blaze was the only one freaking out over this, over being discovered. Or maybe Gabe was freaking out as well, because he and Jasper had been gone an awfully long time—

"Dessert has arrived," said Jasper, sitting down next to Ellis, his focus on the bowl of ice cream in front of him. "What'd you get?"

Gabe slid in next to Jasper, but his eyes were on Blaze, the earlier withdrawal replaced with Gabe's full focus.

The two of them were going back and forth on this, leaving behind a confusing trail in Blaze's chest. But maybe this was part of how it worked, how Gabe worked, having doubts then getting over them. Not in a kiss-kick kind of way, but in a way that told Blaze, seemed to be telling him, that Gabe had enough doubts that his summer with Blaze was intended to be just that. A summer. A fling. A thrill.

Maybe this summer was all Blaze was going to get. Maybe this summer of bliss was all Blaze *deserved*. After that, he would be given his certificate and sent on his way, with nowhere to go and no way to get there.

"Hey," said Gabe, holding his spoon out like he was about to rap Blaze's knuckles. "Can I have a bite of your lava cake?"

The eyes of every man at that table were on Blaze. In the movies, sometimes, and on TV, sharing a dessert and indeed giving someone else the first bite was a cutie-cute thing real couples did when they were courting. When they were first starting out. Maybe Gabe was playing a game for an imaginary audience, and all Blaze could do was go along with it.

"Sure," said Blaze.

He pushed his dish closer to Gabe, like he was going along with it and maybe he was, because he liked this guy, really and truly.

He shouldn't imagine that Gabe was running a scam, even as everybody watched him take a bite of that lava cake, chocolate fudge lacing his mouth before he licked it off. Gabe wasn't like that, wasn't a scammer. He was one of the good guys.

Maybe the end of summer was as far as he could go, and Blaze just ought to back the fuck off and appreciate it for what it was. A little bit of something good to salve his heart so he'd be ready for the next part of his life.

"You okay?" asked Gabe, his eyes dark blue and steady and focused only on Blaze. "You can try my apple pie with ice cream."

"Yeah."

Blaze took a forkful of the pie which, in keeping with the amazing food in the restaurant, was sweet with the bite of cinnamon.

He would never forget this moment, when Gabe had let Blaze have the first bite, like Blaze deserved all the nice things in the world. This moment between him and Gabe where the rest of the table seemed to fall behind a curtain of hush.

Only between the two of them could they interpret the glance between them. The way the edge of Gabe's pinkie touched the curve of Blaze's wrist, leaving behind a faint trace of warmth that burrowed inside of Blaze and seemed to want to stay.

"That's good," Blaze said, finally, resolving to enjoy what he had, and stop wanting impossible things. He shook himself mentally and sat up. "Is there coffee coming?"

The waitress eventually brought four more mugs and a carafe of coffee, and poured for everyone, and they enjoyed their desserts silently amidst the gaiety of the tavern. It was nice, but all Blaze wanted to do was go back to the valley and settle with Gabe on his cot, snug beneath summer bedclothes as the night grew cool.

When they were finished, there was a little argument between Jasper and Gabe as to who would pay, with Jasper insisting, and Gabe insisting right back that Leland Tate himself had authorized the night out for the team, and Jasper and Ellis were also his guests.

In the end, Ellis silently plucked Gabe's credit card out of his hand and gave it to the waitress, arching a brow at Jasper, adding a shrug. There was nothing Jasper could do but mock-punch Gabe in the shoulder, but then he smoothed it with his hand, laughing, threatening *Next time.* That it was how it was between them, it was easy to see—good friends with a long history of give and take.

Blaze didn't have any history like that, not with anyone, and he could taste the envy on his tongue as they left the tavern, spilling out into the parking lot, the warm glow of the lights inside the tavern stretching out over them. And then in Gabe's truck, him in the front with Gabe.

Wayne was in the back seat, hanging over the edge of the front seat, talking about something that Blaze didn't care to give even half his mind to. He just kept his hands to himself all the drive home, through the dark woods of the switchback until they arrived in the parking lot near the mess tent and Gabe parked the truck.

"That was fun, eh, fellows?" he asked, genially, going into good-natured boss mode.

"Sure was, boss," said Wayne, swinging himself out of the truck.

Wayne might have been about to brag about how he'd stuck to his self-imposed two-beer limit, but Blaze didn't have the energy to pretend to be interested, so he tugged on Gabe's shirt and pulled him through the darkness to Gabe's tent.

"Go on," he said, urging Gabe to enter the fully dark tent. "Can you light it?"

Silently, Gabe turned on the overhead bulb, but just long enough to light the Coleman lantern.

When the familiar low hiss sank into Blaze's skin, and the golden glow, turned low, began to soothe him all over, he undressed Gabe. Button by button, cloth from skin, he drew Gabe's clothes off him, and Gabe let him, curving into Blaze's touch, sighing when Blaze drew a hand across his chest, clasping Blaze's hand to him, as though branding himself with the width of Blaze's palm.

"You're sure you're all right?" asked Gabe when Blaze pushed him to sit down so he could draw off his cowboy boots. "You seem awful quiet."

Blaze made a split decision in his head, resolving that maybe they needed to talk, but right now he wanted silence, the silkiness of touch, the velvet of night drawing all around them, shielding them from the world.

Tonight he wanted what was being offered, so he took it with kisses to Gabe's shoulder, the strong line warm beneath his hands, and with touches to Gabe's hips as he drew off Gabe's jeans. Then he pulled off his own clothes, not giving Gabe a chance, and settled with him beneath the sheet on the cot meant for only one man, but which now held two.

"I'm good," he said, draping his arms around Gabe's neck before kissing him hard, the urge to burrow into Gabe's body tugging at him, an insistent thing.

Next to him beneath the sheets, Gabe was all muscle and warmth, his long legs twined with Blaze's, the scratchy hair of his groin, the dusk of his tan where it vanished halfway down his neck. All of this belonged to Blaze, at least for now. Maybe in the morning they'd talk or maybe they wouldn't. But for now, Blaze scooted down, trammeling his hands along Gabe's hips as he sank into the shadow of the bedclothes.

"Hey, now," said Gabe, lifting the sheet. "Who are you hiding from?" he asked.

"From the night," said Blaze without thinking, knowing that what he meant to say was that he was hiding from the world that would, with utmost certainty, take them apart from each other. Gabe to return to his regular, ordinary life, and Blaze to be spat out into that world with nothing to take with him but his empty heart.

"From nothing," he said, smiling up at Gabe, limned in golden light, like he was laughing at himself and some private joke. "Now, will you hush and just enjoy?"

With a grunt, albeit a happy one, sounding suffused with anticipation, Gabe did as he was told for once.

Blaze, his mouth already watering, took Gabe's cock in his mouth and loved on it with kisses and strokes, and throat-strong swallows when Gabe came. Then he crawled into Gabe's arms and let Gabe do the same right back to him, pleasure mixing with darkness, his head thrown back on the pillow, not content until Gabe held him again in those strong arms and curved around him as though protecting Blaze from his own fears.

On Monday morning, Gabe and Blaze took a quick shower together. Then, when the three of them sat down together in the mess tent for breakfast, Blaze ignored Wayne's arch looks.

When Gabe's cellphone rang in his back pocket, he took the call, standing up to go a few feet out of the mess tent, smiling and chatting with whoever was on the other end. When he came back, he was still smiling, though he had an expression on his face that told Blaze he needed to get things done.

"That was Leland," he said, sitting down, pouring himself some more coffee from the metal carafe. "I need to meet with Royce, the new team lead who's coming in this week. You fellows are on your own, so just carry on with what we've been working on. I should be back this afternoon."

"What about the horses?" asked Blaze.

"We'll take care of them now," said Gabe. "Then I need to change and go up to the ranch for this meeting."

They fed and watered the horses, and then Blaze, quite simply, had to watch while Gabe drove off in the truck, leaving Blaze in the quiet that fell as the sound of the powerful engine faded.

Wayne was in his tent, probably jacking off, and the two cooks were in the back of the kitchen. Which left Blaze alone, thinking about how he should get his gloves and his cowboy hat and, at the very least, pretend to work. But he found himself in the mess tent, looking at the landline, which sat there, silently beige, looking right back at him.

Maybe what he needed to do was to call home again. Maybe at the end of summer, they'd let him come home, even if just for a visit. It'd be nice to have the familiar edges of his bunk in the Butterworth trailer brushing up against his shoulders. To hear the familiar sounds of the grind and whoosh of the Tilt-a-Whirl in his ears, the smell of boiled peanuts and wet sawdust in his lungs.

And then the phone rang, like a conjurer's trick. Like it knew what he was thinking.

He picked the receiver up, his heart thudding in his chest.

"Hello?" he asked.

"Hello, Blaze?" his mom said in a tone that told Blaze she was busy and irritated, even before she said another word.

"Hey, Mom," he said, holding onto the receiver with both hands. "How'd you get this number?"

"You gave it to me when you were begging us to come visit you," she said, terse. "Where are you now?" she asked.

"What do you mean, where am I?" He blinked, confused. "You called *me*. I'm in Farthingdale Valley, serving my parole."

"Well, you need to come home." There was a bit of silence in which, in the background, Blaze was sure he could hear the screams from the Tilt-a-Whirl. "You need to come home now."

"I can't come home, Mom. I'm doing *parole*." He emphasized the last word, as if he stupidly thought she wouldn't remember where he'd been for the last two years.

"Well, your brother's been arrested, and while we're waiting for him to get released, you can help out. Run the stand. Pick up the slack."

"I'm not picking up his slack," he said, making his words as clear as he could manage with the rage tumbling over and over in his chest. "I can't just *leave*—"

"You sure can," she said. In his mind's eye, he could see her nodding. "I checked it out. You can do parole while living with us. We'll vouch for you. Make sure you meet with your parole officer each week and whatever. You need to help your brother out, that's the main thing. If there's a trial, you can testify on his behalf."

"You want me to testify on his behalf." He felt like he'd been hit in the head with the rubber hammer from a high striker game. "Mom, I already served two years protecting him. Two *years*. What was he arrested for this time?"

"Drugs," she said. "Which I'm sure someone else planted on him. Or maybe the cops did. Someone with a grudge against your dad, who thought to frame Alex."

There would be plenty of people with a grudge against Blaze's dad, but if Alex had drugs on him, it was because he'd bought them himself, or had been dealing them. He'd probably been involved with drugs this whole long while.

Day after day, when Blaze had been behind bars, Alex had been out in the free air, doing what he wanted, helping out because it suited him.

Well, right now, it didn't suit Blaze at all to try to rescue his brother from his own self-built trap. But try to explain that to his mom, and the argument would rage and boil, leaving Blaze confused about what he needed to do. She was just that good at manipulating him. He needed to move away from this conversation, fast.

"I can wire you money for the bus," she said. "You can be here by morning."

Here by morning meant that his family was maybe a ten or twelve hour bus ride away. Mentally, he drew a map in his head, thinking they could be anywhere from New Mexico to Iowa, though at this time of year, Iowa was more likely. And the perfect place for a summer carnival, all those farmer kids with dollar bills folded in their earth-stained hands, ready to hand it over for some fun. *Step right up, the carnival's in town!*

Blaze shuddered.

"I can't leave," he said, his mouth dry. "And I'm not going to. I saved him once. Gave up two years of my life. I'm not giving any more."

He hung up before she could say anything, and though she might be able to find him, there was nothing she could do to drag him home. Which sent sad, confusing spirals all the way through him.

When only a short while ago when he'd been in prison, he'd been desperate for a visit from them, or would have liked a phone call or care package. He would have loved a visit from them now, while he was at the ranch, but maybe it was better that never happened, because they would have tracked their poison all over the place.

Still, he was shaking as he stood up because even from miles away it still affected him, that he came from a family of not just carnies, but criminals. Maybe he'd deserved those two years for all the crappy stuff he'd helped his dad do to those old people. For all the cheats and tricks he'd used to swindle people out of their weekend fun money. Promising a good time, an easy win, and just taking that away from them, along with all the money in their pockets.

He ran his fingers through his hair, almost tearing at it.

This was why he was barely going to get a summer with a nice guy like Gabe. Gabe, who probably never even jaywalked or cheated on his taxes or left in the middle of the night without paying rent or the electricity bill. Who even now was probably continuing to overthink the idea of him and Blaze being together.

Nice guys like Gabe never ended up with ex-cons.

Maybe Blaze should cut and run, not to go home, but simply to light out for whatever distant horizon he could point himself at. That way, at least, he wouldn't have to wait to have his heart torn out. He could have it torn out now, quick as anything, and get it over with. Lick his wounds later. Recover never.

At the very least, he was going to need to learn how to sleep alone.

CHAPTER 26
GABE

As Gabe sat across from Royce in the dining hall of the main lodge at the guest ranch, he wished he had brought his laptop, or even a notebook, to take down everything Royce had to say, because all of Royce's ideas were good ones. Like building a series of shelters for the horses in the pastures, rather than one big barn, since the horses would only need to shield from the sun and heavy rain, rather than snowstorms.

Another idea Royce had was to spread pea gravel on the paths, and plant low ground cover pretty much along every inch of those paths, to help with wear and tear. Gabe could see dollar signs piling up around every word Royce said, but then Royce's family had money, which, again, made Gabe wonder why Royce was even working at a guest ranch in Wyoming.

But Royce had been polite and grateful for the meeting, so Gabe was pleased to describe to Royce a template for how his first week might go, even though it'd taken him away from his own job, his own Sunday at rest. And Blaze.

"If you have any questions once things get underway," said Gabe as they stood up and shook hands. "Don't hesitate to reach out. I'll have my two-way radio strapped to my belt, as will you, so I'll always be within shouting distance."

"That's very kind of you," said Royce. "I'm looking forward to working with you and the parolees. It'll be like an adventure."

Pleased that the meeting was over at last, however pleasant it might have been, Gabe hopped in his truck, and headed down the switchbacks, back to the valley. When he parked his truck and got out, he went to the mess tent to see if Blaze was there. He wasn't. He wasn't at Gabe's tent, nor was he by the pasture.

The last place Blaze might be was in his tent so, heading that way, the dry grass crackling beneath his feet, he came up to Blaze's tent, and there, yes, sitting on Tom's former cot, was Blaze.

He was hunkered over, elbows on his knees, hands clasping his head, his dark hair falling lank over his fingers.

"Blaze?" Gabe came into the tent slowly and sat on Blaze's cot and, hands on his knees, waited a good long moment. "What happened?" he asked. "What's going on?"

Blaze looked at him with eyes red-rimmed from scrubbing, his lips pale, a kind of shocked white all over his features.

"Are you hurt?" Gabe asked, trying again.

"It's not that," said Blaze. "It's you."

Gabe sat up straight, shock rippling through him as he reached back over the last two weeks, thinking of mistakes he might have made, the first one being giving into that first kiss. Which he didn't regret, but maybe Blaze did.

"You," said Blaze again, his voice wobbling as he scraped his hair back from his face, sitting up. "And this place. And my mom, who just called. She wants me to come home because my brother got arrested for drugs and is in jail. This time, it's him who got arrested instead of me. But this time, instead of letting *him* rot in jail like they did me, they want me to testify on *his* behalf."

Anger suffused the air around Blaze's shoulders, settling on everything it could touch while the sun heated up the overhead canvas, giving the air a warm, musty, still smell.

"As for you and me, you don't want to be with someone like me," said Blaze, the words heavy in the air. "My family is nothing but carnies and drug dealers. We're not good enough for the likes of you."

"You don't trust it," said Gabe, grabbing onto the first thing he could find. "You committed a crime and spent two years in jail, so you don't think anyone trusts you. So you, in turn, don't trust anyone else. But I trust you—"

Blaze stood up so fast, he loomed over Gabe, teeth bared, hands curled into fists, face even whiter now.

"I was never guilty, I told you that," said Blaze in a voice so quiet it belied the tremors in his hands. "My folks made me take the fall for Alex and I know every ex-con says they're not guilty, but I'm really not. Now they want me to testify so he can get off Scott free. Hell no."

"You don't have to do it." Gabe stood up, holding back from reaching out to touch Blaze by the barest inch. "You don't have to go."

"I'm not going, and I'm not doing it," said Blaze. "I'll be good God damned if I ever go back to them. But I sure as hell don't belong here. With you."

Pushing past him, Blaze walked out of the tent in long strides, as if he couldn't get away from Gabe fast enough, far enough.

What had he done to earn such anger, that Blaze would mention him and the mess with his family in the same breath?

He followed Blaze, catching up, snagging Blaze's shirt sleeve with his fingertips, not enough to make Blaze stop if he didn't want to, but to make sure Blaze knew he was there. Right next to him, beneath the warm sun blazing down on their heads as they stood in a small clearing.

Blaze stopped, turning to look at him, half a second away from turning to go.

If he truly wanted to go, then Gabe would not only let him, he would take him there, however long the distance. But he wanted him to stay.

"I do believe you, you know." Gabe let go and nodded, wanting Blaze to focus on what was between them, something so newly begun it hardly seemed real. "I didn't at first, because yes, a lot of ex-cons say they're innocent when they're not. But you are."

"You *don't* believe me." Blaze's eyes were frozen, a deep underwater green. "You never have."

"But I *do*," said Gabe, putting everything he had into the words. "You don't act like you've ever been on drugs—"

Blaze pushed past him, a rough shoulder thumping into Gabe's shoulder, and though he knew he could chase after Blaze and stop him, he needed to let him go. Which was the worst feeling, a poisonous uprising in his chest, a weightless lack of solid ground beneath his feet.

In his heart, he knew he hadn't quite believed Blaze when he said he'd been innocent and that he shouldn't have gone to jail. At least in the beginning. Over time, however, he'd come to know Blaze, the kind of man he was. A good man with a good heart, not some junkie jonesing for his next fix.

And, except for a few wobbles, he'd not questioned his own feelings or doubted what they had between them, as new as it was. Perhaps he should have made more sure of how things were for Blaze, though certainly the phone call from his mom had been totally out of the blue.

He'd always wanted the best for Blaze. He knew he had. He'd thought Blaze knew that. Only now what?

The new parolees would be arriving in a day or two, and Gabe would have to step up to the plate and help Royce set the right tone. That he should be wary, that some ex-cons weren't to be trusted. That guys like Kurt would seem okay on the surface, but below that, sometimes right beneath the skin, they were not docile. They were wild, and some of them wanted to stay that way.

Blaze had never been like Kurt, not even for a second.

Gabe looked up at the pine trees, a brilliant green against the blue in the bright sunshine. His heart was racing and, in the clearing between the trees, he stood totally alone. Wayne was probably snoozing in his tent, and as for Blaze—

He pulled out his cellphone and walked toward his own tent, going past it to stand on the slope beside the no-name dirt road, looking at the display to see how many bars he had. Three. It was enough.

THE COWBOY AND THE RASCAL

"Hey, Jasper," he said when Jasper picked up, and he was grateful for Jasper in more ways than one, though he was kicking himself because he couldn't figure this out without help.

"What's up?" asked Jasper, and it sounded as though, in the background, Ellis was there, asking questions about dinner, and whether there was enough ice cream.

"I fucked up," he said.

"How so?" asked Jasper.

"It's Blaze and me—" He paused to take a deep breath. "It was going good. Seemed like it would keep on doing that, only his mom called him and wants him to come home—his brother got arrested, and the way he told it, his mom thinks Blaze is the only one who can get the brother out of trouble."

Gabe paused again, wondering how someone he'd never met and was never likely to, who Blaze didn't even seem to care for at all, could wreak such havoc.

"Now he thinks he's bad news, and I shouldn't want to be around him. I had to let him walk off, but it killed me. He acted like he was going to leave the valley."

Gabe needed advice and needed it badly. Jasper had been through this, a relationship with someone whom society might not approve of, who had a grotty background. But Jasper, his own man in so many ways, probably never gave a rat's ass about what society thought. He only cared about what he wanted and what Ellis wanted.

"C'mon, talk to me." Gabe held the cellphone with both hands, turning away from the sun so he could duck his chin in his own shadow.

After a moment of silence, he could hear the change, the level of noise behind Jasper rising. As though Jasper had stepped outside, amidst the wind and the group of trees around his stone cabin.

"Here's the thing," said Jasper. "You're kind of going about this like this guy is a criminal and needs to be handled that way. But he's done his time, so—"

"He is innocent," said Gabe, cutting into whatever Jasper had to say. "He said that from the beginning, and I didn't quite believe him.

Maybe I acted like I didn't believe him even though I could see, day by day, through everything he did and said—he's as innocent as the day he was born."

Gabe waited, feeling like he could feel Jasper thinking at the other end of the line.

"Someone who went through being in prison," said Jasper, slowly. "It's like a horse that's been abused. Horses can be violent or out of control, but not a one of them deserves to be lashed to a hitching post so tight they can't move."

Nodding, Gabe knew what Jasper was getting at. In the old days, to break a horse, you punished it, you whipped it, you made it impossible for the horse to move until they submitted to your will.

It was a bad way to tame a horse, a horrible, cruel way, as it only made the horse angry and miserable, in spite of its seeming docility and obedience. One wrong move, a twitch, some days, and the horse would lash out, tearing at whoever was closest.

"So if you get a horse that's been through that, some days, hell, sometimes every day, you have to go back to square one. Like you just got the horse from someone who broke him that cruelly. In your case, with Blaze, tell him the truth. Treat him gentle, the way he deserves it, even if he doesn't know it yet. Bare your soul. That's the only way he'll know that you mean it."

"Go big or go home," said Gabe, half to himself, half to Jasper.

"That's it right there." With a low huff, maybe a half-laugh, Jasper said. "Spill your guts to him. Tell him how you feel and make it stick. Tell him your dreams. Your hopes. Get him to tell you his. Most importantly, ask him to stay. Otherwise, you're going to have to watch him walk away forever. You want that?"

"No."

"Exactly. Now, I got to get some dinner on or Ellis will starve."

Gabe laughed, his heart lightening a little bit.

"And we still need to shoe the rest of those horses, so call me tomorrow and we'll set a schedule. Okay?"

"Okay," said Gabe. "And thank you. I'm going to try. I don't know how, but I'm going to try."

"Good man," said Jasper. Then he hung up.

Which left Gabe standing there, his silent cellphone in his hands, the wind across the grasses on the slope, the sun a hard yellow circle in the sky.

He wasn't a grand gesture kind of guy, though he did believe that actions spoke louder than words ever could. Somehow, maybe, he'd given Blaze the idea that he couldn't come to Gabe just to rant or complain about things. Or that his family was a stain burned into his skin, a dark tattoo for everyone to see and judge him by.

If Gabe had sent out silent signals, even without knowing it, and if Blaze had interpreted those signals as judgment, then Gabe was going to fix it and make sure Blaze knew what was really in his heart.

CHAPTER 27
BLAZE

Blaze strode beneath the shade of the pines to the switchback road, which he followed all the way up to the top of the hill. His lungs were bursting by the time he stopped to turn and look out over the valley, the lake a blue cobalt beneath the blazing sun, slanting lower in the western sky, the dust from the low foothills beyond sifting over the pine trees.

It was such an odd spot, windblown, almost bare except for the new-looking cabin near the topmost part of the hill, that Gabe had told him used to belong to some old guy named John Henton. All around the cabin, there was nothing. Nothing for miles.

If he had his cowboy hat, he wouldn't have to shade his eyes to look out over the valley, though even with it, the search for Gabe would have been futile; the trees were too thick to see much but the very edge of the mess tent, the tops of the row of tents just beyond that.

Beyond that, he could locate nothing, and certainly could find no sign of Gabe. Who, because he was such a responsible guy, was hard at work, or making mental notes about that guy he'd met with, Reece or whoever. Taking stock of the first aid supplies in case someone, one of the new parolees, was dumb enough to get himself hurt again.

Now that Blaze's body was cooling down, as well as it could in full sunshine, he could see how stupid he'd been to react that way to his mom telling him to come home. Alex had always come first and Blaze always came last, though this had not been obvious to Blaze until he'd had time to figure it out in prison.

Even if Blaze didn't go home, they'd probably find a way to get Alex out of handcuffs and safely back inside the Butterworth trailer. A place where Blaze had never truly belonged, though why had it taken him this long to figure out?

On the other hand, did he belong here in the valley? Did he belong with Gabe?

He'd certainly shoved Gabe away hard enough to leave emotional bruises. That was, if Gabe cared about him at all, to be even the least bit affected by Blaze's rejection.

The sun, which was giving him a headache, and made heading toward the growing shade in the lee of John Henton's remade cabin a good choice. When he got there, he hunkered in the shadow of the south-east corner. Now, from this angle of the hill, he could see the slant of land as the foothills rose to the west, see the hard, gray line of Guipago Ridge, and watch the sun slant lower, sending shards of light through the tall prairie grasses, sparkling gold along the edges.

If Gabe had been there, he'd know what kind of grasses there were, and why only the tops of them shook in the slight, growing breeze. If Gabe had been there, the growing shadows would have felt less lonely, and the anticipation of the walk down the switchback would have seemed less like a chore and more like a mini-adventure, complete with birdcall and the heady scent of pine, spicy as it cooled.

Bending to rest his forehead on his folded arms across his knees, his brain flashed images at him of the last time he'd sat this way. Pressed against a pine tree in the dark because he'd been lost in the dark and couldn't find his way back to his own tent.

That time, Gabe had rescued him, though it didn't look like there'd be a repeat rescue this time around. Blaze was on his own and he'd done it to himself on purpose, leaving himself no other option but to figure out how to do his parole another way. Because Gabe wouldn't want him around anymore, right?

Head down on his knees, he'd dozed for a while and awoke to a change in the weather. A good cool breeze was coming off the mountains, clouds on the horizon, low and sweeping. He shivered as he stood up and realized that if he planned to leave, he needed to be sensible about it.

He had no cash in his pocket, since he'd not been paid. At some point, there was supposed to be a bank account the program had set up for him, with a bit of money coming in each week. That hadn't happened yet, but it would be too painful to wait around.

He needed to pack, and get organized, and then leave. Which meant going back down into the valley, getting some dinner, having an early night. Look at it all again in the morning.

Walking beneath the pines as he made his way down the switchback chilled him all over, but he was warm again once out in the sunlight. He could smell that dinner was already underway as he made his way across the parking lot to the mess tent, but when he got there, only Wayne was sitting at the long table, while Del placed a platter full of lasagna on a hot pad in the middle of the table.

"Where you been?" asked Wayne, serving himself the biggest corner piece. What did that matter? There were three other corners, and Blaze wasn't all that hungry.

"Walking around," said Blaze. He grabbed a slice of garlic bread from the basket and sucked on the edge of it for a minute, and knew full well and good that he couldn't trust Wayne enough to tell him any of what was going on. That, in fact, without Gabe, Blaze had nobody to talk to.

"There are new guys coming this week, Gabe said," said Wayne, talking with his mouth full. "Tuesday or Wednesday, he said."

Blaze quelled his jealousy that Wayne had had any of Gabe's attention at all, and reminded himself that he was lighting out in the morning. Bags packed.

He still had his gate money, so he could at least buy a bus ticket to somewhere. He'd leave his cowboy hat and boots behind, buy a burner

JACKIE NORTH

phone, first chance he got, and just go wherever. Who cared anyhow? Not him, that was for sure.

"Maybe you'll get a new roommate and won't have to sleep with Gabe anymore." Wayne looked smug as he grabbed more garlic bread than one man could eat and Blaze couldn't figure out whether he was being mocked for needing a roommate to keep away the scary darkness, which Wayne didn't know about, or whether Wayne was harassing him because he'd been sleeping with the boss. Either way, it was best not to reply to a guy like Wayne. Ever.

Blaze got up and went out of the mess tent, knowing he'd regret not eating when he got hungry later, only now his stomach was in knots and he felt more lost than he had in a long time. With long strides, he crossed the distance to the clump of trees where his tent was. Now empty, of course, except for two cots, one made up, the other one bare. The white shelves, one with his stuff crammed into it.

But there, sitting on the left-hand cot, his cot, was an envelope with his name on it.

For a long moment, not enough for his thumping heart to slow down, he stared at before he went to it, picked it up, and sat down.

He didn't think he'd ever received a letter in his life. Certainly not a hand-delivered one. He was almost caressing it as he touched it, tracing the letters that spelled his name in careful, simple cursive. *Blaze.*

Opening the envelope, he found a single sheet of notebook paper, rough at one edge, crisp along the other. It read:

Dear Blaze,

When it gets dark, please come to the fire pit. What I want to say is too complicated for paper, and I hope you'll let me explain.

Yours,
    Gabe

The sun hadn't quite set, so it wasn't dark yet, and even when the sun went down, the angle of the mountains would create a deep purple twilight that would go on for quite some time. That much, at least, Blaze had learned by coming to the valley.

In prison, the lights went out, and that was it, you were surrounded by half-pitch darkness. Doing your best to sleep, except you couldn't on account of the light in the corridor never went out, a permanent reminder that you'd fucked up and nobody liked you and you were trapped inside forever.

He wasn't in prison any longer and was free to make up his own mind about what to do, in spite of the fact that there was no demarcation between night and day, only a shifting, shadowy space between them.

Folding the letter quite carefully, hissing when he accidentally tore the ragged upper left corner, he put it in his pocket. And then walked, without looking right or left, to the fire pit. Knowing his heart wasn't quite prepared to get broken all over again.

He came upon Gabe next to the fire pit, one knee buried in the dirt, building what looked like it would turn out to be a giant bonfire, like he wanted to light up the night with it. On one of the Adirondack chairs was a paper bag with sticks poking out of the top, and Blaze didn't need to look to know that the bag contained everything they needed to make s'mores.

Only s'mores weren't going to cut it. Not when after the marshmallow and chocolate were washed off, graham cracker crumbs fed to the squirrels, Blaze would still be who he was, and Gabe would still look like he was staring down a whole host of ramifications about who his heart wanted him to care about. To love.

Blaze opened his mouth to make cheerful patter to break through the silence as Gabe, hearing Blaze behind him, stood up and brushed his palms on his bejeaned thighs.

Blaze wanted to say *You're going to burn down the forest with that*, but then Gabe might take that as a signal to explain how the fire pit was lined with stone, and that there was at least a two-foot diameter of gravel all around the fire pit to keep that from happening.

Blaze didn't want that. He wanted Gabe to have his say, and then

Blaze could say no to whatever, get his stuff from Gabe's tent so he could pretend to be brave as he spent his last night in his own tent before leaving in the morning. That was the plan, anyway.

"I was going to wait till full dark," said Gabe, gesturing at the fire he'd built, ready to be lit.

There was dust on his cowboy boots, his head was bare, and he looked like he'd crawled through the woodpile looking for the most perfect logs and kindling because there was a small gathering of wood chips on his shoulders.

"Say what you got to say," said Blaze, stuffing his fists into his pockets, not coming any closer than the Adirondack chair farthest from the fire pit. "And maybe you won't need to light it."

Blaze regretted the words the instant he said them, because they made Gabe's eyes bloom with sadness, made him look away, toward the mountains.

"Or maybe just light it now," said Blaze, thinking of the when Gabe had lit his Coleman lantern just for Blaze, just because Blaze wanted it lit. "Just light it. Then tell me."

He was pretty bossy for an ex-con with absolutely no rights whatsoever. Except Gabe had taught him that he did have rights, and that his feelings mattered, only not all the time. Only when Gabe was up to the task of not being dubious about what had happened between them.

"Okay," said Gabe. He took a single match from his pocket and lit the kindling, which, of course, smartly started the logs to pop and glow orange along their ax-sharpened edges. "Here goes."

Gabe paused before turning his attention away from the fire and toward Blaze. He rubbed his mouth with one hand, and tucked his other hand in his pocket, an echo of Blaze's hands.

"I know it must have seemed like I sometimes changed my mind about you, about us. And I did. But you have to know I was trying to figure out what was best. For the valley, for myself. And in the end, I realized that the most important thing—the only thing that mattered —was what was best for you. For you and me together."

Blaze could only blink. He had no idea where Gabe was going with any of this, except for the part that made some part of him snarl, where Gabe had figured it was up to him to decide what was best for Blaze. When Blaze was fully capable of figuring out what was best for himself.

"Your family is shit," said Gabe, almost spitting the words. "And if they could make you think that you were just there to save your brother this time around, then, yeah, I can see that's what they did before and what got you arrested. I believed you when you said you were innocent, but maybe not all the way. I do now. Not that it matters to me that you were in prison."

"Oh, it sure as hell does." Blaze snapped his mouth shut before he could say any more.

"It only matters because you suffered for it." Gabe shook his head slowly, as if he wanted Blaze to echo the motion and agree with him. "I could tell by the way you talked about it all, about the driveway scam, that it didn't sit right with you, even if when you were a kid, it just seemed natural to steal from folks. To trick them. But that's not you now, even if it ever really was. And all I want—"

Gabe moved a step closer, and the twilight, grown purple around them, made it dark enough that the growing bonfire outlined him in gold lights.

"All I want is just to be with you. Even after summer ends. Especially after summer ends."

The end of summer seemed miles away. Between now and then was a distance filled with rocks and ruts and things that would trip Blaze up and make Gabe doubt all over again. The end of summer felt too long away and yet not long enough for him to figure out how he felt about all of this.

"I've always felt like a second-class citizen," said Blaze, never able to keep his mouth shut for long. "With my family. In prison. Even here, in the valley."

Watching the sparks fly up from the tops of the logs, shots of orange and gold in the growing darkness, distracted him while he willed the thumping of his heart not to hurt so much. His feet moved him closer to Gabe in spite of his own good intentions.

"I don't want to protect Alex. I don't want to feel like that anymore. I spent two years behind bars for no reason. Being with you, at least most of the time, taught me that I didn't deserve a single minute of those two years. I wanted to feel like I was good enough to deserve you, and most of the time, I did. I want to keep on feeling that way, only I don't think you want to. There was doubt in your eyes. Not all the time, but sometimes."

"I don't doubt you." Gabe came closer too, his voice raised, sharp-edged.

"Yes, you *do*."

"I *don't*," said Gabe, more softly.

Reaching up, Gabe was close enough to tuck Blaze's hair behind his ear, a simple touch that made Blaze shiver all over.

"And if I did, I don't anymore. Truly, not anymore."

Blaze could feel Gabe's body heat, even surrounded by the warmth of the fire. Could smell the woodsmoke in the air, and the sweat from Gabe's exertions getting the fire built, getting s'mores supplies, getting everything ready for when Blaze would read the letter and come to the fire pit. As to how long Gabe had been willing to wait—

Up close, there was sweat along Gabe's jaw, his dark hair sticking to his temples. His eyes glittered, not with firelight, but with something else, coming up from deep within him, looking like tears, making Blaze's heart feel like it had been ripped open wide.

For Gabe to come to this point, vulnerable, as if he'd been devastated at the thought of never being with Blaze, was enough to undo Blaze to the point where he moved closer till his work boots touched Gabe's cowboy boots, and he stopped.

He leaned into Gabe's touch until the touch became Gabe's palm cradling his cheek. Warm skin, rough-edged, calloused fingertips. That tremor. Gabe's breath along his jaw as Gabe leaned in for a kiss.

But he was watching Blaze, his eyes fully open, as if he was wary of Blaze leaping away like a wild thing that did not want to be tamed.

If Blaze let anyone tame him, it would be this man. Who, kind of quiet and even tempered, waited for permission for a kiss between them. He looked like he might wait forever, a sheen of tears in his blue eyes out of fear that the answer might be no.

"Okay," said Blaze, letting the breath rush out of his body as he stood as still as he could for that kiss, the soft, velvet touch of Gabe's lips upon his. The warm circle of muscle and bone as Gabe's arms came around him. "Okay," he breathed, half panting as they parted.

"I'll teach you anything you want to know," said Gabe, sounding breathless himself. "Tell you anything about me that you want to know. And you can tell me anything. I just want us to be together when summer ends and then forever after that."

"You're such a romantic, Gabe," said Blaze, parts of him trembling as he circled his arms around Gabe's neck, the earth solid beneath his feet for maybe the first time in his life. "I think I'm the only person who knows it, but that's okay. It means that part of you is for me alone."

Maybe he was being greedy, demanding this from Gabe, wanting it for himself, only for him. But maybe it was okay, because Gabe's smile grew soft as he clasped Blaze's face in his warm palms, and kissed his chin, his cheeks, the corners of his eyes.

"You can have it," said Gabe. "You're the only one who's ever seen it anyhow."

Blaze took those kisses and absorbed them inside of himself where he would keep safe them forever.

"So I'm not moving out," he said, tipping his head back, looking at Gabe like he was examining him. "And everyone will have to know about us, since it'll be less easy to hide it, what with Wayne already onto us, and more parolees coming this week."

"And Jasper knows," said Gabe. "And Ellis, I'm thinking."

"Do you care?" Blaze asked, demanding it.

"No." The answer was solid and sure, and there was no hesitation in it. Only Gabe, his arms around Blaze's waist, tugging him close. "I never will."

Blaze's throat was too full for words, tight, almost too tight to breathe. But when Gabe brushed a soft kiss across his mouth, he drew in Gabe's breath, his energy, and it filled him from the bottom all the way to the top of his head, and he tucked that head into the curve of Gabe's strong throat.

"I only care about you," whispered Gabe in his ear. "Only you."

Over Gabe's shoulder, Blaze could see gold and yellow and orange sparks flying up into the purple twilight, the warmth of it reaching him, but never coming close to the warmth of Gabe's shoulders, his body, the nearness of him. Blaze closed his eyes.

This was all he'd ever wanted, only he'd not known it until now.

CHAPTER 28
GABE

After they carefully put the fire out and after they'd gone to Gabe's tent, Gabe had been unable to light the Coleman lantern before he and Blaze had tumbled into bed.

Thus the overhead light had blared upon them as they exchanged kisses and sweet promises, and Gabe had lingered over each touch, counting his blessings, savoring the warmth of Blaze's body, the closeness between them. The taste of Blaze on his tongue, the silky sweep of Blaze's hair against his neck, as they rested, languor overtaking them both.

"Do you want me to light the lantern?" asked Gabe. He sat up, gently drawing Blaze's arms from his neck, knowing already that the answer was yes.

He pulled on his boxers and crouched in front of the shelf, looking for the box of matches, which he must have moved from their usual spot. As he did this, the hatchet Jasper had given him slipped from its nook and clattered to the wooden floor. Luckily, it had a leather blade cover and luckily it missed his toes, saving them from a good banging.

"What's that?" Blaze propped himself on his elbow, the sheet draped around his hips in a come-hither way. "Do you have an actual axe in your tent?"

JACKIE NORTH

With a small huff of a laugh, Gabe found the box of matches, and stood to light the lantern, and when, finally, the lantern was lit, he turned off the overhead light.

Now the tent was as it should be, the way they both liked it. Bathed in golden light, the low hiss of the lantern accompanied by the nighttime sounds of owls, the wind in the pines. A lone cricket, or maybe two, singing a sad but hopeful chorus in the darkness.

"It was a gift from Jasper," said Gabe as he slithered beneath the sheet, taking Blaze in his arms. "For my cattle ranch."

"I didn't know you owned a cattle ranch," said Blaze, leaving sweet kisses along Gabe's neck, the line of his jaw.

"I don't," said Gabe. "At least not yet."

It felt good to tell Blaze about his someday ranch. It felt comfortable to talk about his dreams, and the life he envisioned for himself. One day. Some day.

In his chest, of course, sprung the hope that maybe Blaze would want to be a part of that. But maybe he should *say* that, rather than playing it so close to the vest.

"You ever think about working on a cattle ranch?" asked Gabe. He trailed his fingers through Blaze's hair, the feel of the silky strands making him shiver with pleasure.

"With you?" asked Blaze. "I would want nothing more." He smiled, his warm mouth moving along Gabe's shoulder, as if he were already ready for round two. "But why did he give you the axe?"

"It's a hatchet, really," said Gabe. "It's for when I have to go out at four in the morning in the middle of winter and break the ice on the water tanks for the herd." He tucked his chin to kiss the top of Blaze's head. "Still interested?"

"Always," said Blaze. "But if that's what you want, why are you here and not there, on this ranch of yours?"

"Can't afford it," said Gabe. "Still saving up."

"Well, ask Leland for help."

In the midst of scooting lower, taking Blaze in his arms, his body warming up to the prospect of pleasure, Gabe went still for a heartbeat, then continued scooting down until they were face to face.

"I can't ask Leland for money," he said, the words a whisper as he swept his lips across Blaze's.

"Not money," said Blaze. He clasped Gabe's face in his hands, his expression steady. "But, you know. Something. I'm no financial expert, but he thinks a great deal of you to put you in charge of this project, right? So maybe ask him for a co-sign. Or if he could talk to his bank manager, put in a good word. Otherwise, it'll always be a dream. Far away and unreachable."

"It always seems far away," said Gabe, then a little silence fell, feeling weighty and deep.

"Just think about it," said Blaze. "Why wait on your dreams if you could do something about it. Hell." He laughed, pressing his temple to Gabe's shoulder. "I'd even get up with you. Yes, that early, just to break that ice. Can I get a hatchet of my own? From Jasper?"

"Yes." In his mind, he knew Jasper would make a second hatchet, identical to the first. And in his heart, he absorbed Blaze's straightforward advice into something that could help him be bold enough to approach Leland about this.

Of course, he would work making the valley ready for paying customers the rest of the summer, but after that, when autumn came, he and Blaze could drive north to look for some land, with Blaze hanging out the window, as he liked to do, the cool air whipping through his hair, the smell of tall grasses and fresh air circling inside the cabin of the truck.

With Blaze by his side, he now had a future worth working for, a future better than he'd ever imagined.

The End

Thank you for reading!

If you enjoyed this book, please consider leaving a rating (without a review) or leaving a rating and a review!

Want to read more about the romance between Gabe and Blaze? Search on "Prolific Works Jackie North" to display the list of my free downloads.

Would you like to read more of my m/m cowboy romances? I've got a whole series you can binge on! Start with *The Foreman and the Drifter*, Book #1 in my Farthingdale Ranch series.

JACKIE'S NEWSLETTER

Would you like to sign up for my newsletter?

Subscribers are alway the first to hear about my new books. You'll get behind the scenes information, sales and cover reveal updates, and giveaways.

As my gift for signing up, you will receive two short stories, one sweet, and one steamy!

It's completely free to sign up and you will never be spammed by me; you can opt out easily at any time.

To sign up, visit the following URL:

https://www.subscribepage.com/JackieNorthNewsletter

- facebook.com/jackienorthMM
- twitter.com/JackieNorthMM
- pinterest.com/jackienorthauthor
- bookbub.com/profile/jackie-north
- amazon.com/author/jackienorth
- goodreads.com/Jackie_North
- instagram.com/jackienorth_author

Author's Notes About the Story

Back in 2020, when I first began writing my Farthingdale Ranch series, I knew I would be writing a six-book series. What I didn't know, couldn't have known, was that I would be inspired to start another six-book series — my Farthingdale Valley series, the first book of which you hold in your hands.

Did you ever wonder how I came up with the idea for Farthingdale Valley? Then read on.

Of all the books in my Farthingdale Ranch series, *The Blacksmith and the Ex-Con* has been by far the most popular, far outselling all of my other books with the exception of *The Foreman and the Drifter*. Which only makes sense, as *Foreman* is the first book in the series.

The Blacksmith and the Ex-Con has the most star ratings, the highest number of glowing reviews and, most importantly, the strongest, most intense readership of any of my books.

Sure, I have my own personal favorites among my books, even though authors aren't supposed to have favorites, but readers, quite simply, LOVE *The Blacksmith and the Ex-Con*.

I could write an article about why I think that is, but I think I can summarize much faster than that:

AUTHOR'S NOTES ABOUT THE STORY

- First, like *Honey From the Lion*, *Blacksmith* is about two men living in relative isolation.
- Second, there is a teacher/student dynamic, which is one of my favorite tropes.
- Third, Jasper is a little grumpy and very patient, and Ellis is traumatized.

The tagline for the book says it all: *"If anybody ever needed him, Ellis did. Ellis was broken. Jasper liked to fix things."*

When I was finishing up my Farthingdale Ranch series, the positive reader response to *Blacksmith* kept coming in, both surprising me and delighting me.

But why was this happening when the tropes in *Blacksmith* were in so many of my other stories? What was the difference?

The difference, I think, was Ellis' character. He's a criminal (for all the right reasons, I believe), he went to prison, and then he got out on parole, a broken man.

Is it sexy being a parolee? No, I don't think so. But there was a compelling dynamic that developed between Jasper, the "man in the field" and Ellis, the guy who's expected to start his life all over again with nothing but his gate money and a heart full of grief.

Readers ate it up, and I had such a good time writing that story that I wondered if I could write a whole series with that exact same setup. And thus the idea for Farthingdale Valley was born.

My notes from October 2021 read something like this:

- Series in a controlled space
- Series w/ ex-cons in rehab
- Series connected with Farthingdale Ranch
- Leland wants to expand the ranch to include retreat/adult day camp on land south of ranch
- They (the ex-cons) could built that retreat

That's how it all started — and when I was writing the end of *The Wrangler and the Orphan*, knee-deep in the rescue scene, I already

AUTHOR'S NOTES ABOUT THE STORY

knew that Brody was riding Diablo across the hills and among the pine trees where the retreat would one day be built.

Imagine if you will having to keep that idea alive for over a year, and you will know how glad I am to finally be able to share these stories with you.

A Letter from Jackie

Hello, Reader!

Thank you for reading *The Cowboy and the Rascal,* the first book in my Farthingdale Valley series.

If you enjoyed the book, I would love it if you would let your friends know so they can experience the romance between Gabe and Blaze.

If you leave a review, I'd love to read it! You can send the URL to: Jackienorthauthor@gmail.com

Best Regards,

Jackie

- facebook.com/jackienorthMM
- twitter.com/JackieNorthMM
- instagram.com/jackienorth_author
- pinterest.com/jackienorthauthor
- bookbub.com/profile/jackie-north
- amazon.com/author/jackienorth
- goodreads.com/Jackie_North

About the Author

Jackie North has written since grade school and spent years absorbing mainstream romances. Her dream was to write full time and put her English degree to good use.

As fate would have it, she discovered m/m romance and decided that men falling in love with other men was exactly what she wanted to write about.

Her characters are a bit flawed and broken. Some find themselves on the edge of society, and others are lost. All of them deserve a happily ever after, and she makes sure they get it!

She likes long walks on the beach, the smell of lavender and rainstorms, and enjoys sleeping in on snowy mornings.

In her heart, there is peace to be found everywhere, but since in the real world this isn't always true, Jackie writes for love.

Connect with Jackie:

https://www.jackienorth.com/
jackie@jackienorth.com

facebook.com/jackienorthMM
twitter.com/JackieNorthMM
pinterest.com/jackienorthauthor
bookbub.com/profile/jackie-north
amazon.com/author/jackienorth
goodreads.com/Jackie_North
instagram.com/jackienorth_author

Printed in Great Britain
by Amazon